THE CHAPTER OF ST CLOUD

Also by Marcus Attwater

St Oda's Bones
The Gift
The Secrets of Greystone House
Four Stories
Serendipity: A Tale in Four Reconstructions
Spindlewood
The Ruins of Cair Nynian

THE CHAPTER OF ST CLOUD

MARCUS ATTWATER

ISBN: 9798846608795
Copyright © Marcus Attwater 2019
This edition published by Attwater Books 2022
Cover design by Attwater Books, photograph by the author

www.attwaterbooks.nl

1

The voices of the choir soared into the arched spaces of the cathedral.

Lux æterna luceat eis, Domine,
cum sanctis tuis in æternum,
quia pius es.
Requiem æternam dona eis, Domine;
et lux perpetua luceat eis;
cum sanctis tuis in æternum,
quia pius es.

DI Collins looked at the singers so he would not have to look at the mourning parents in the front pew, or the tearful schoolfriends sitting across the aisle from him. It was almost too beautiful, this music. It gave voice to things that weren't there yet, perhaps never would be. Acceptance, serenity, strength. The broken couple staring at the coffin knew nothing of all that. All they had was the gaping emptiness where their daughter had been. Collins wondered who had chosen the music, who had organised this sad and dignified ceremony. Certainly neither Mr or Mrs Miller would have been capable of it, he had seen what their grief did to them.

There had been no need for him to come. The girl's death had been only briefly suspicious, and the inquest ruled her overdose an accident without any questions asked. The police were no longer involved. But he had been the one to tell the parents, breaking their world apart in one shocked moment, and later he had been the one to bring them the useless reassurance that she had not died at someone else's hands. Somehow he felt responsible. So he had come to pay his respects, on his own, to listen to the choked-up tributes to a girl he had never known, and now never would.

Death by misadventure. What an odd phrase it was. It must have been an adventure for her, seventeen years old, out with her friends, something new – 'go on, try it, it'll be fun'. But she had been a wisp of a girl, and the pills in combination with the amount of alcohol she had already drunk stopped her young heart. Death by misadventure. She had been no more stupid or reckless than many of her contemporaries, just unlucky. But of course the neutral finding of the inquest did not stop people from apportioning blame. In newspapers, during coffee breaks, on web forums, people dealt in reasons and opinions. It was the drink, the drugs, the parents, the schools, young people today. It was all or none of these things. Sitting in his hard pew listening to the singing, Collins knew it was never so simple. The only way to prevent accidents like these was for parents to lock up their children until age twenty-five, and then they'd probably still break their necks trying to climb out of the window. The hardest thing of all was facing that there was no one to blame, nothing you could do. Naomi Miller died, the world went on without her, and the heavenly assurances of the choir could never change that.

2

Claire sang as she drove away from London. It was a perfect late-August day, with sunshine and clouds chasing each other across a big sky, but Claire would have been just as happy if the weather had been dismal. She was on her way to see Simon, and that was enough to make her sing. She would be staying with his family for a week, a good end to her holidays. Next year they would travel, they had promised each other, have three or four weeks in Italy. Simon wanted to show her Florence and Siena, show her the country that gave life to the art he loved. In preparation for this far-off prospect, Claire's luggage contained a teach-yourself-Italian course and a brand-new dictionary. She had even, schoolgirlishly, bought a new pen and a bright green exercise book. If she got bored during her week in the country she would know what to do. She couldn't stand it that Simon spoke a language she didn't, and she was determined to catch up with him.

She had met him at her best friend's wedding. Such a cliché, really, but one she was happy to embrace. Only last June, it was, and she'd been feeling old and left-over and not very generous towards her friend, who was trying to outdo the Duchess of Cambridge in radiance. Bryony had been the third of four friends to hook up. Gina was living with her boyfriend, and Julia was married ages ago. Only Claire was still single, and she was two years older than Bry. She'd been reflecting on this, watching the chattering couples around her – and they had all seemed to be couples

– with a jaundiced eye, when a good-looking young man materialised beside her and started talking about the architecture of the church, of all things. They had introduced themselves: Simon, art historian; Claire, medievalist. She noticed he had the same combination of dark hair and blue eyes she had herself, but although she did not consider herself particularly striking, in him it was startling and attractive. They had continued talking until Bryony broke them up, clearly feeling that one of her husband's guests was monopolising her friend. 'Who is he, Bry?' Claire had asked, but the bride just shook her head. 'Must be one of Paul's friends, I don't know half the people here.' Claire resolved on the spot that when she got married, they would have just a small party for people they really knew. Suddenly, it hadn't seemed such a strange thought. Especially not when Simon sought her out again after the best man's speech. She found herself telling him all about her research, her ideas for a book. He was the first man she'd ever met who didn't glaze over at the phrase 'feminine theologies'.

They continued to meet in the weeks that followed, until he was spending almost as much time at her flat as she was. Her friends were doubtful, but she ignored them. All right, he was younger than she was, but so what? There were horrible men of all ages, why discriminate against the nice ones? And sometimes they were just being silly.

'You're not going to marry one of Paul's posh friends, are you?' Gina had said, 'One public schoolboy among one's acquaintance is enough, thank you very much.'

'Simon's not like that at all,' Claire had protested, wondering what this implied about her opinion of Bry's new husband. Still, for all her casual reply, she was glad she hadn't told the others precisely where he lived. The first time he had taken her home she'd thought 'you have got to be kidding me'. Maybe she had even said it aloud, as they had approached his parents' house on the long drive.

'It's a former bishop's palace, built in the early seventeenth century,' Simon had explained, with art-historical detachment, 'It's been our family home for a long time.' If she hadn't been apprehensive about meeting his family already, she would have been then. But her fears were groundless. They were the most welcoming family in the world, and she felt at ease almost at once. And there was a lot to feel at ease with. When Simon said 'family home' he didn't just mean his family had been living there for generations, he meant that most of it was living there right now.

Claire grew up the eldest of two daughters, the gap between her and her sister just too big for them to be company. Her grandparents died early, her only set of cousins had lived too far away to visit often. She had dreamed of a large family as a girl, she wanted aunts and uncles and lots of cousins like other children had. Later she thought she would have a large family herself, she would have four children at least. That was pushing it a bit by now, half a year after her thirty-first birthday. She'd settle for two, if she had to. But arriving at Simon's parents' for the first time, she thought she had found her large family.

'It would be a wicked waste, for just one couple and their children to live in a house like this,' Simon's ridiculously young-looking mother Anna had explained to Claire, while giving her the tour. 'And each, um, sub-family I suppose you could say, has their own space, we don't have to be in each other's pockets all the time if we don't want to.' All this while ascending a staircase that would have made a comfortable house on its own. There were portraits on the walls, and some of them looked like Simon.

'So how many of you are there?' Claire had asked. She'd only met Simon's parents and his great-grandfather as yet, though she had been promised brothers and sisters at supper. Anna had counted on her fingers, she had actually counted on her fingers. 'Twenty, give or take.'

'You're not *sure*?'

Anna had laughed at her astonishment, 'Oh, it varies a bit with the seasons. We home-school the children, you see, until they are eleven, and in term time we have some nieces and nephews staying who live away with their parents in the holidays.'

Now, on her way to visit the house for the second time, Claire still wasn't sure she'd met all twenty of them. Simon would keep saying things like: 'Oh that's Ezra, my cousin' or 'my aunt Martha' or 'Abby' or 'Luke' or 'Joshua' or... she despaired of ever getting to know them all. But they were certainly worth knowing. She had been impressed with how unashamedly intellectual they were, the wide array of professions they had chosen. It was so different from her own family home, where watching University Challenge on the telly was considered suspiciously highbrow. Here the children were precocious, growing up as they did amidst a bunch of incredibly knowledgeable adults. Maybe that was why Simon sounded so wise for his age. He was younger than she was, yes, but she often felt he had somehow managed to squeeze a lot more wisdom into his years than she had into hers.

'So you're in love with his beautiful mind, then?' Julia had asked, when she tried to explain this.

'Not just that,' Claire had said, 'But you know what I mean, don't you? It's a relief to meet a man who knows how to talk about other things than the footie and the property market. I've never met anyone who wasn't a colleague who could challenge me in my own field. There aren't that many people who know enough about medieval Christianity to try.'

'Okay, with me it's more the cricket and the stock exchange,' Julia had conceded, 'But I see what you mean. Good for you, Claire.'

She got off the motorway after she passed Oxford and continued her journey on the friendlier country roads. The place names of tiny villages peeled off at either side, and her historian's mind automatically set them in their proper place in time. All those names recalling ancient fords and woods and settlements. No *thorpes* or *bys* here, this was pure Anglo-Norman, Domesday country. Well not 'pure' obviously, she corrected herself, Anglo-Norman already being a mixed breed. Away to her left, the square tower of the cathedral marked the presence of a town that had sat in this valley for ten centuries at least. The cathedral whose bishop had once seen fit to build his splendid residence in the next village along. She was getting near now. From the next bend, she caught her first sight of the house, deceptively close. She knew it would be nearly twenty minutes yet on the winding lanes, but already she felt she was coming home.

3

They came to her house, her sons' messengers, and offered her a set of shears and a sword – one blade or another. Clothilde, queen-mother, guardian of kings to come, looked at the gifts with perfect understanding. Would she let her grandsons be tonsured and put away safe in a monastery? Or would they be killed, and not trouble her sons' conscience anymore? It was a choice between the mildness of the religion she brought to her husband's family and the cruelty that was theirs by right of inheritance. Clothilde understood, and wretchedly, fatally, she chose...

Dominic chewed on the end of his pencil and looked down in mild horror at what he had written. What did he think he was, a novelist? This was no way to start a sober history of a monastic order, though in truth, it was how the order had begun. Instead of this colourful story, he should be writing an introduction carefully outlining his aims. But those aims were no longer as clear-cut as he would like. Sometimes he wished he'd never started on this project, especially lately, now it came to actually writing the book. Uncharacteristically, instead of working on his tiny, shiny netbook, for this study of the Chapter of St Cloud he had bought a handsome bound notebook, which he had gradually filled with pencilled lines. And now this flight of fancy. Maybe he had written it because at least this harsh scrap of legend went uncontested. The two eldest sons of King Clodomer were killed. The youngest child, Clodoald, entered the church, and later established his own abbey, which was renamed St Cloud after his death in honour of the founder. It was from that abbey that the order known as the Chapter of St Cloud had grown. Dominic had thought it such a perfect subject when James dropped it in his lap. Right up his street, encompassing both the history and the historiography of a monastic order, and no one had done it before. Should he have been worried about that earlier? The Chapter of St Cloud still existed, and he had anticipated some resistance at the idea of a scholarly study. Information about it was hard to come by, he had found, sometimes even the written sources seemed cagey. People associated with the chapter were difficult to find and unforthcoming when tracked down. Its abbot was so completely unavailable that Dominic had started to doubt his existence. Or maybe he was just being paranoid. Maybe he should stop shilly-shallying and just write this straightforward monograph that any university press would be happy to publish at a small loss. With a clear, simple title, he had imagined it. *St Cloud: a history*, something like that. And sometimes he could almost convince himself that that was all there was to it.

He pulled Alfred Poole's book towards him. It wasn't actually very useful, belonging to the kind of history that reflected its own time more than its past, but it had the distinction of containing one of the very rare printed summaries of the development of the chapter. The spotty Victorian volume, printed in an age with a realistic attitude to the selling value of true crime, contained a lurid account of the author's murder in the back pages. A botched robbery had done for Alfred Poole before he could start on his projected history of the Chapter of St Cloud. It was as if the enterprise was cursed.

'Excuse me, is this place taken?'

'No, no. Please, sit down.'

A pretty dark-haired woman took the seat across from him. Noticing that his books had begun to take up more than their share of table, Dominic made room for her. They worked in silence for a while, the woman at her laptop with a neat stack of linguistics texts beside her, Dominic increasingly frustrated by the lack of information in his hoard. He noticed the woman was taking peeks every time he picked up a different title. 'I'm sorry,' she said eventually, 'I'm hopelessly curious, always looking what people are reading. What is your subject? That's an odd collection you have there.'

Dominic was happy to have an excuse to talk. 'I'm not making much headway,' he said, 'But it's the history of a religious order. It's a long history, hence the combination of Carolingians and twentieth-century Catholicism.'

'Oh. Is it interesting?' she asked, sounding mildly disappointed.

'I think so.' He was used to that reaction. Monks and nuns were inherently boring to the general public, even if the general public in this case – he'd taken a peek of his own – could be fascinated by *The Construction of Noun-Phrases in the Indo-European Languages*. But the woman was still looking at him expectantly, so he tried to explain a little more. 'I think even historians sometimes tend to forget that for a long time the religious wasn't part of everyday life, it *was* life. We think of the cloistered as missing out on something – this age abhors celibacy – but a monk in the twelfth century was fully part of life, and performing an important function. The concerns of a religious order were the concerns of its times.'

'I see.' She appeared amused by his insistence, and perfectly content to continue talking. He hoped she could be engaging on the subject of Indo-European noun-phrases. 'But what makes this particular order your fascination of choice?'

'Partly, I'm afraid, that it has been the least studied of them. The mendicants, the white monks, the military orders especially, they've all been researched to death. The Chapter of St Cloud is obscure, but it's been obscure for a very long time. And it seems to have kept its character remarkably well, through the centuries. There's always the same focus in its religious thought, which is odd, given the number of reforms and renaissances it's gone through. And it has a history of strong, charismatic abbots. That is, as far as I can tell.' Was he explaining too much?

'Why? You seem uncertain.'

'It's very hard to find primary sources. There are some charters, chronicles written after the fact, a seventeenth century copy of the Rule. But there is little original material, and modern scholarship is very insistent on primary sources. Something that didn't bother him yet.' He patted Alfred Poole. 'He made all kinds of connections that seemed eminently reasonable to him, and now I'm having to go over it all again to see if his assumptions were warranted.'

She smiled. 'Don't you love those self-confident Victorians? Mind you, we wouldn't have been anywhere without them. We owe the whole historical-linguistic edifice to their willingness to make assumptions.'

Here we go, Dominic thought, *noun-phrases*. They turned out to be unexpectedly entertaining.

On his way home he bought an evening paper at a newsstand. The lead article was about yesterday's murder. A young man, the barman of a local pub, had been shot in his home. No motive, no suspects. Not very cheering, but at least it put Dominic's own worries in perspective. Murder was still rare enough in this town to make headlines. He had moved here only a few months ago, but Dominic knew the young man's – the boy's, really – place of work, knew he must have seen him around. And now he was dead. An Inspector Collins was quoted as saying the police were keeping an open mind as to the motive and identity of the perpetrator, which presumably meant he hadn't a clue.

Dominic's steps had automatically brought him into the Close, and he tucked his newspaper under his arm and went through the church's small south entrance. There was no choir practice today, but he still liked to go home by the cathedral, even through it, on most days. It was nearly closing time, and the tourists had left. He loved a big church when it was quiet, even though he knew that in the days when it was built it wasn't meant to be. Now he moved silently through the south aisle until he reached the westernmost bay. There he leant companionably against a massive compound pier and looked upwards to drink in the cathedral's towering gothic beauty. It never ceased to amaze him, the proportionate perfection of the arches, the clear lines of the vaults, the little builders' quirks he was only beginning to notice. The cathedral had been one of the reasons he chose to come here. He would never have taken a job at a university in a town that didn't have a proper gothic building at its heart. He had grown up in a cathedral town, and he was determined he would eventually die in one.

He crossed the nave and went out on the north side, through the devil's door. The door that would have been kept permanently closed in former days now sported a practical wheelchair ramp, and Dominic felt no compunction about slipping out where the devil once slipped in.

4

He remembers the building of the abbey. He remembers the great blocks of limestone that went into raising the walls, the churning watermill and the terrible draught in the refectory when the wind blew from the east. He remembers the chants and the prayers in the night; the simple life of the monks, away from the world, before greed and doubt and ambition returned. He remembers the scholars of the emperor's court, many years later, when the scriptorium was never empty, and how the name of the abbey spread far and wide. He remembers the return to the Rule, and the first daughters and their priors, bright and zealous. Weren't those days the best? With houses all over France and England, with scholars at Paris and a voice in the curia. Oh, the books and the good works he remembers, and the great number of monks and nuns who sheltered under the abbey's wings. He had been proud of his flock. He had shrugged at the rise of the new preaching orders, he had felt rooted in that ancient house on the Seine. Safe, he had believed they were, safe for years, even when they grew smaller, just a few abbeys, a priory here and there. Those years all run together now. They must have been happy. There must have been peace, for he remembers the violence that ended it. He remembers the king's soldiers who took away the plate and the reliquaries. He remembers the abandoned cloisters, the years of hiding, of furtive meetings and unspoken words. Years of fear and silent prayer, right until the creeping words exploded into blustering debate, every man shouting for his own god. He remembers the stones of the kingless rabble that smashed a church's windows into painful shards, and the pamphleteers' dripping poison. But they had come out of that ordeal strengthened, renewed. They had learned to be quiet, had learned patience and wisdom. No worldly ambition marred the abbey's new face. No blocks of stone marked its place now, nothing that could be pulled down. It lived in his mind, and in the souls of his followers. And the years that succeeded were strange, but they have brought him here, to this place and time, where he can survey history and maybe make sense of it, all the way from that first course of masonry until now. But there is so much he remembers, there is too much. The abbey is there, the abbey is eternal, but he knows there were thoughts before he knew even that.

He recalls, but dimly, his proud, long-haired brothers, his stern-faced grandmother, who loved him. His memory of that time is confused and its colours are crude. He is not sure what really happened, what he was told later, what is true or false. He knows they were his older brothers, and they died where he was spared. It's not so strange that he doesn't remember them well. He was only a child. And after all, it was nearly fifteen-hundred years ago.

5

When he got home Dominic put on a recording of Allegri's *Miserere*. They had just started rehearsing it with the choir, and he liked to get a feel for the music as it was performed by others. A large production together with St Oda's Singers, it would be his first big project since he joined the Cathedral Choir. Now he hummed along bits as he started getting supper together. *Asperges me hysopo...*

He had been living in the flat for five months, having taken over at the history department during a lecturer's pregnancy leave. From the new term onward he would be teaching his own courses full-time. It had been a good move. Things had been all right in Canterbury, but while he was there he would always feel like half of a couple that no longer existed. It was the place of his life with Blake. They had broken up nearly two years ago now – two years! – but only since he moved had Dominic felt all right with that, here in his own place. Now, when he took stock, he could be content. Dominic Walsingham, 36, lecturer in the history and historiography of the middle ages, reasonably accomplished tenor voice, unreasonable fondness for gothic architecture, nice brown eyes. Not bad, really.

It was James Sutherland who had supported his candidacy for the post, he suspected. James had been his thesis supervisor when he was still at university, he owed him a lot. It must have been the conference last year that put him in mind of Dominic again. *The Third International Conference of Monastic Life in the Middle Ages* at

Kalamazoo, Michigan. He'd laughed when he saw that incongruous place name tagged on. But he had never been to the States before, and he had been invited to present a paper, so he went. The conference was held on a large everything-provided campus, which seemed to exist without any relation to the outside world. There were medievalists from all over the world, with the largest contingent from the home university. There was a lot of top quality work coming from there, Dominic knew, and yet it always struck him as a little unlikely, that someone, a lot of someones, in the American Midwest had chosen to study the history of another continent. Where he grew up, the next medieval church was five minutes' walk away, ten minutes on a bus brought you to a full-scale castle. How did you get interested in the European Middle Ages when there weren't any physical ties to that time? He always planned to ask the question when he met a real Midwestern medievalist, but they all proved more interested in talking about the paper he read. He'd been quite proud of it. *The Monastic Rule in History and Memory: Creative Contradictions*. There were some vociferous disagreeing voices during question time, which was always good. The essay was to be printed in the proceedings, they assured him he'd have a copy any month now. He had enjoyed the conference. In the evenings, when there were no discussions or lectures, the Brits had tended to stick together in the bar, exchanging university gossip and bemoaning the transatlantic inability to brew a proper cup of tea. It was on one such evening that James had mentioned the Chapter of St Cloud. They were at their table as usual, James and Dominic, Claire Althorpe, and Stuart Tanner from Aberdeen. They had been listening to an address about monastic filiation that afternoon, maybe that was what brought it on.

'I assume you've heard of the Chapter of St Cloud?' James asked, 'French order, grew from an abbey founded in 550. Joined the Cistercians in the twelfth century, founded abbeys in England and all over the place, the usual story. Except that it still exists. A student of mine was going to write a thesis on its history, but he decided against it at the last moment. Went for teacher's training instead.' James grimaced. 'But you know, a history of the chapter has not been written yet. So there it is, up for grabs.'

'Why don't you write it yourself, James?' Claire had asked.

'Not my thing, dear,' he had shaken his head, 'No, this is stuff for an up and coming young academic to make his mark with.' James had never learned to modify his speech on feminist principles, and Claire had winced, but only a little.

'St Cloud was Clovis's grandson, wasn't he?' Stuart had said, 'I know my Merovingians. I wouldn't be much good at the later stuff, though.'

Dominic hadn't said much then. But the name stuck in his mind, and when he got home he had, idly at first, then with more sense of purpose, started to find out about the chapter. James had been right when he said it still existed, but only up to a point. There apparently still was an organisation calling itself the Chapter of St Cloud, *Le Chapitre de St Cloud* in France, though how much it had to do with the original order was unclear. But as a medievalist, he was more interested in the earlier centuries anyway. After he moved house, Dominic had seriously started to research the history of the chapter, from the founding of the first abbey onward. It was mentioned in secondary sources fairly often, but very little in the historiography of the monastic orders. Dominic had started to wonder why historians had kept away from it. There was little material for the early years, but that hadn't stopped people writing books about things whose existence was even more doubtfully documented – the Holy Grail sprang to mind. And it wasn't as if the chapter had been insignificant, some respectable scholars had emerged from behind its walls. Every student of medieval thought knew Thomas of St Cloud's *De Vita Sancta*, mostly in James Sutherland's translation, and religious historians still read Judith of Paris. But something stopped earlier students of the chapter from getting very far, and no book about it ever appeared.

Dominic dished up his supper and took it through to eat on the settee. He put an end to the repeating *Miserere* and put on a Tallis CD instead. Maybe that friendly linguist would be in the library again tomorrow. It had been nice talking to someone new, he hadn't proved very good at making friends in this new town so far. He hadn't asked her name, he now realised, nor she his. How typical.

6

The prior stood looking out of the window, his back to the young sister who had come to report to him. This part of the Chapterhouse overlooked the apple orchard, and he could see the abbot there enjoying the dappled sun, as yet unaware of any threat to his peace. If only it could stay that way!

'You are sure, Sarah?' he asked.

'Oh yes. It's gone beyond a proposal now. I spoke to him in the library today. He thinks he's not making much progress, but he's gone too far to stop.'

'Then we must make him stop.' Already his mind was looking for ways and means. This wasn't the first time they had been confronted with something like this, and usually it was easily dealt with. 'Could you scupper his chances with the Press?'

'I could try,' she said doubtfully, 'But that would not eliminate the risk, you know. It's an attractive project, on the face of it. He would take it to another publisher, and then I would not be there to keep an eye on it.'

Sarah was advisory editor to the local university press. Recently, a proposal had been received for a history of the Chapter of St Cloud. Their chapter. And for a variety of reasons, none of them were eager to ever see it in print. The prior was taking this very seriously.

'What does he know?'

'The usual stuff. He has read that old book of Poole's. He knows James Sutherland personally,' Sarah replied, 'And he has reached the point where he starts to find it strange that there isn't more to be found.'

'Will that discourage him sufficiently?'

'I'm afraid not. I think this one is good at what he does.'

The dangerous ones always were. That's what made them dangerous. The prior had rather hoped a little discouragement would go a long a way. But he had to make sure.

'We'll have him watched,' he told Sister Sarah, 'See what we can do about it.' Even to her, one of the most trusted, he would not give away too much of his thoughts.

'Do you want me to talk to him again?'

'I don't think so. Let him live in ignorance for a while.'

'All right. I'll send Lucas and Joseph to see you about this.'

Sarah left. The prior followed a moment later, knowing he had better inform the abbot of this development.

'Trouble brewing, my son?' the abbot asked, when he joined him in the orchard. The old man still had a sharp mind, he didn't miss much.

'Father,' the prior inclined his head politely, 'Just another inquisitive historian.'

'You think he is a threat?' The abbot did not appear to be much troubled.

'One that will be taken care of, I assure you.' As it always had been.

'What's his name?'

'Walsingham. Dominic Walsingham.'

7

Claire added her Ford Ka to the motley collection of cars parked in the drive and contemplated the house. It looked like something that should be administered by English Heritage, with its façade practically unaltered since it was built, and the handsome wings added in a later century harmonising rather than clashing with the original building. Architecture wasn't her strong point, but she knew she liked this. As she was getting her bags from the boot, Simon came running down the steps to catch her in his arms. That was one of the things she loved about him, that he would give her a full-on snog even though he knew half his family must be watching. He wasn't easily embarrassed.

'*Ciao cara*, I'm so glad you're here.' He took one of her bags, and together they walked up to the front door, where his mother was waiting, a smile on her face. 'Hello Anna,' Claire said, kissing her on both cheeks, 'Good to see you again.' She marvelled again at how young Anna looked, more like Simon's sister than his mother. And she was always so unruffled and smartly turned out, you wouldn't say she was raising three adolescents either. Sometimes Claire felt like a frump in comparison.

'I've put you in the same room as last time,' Anna said, 'You remember the way? Then I'll leave you to your own devices. See you at dinner, my dears.'

'She thinks you're one of the family now,' Simon grinned, 'So she's not going to play hostess. Do you want to change for dinner?'

'How much time do we have?'

His grin became even broader. 'Time enough.'

There were four generations living in the house, from Simon's octogenarian great-grandfather Toby down to his eleven-year-old brother Titus. Simon was the first to admit that it was an odd arrangement.

'But I suppose the house sort of asks for it, and we've always been close, as a family.'

'Yes, you said so before. I still think it's wonderful,' Claire said, 'Is everybody here now?'

They were lying side by side on the wide guest bed, listening to the life of the house going on behind the door.

'Bennett and Maisie are still on holiday. And dad's been in France for a while, but he'll be back any day now.'

'You'll have to explain a bit more, you know,' Claire said, rolling onto her side to smile at him, 'Who are Bennett and Maisie?'

'My great-uncle and -aunt. You've met their daughter, my cousin Bethany.'

'Of course, I liked her. So what's your father doing in France?'

'Oh, I'm not sure. Something to do with property we have there, I think.'

They were so easy to get along with, Claire sometimes forgot that Simon's family must be, by her standards, quite ridiculously rich. She couldn't imagine not being sure about whether her family had property in France or not. But they didn't act rich, and they all had quite normal jobs. Except for Anna. It had come as a complete surprise to

Claire that Simon's mother was better known as the chick-lit author Laura Garnett. She had found out by accident during her last visit, when she had picked up a bundle of letters addressed to the author.

'That's you?' she had asked Anna, 'I know the books, of course, but I thought Laura Garnett...'

'...was a cheerfully single thirty-something?' Anna smiled, 'The publishers are very careful not to let on that I'm married with five children, it would spoil the image. And 'Laura Garnett' works so much better than plain 'Anna', don't you think? I always wanted to be a Laura as a girl, and Garnett's my maiden name.'

'And my sisters would die if their mates found out their mother writes chick-lit,' Simon had put in.

They had chatted on about her books, until Claire suddenly caught up with what Anna had actually said.

'*Five* children? But there's only Simon and the two girls and Titus...'

Anna suddenly looked older.

'Jacob's no longer here,' Simon said shortly.

'Oh! Oh, I'm so sorry.'

He shrugged. 'You couldn't know.'

'It's not–' Anna began, but she thought better of what she had been going to say, and with a visible effort, had returned to the subject of writing. Simon's other brother had not been mentioned again.

'I'm so glad you're visiting us again, Claire,' Bethany said, as they sat down to dinner, 'Simon doesn't know how lucky he is. What will you do while you're here? Sightseeing?'

'Some of that, I suppose,' Claire replied with a smile. She had taken to Bethany at once when she met her, she was easier to get along with than Simon's two sisters, who seemed to live in a teenage world Claire was carefully excluded from. She told Bethany about her plans to learn Italian.

'Rather you than me,' she said, 'Simon speaks it fluently, of course. He went there for four months during his last year at uni, and came home chattering away like a native. Don't know how he does it.'

'I hope it helps that I know Latin. Vocabulary shouldn't be a problem, at least.'

'You know Latin? But of course, you'd need that for medieval history. I had Latin at school for a year, hated it.' She pulled a face. 'Noun cases.'

'Medieval Latin is quite fun,' Claire replied, knowing this sounded unlikely, 'You can see the other languages coming through, sometimes.'

All through the conversation she had the feeling she was being watched. She knew the younger members of the family would be stealing glances at Simon's girlfriend, but it wasn't that. Sometimes, when she looked around, she saw Simon Peter's piercing blue eyes regarding her. Simon's grandfather – why, if they were all going to live in the one house, did they insist on naming all the eldest sons Simon? – was a quiet man, not given to heartiness or jokes. When he said something, it was meant to be listened to. Claire was sure that had she been a few years younger, she would have been frightened of him. But there was also a familiarity about him, because he and Simon looked so much alike. When she was introduced to Simon Peter, Claire had thought: so this is what he will look like when he's in his sixties... it could be worse. His wife Edie was a self-effacing woman who had clearly handed over lady-of-the-house duties to Anna with a big sigh of relief, but Simon Peter was very much the lord of the manor still.

'So, Claire,' he said, when Bethany turned to her other neighbour. 'You and I never really had a chance to talk the last time you were here. Tell me about your work.'

'I lecture in medieval history at Royal Holloway. I specialize in gender and Christianity,' she reeled off.

He narrowed his eyes. 'Female monasticism?'

'Not only,' she said, slightly taken aback, 'But I did publish an article on that, as a matter of fact.'

'Yes, *Queens of the Cloister*. I thought it interesting.'

'You've read it?'

'I thought I would see what Simon's girlfriend got up to. Do you like teaching?'

To be or not to be honest? With this man, it was hardly a question. 'Not really,' she admitted, 'It's part of the career, but I'd prefer to do only research, if I could. Take the time to write a full-length book instead of trying to get an essay published here and there. I would like to develop the idea of the convent as liberating rather than constricting.' Feeling she had said enough on that subject, Claire switched tracks. 'And what do you do? Or used to do, maybe?'

'Yes, I suppose you could say I'm retired now. But I still sit on the board of the scholarship fund, together with my son. Your Simon will take my place there eventually.'

Your Simon. If even this patriarch conceded that Simon was hers, she was home and dry. Just imagine, if she and Simon should marry, she would come to live here. Maybe she would not have to teach anymore, she could write her book, in one of those charming smaller rooms on the second floor... What a very unreconstructed fantasy, Claire, her inner feminist scolded.

'Scholarship fund?' she said.

'Hasn't he told you about that? The family fund two scholarships every year, for one girl and one boy to take the honours degree of their choice at the local university. My grandfather set it up in the thirties, just for talented girls to start with, because back then it was so much harder for them.'

'No, Simon didn't say. How lovely. Simon! Why didn't you tell me?'

'Tell you what?'

'About the scholarships.'

'There's so much I don't tell you,' he joked, 'But the scholarships are dad's baby, really. You should ask him about it.'

Claire was glad that the family wealth was being put to such a good use, especially now it became harder and harder for bright students to get university places, and she said so.

Later that evening, while Simon was doing his share of the housework, Claire called her friend Gina. She just had to tell someone about it all.

'The whole family in one house?' Gina exclaimed, 'Christ, I'd hate that.'

'They're not like your family, Geen. And the house is enormous.'

'But how do they manage? The shopping alone...'

'There's a cook. And aunt Rhoda functions as a kind of, well, matron, I suppose. There's cleaning duty rosters and everything – but you only get put on them when you stay longer than a week. And dinner's in two sittings – in the morning you put yourself down for six or eight o' clock, so the cook knows for how many she should, um, cook.'

'Sounds dreadful.'

'It isn't. It runs like clockwork, actually. And apart from dinner and housework the families have their own apartments. It isn't as if I can just clump into Simon's grandmother's sitting room without knocking.'

'Hm. But don't the kids want to move out? I couldn't wait to be on my own, when I was eighteen or so. Neither could you, Claire.'

'Sure the kids move out when they go to university. And they don't all move back to live here. They don't *have* to. But I suppose a house like this is hard to leave. You and I never had a home like this. I wouldn't have wanted to leave here.'

'Yes, I noticed that.'

'Look Geen, why are you being so sceptical? I'm trying to tell you I like it here.'

'I'm your friend, it's my duty to be sceptical. Remember when Julia was dating that creep Rory?'

Claire snorted. 'I'm a lot older and wiser than Julia was then. No wacky Christian sect here, I promise you. Just plain, non-attending C of E.'

'Glad to hear it. You take care.'

'You too, Geen. Catch you later.'

8

He had almost decided it was too hot to work. It was still quite early, but the flat hadn't cooled down much in the night. He should go out, get some colour on that white English skin of his. But he suspected that that would really be just another excuse for not admitting he was stuck with his research, so he persisted. Thank heaven for the internet, Dominic thought. A Victorian clergyman-writer, an Oxford don from the fifties, a Ph.D. student in 1986 – how else did you go about finding them?

The thought had come to him quite suddenly, in the middle of a sleepless night. Why had no history of the chapter ever been completed? What had discouraged his possible predecessors? James's student hadn't been the first to abandon a projected thesis on the order, there had been Barry Skinner, in the eighties. And earlier still, Alice Wright, who had written a monograph on Judith of Paris, never published her intended book on the order to which Judith belonged. So what happened? Conscious that he was indulging in the most flagrant procrastination, Dominic set about finding out.

About Alfred Poole he knew more than he liked already, thanks to the Victorian's enterprising publisher. Finding Alice Wright was easy. She had a Wikipedia page of her own, which praised her revolutionary – in the field – work on feminine mysticism and mentioned her long friendship with Shakespeare scholar Charlotte Harmondsworth. It also informed him that the poor woman had been poisoned not long after the publication of her book on Judith of Paris. The wording did not quite eliminate suicide, but he had the impression she had been killed. Arsenic in her tea – how very Christie. The knowledge disturbed him more than he liked. Who would kill a completely inoffensive historian? And why did he have to go and look this up? It only upset him, and it didn't actually teach him anything he wanted to learn. The Chapter of St Cloud was not even mentioned. He abandoned Wright and went on to try and find out about Barry Skinner. The problem here was that there were too many of him. 102 of them in the UK alone, if you believed Google. But how to find the one whose Ph.D. proposal was filed under the title *The Rise of the Abbey of St Cloud*? That thesis never appeared, he had looked for it, and none of the Barry Skinners published on medieval or religious history. Of course, Barry Skinner might be dead by now as well. That thesis proposal dated from 25 years ago. Anything could have happened. He tried a few more searches, with various combinations of words, and finally just added 'murder' to the mix. What he found, among a lot of trash, was a sensationalist magazine article about unsolved murders. On 21 April 1986, at his home in a student flat, one Barry Skinner's head was bashed in with a paperweight by an unknown, but most likely male, assailant.

It might not be the same Skinner, Dominic told himself, there's loads, you saw. But the article said he was a history student, and he never did finish that thesis, did he? He printed out the article, which didn't really have much to add. It looked like the author had just used the case as padding for two much more spectacular murders. Dominic noticed his hands shaking as he stuck the print-out in a file.

With Alfred Poole, this made three historians of the Chapter of St Cloud and three violent deaths. And as his ex was wont to say 'two is coincidence, three is a pattern'. This was too much. These murders couldn't have anything to do with each other, could they? He told himself he was just having another attack of imagination. And yet. There had been no apparent motive for any of the deaths, certainly no murderers convicted, as far as he could tell. But that did not necessarily mean they had anything to do with the chapter. His thoughts went around in this circle for a while, until he decided he needed to talk about this, and not just have a chat with a colleague. There was only one thing he could do, and, hands still trembling, he called the police. He worked through the 'if you want to report a crime dial 1' routine until he got to talk to a real person.

'I think I may have information about an unsolved murder,' he said, trying not to sound like the kind of person who made calls like this for entertainment, 'I would like to talk to someone about it.'

'If you have information about the death of Sean Whiteside, you should talk to Sergeant Walter in CID–'

'No, no. This isn't about that. It was much longer ago. Look, could I just make an appointment?'

His urgency must have come through, because now he was offered a meeting with a DI. He made a note in his diary – *4 pm: police*, as if he was likely to forget – and thanked the officer politely.

Four o'clock. If he hurried, he could nip over to check the newspapers in the Oxford city archives and see what he could find about the murder of Alice Wright.

9

Detective Inspector Collins stared at the whiteboard in his office. He hated the thing. It had photos of the murder victim stuck to it with little magnets, and his name in a big red circle in the centre. There were arrows to various other names. There were a lot of questions marks, in blue. The whiteboard was there to help him 'visualise connections and think things through spatially, as it were'. Or some such crap. Apparently they needed that, now practically all information came in electronically and nobody used old-fashioned notebooks anymore. The things were all over CID. But there was nothing on the whiteboard that he couldn't just as easily remember. Other people had pictures of their family in the office. He had a boy in a blood-soaked T-shirt.

The reason that he was looking at it anyway was that he was, as they put it so nicely in the local paper, baffled. Sean Whiteside, twenty years old, chemistry student, barman of the Hollow Crown, had been found dead in his room by his father, shot through the heart. No witnesses, no suspects. No enemies. Apparently he had been popular, but not so popular as to raise deadly jealousies. He left one devastated girlfriend, two heart-broken parents. And one police inspector at a loss. It was an odd crime. Not, by CID standards, very violent. Just one shot, precise and lethal. There seemed to have been no struggle, no drama. Not in Sean Whiteside's death, and little in his life. His parents had told him he was a hard-working student, a scholarship boy of which they were rightly proud. Even allowing for the rosy view fond parents tended to take of their children, Whiteside's life did not appear to have invited danger.

His phone rang. DS Walter. 'Yes?'

'Sir? We have a lead.'

He almost admired the man for the way he could make 'sir' sound insubordinate. Sergeant Walter was having a hard time getting over the fact that his younger colleague had jumped ahead in the promotion stakes.

'Yes?' he said again, neutrally. He had promised himself never, ever, to lose his temper with Walter.

'You'll love this. The kid was pushing Oblivion.'

'Right. That changes things. How did you find out?'

'Fellow student of his told me. Bought some of the stuff off him a month back. Couldn't tell me where he got it from, though.'

'We'll find out. Thanks, Walter. I'll contact the boys in Narcotics.'

If Whiteside had been a dealer, things were suddenly looking a lot more messy than the whiteboard suggested. Collins didn't like this at all. There wasn't much drug-related crime on his patch, but there was always some, of course. And things tended to get confused pretty quickly when dealing with it. Organised crime didn't stay neatly within CID approved boundaries. He tried to reassure himself that Sean Whiteside couldn't have been a big-time dealer, otherwise Narcotics would have contacted him by now. Wouldn't they? The name had been all over the papers. Yes, surely even those dopes would have made the connection. He called his opposite number in the drug squad and asked for a list of all sources of Oblivion in the neighbourhood.

'Nasty stuff that, Oblivion. Remember the Miller girl?' Jim said, 'Your dead boy a user?'

'Dealer. Nothing big, I think.' Meaning: nothing for you to worry your pretty head about.

'I'll email you a list. But I would appreciate it if you'd give us a heads up before talking to any of them. We've got some delicate operations running.'

'Of course. Thanks, Jim.'

He got up, selected a purple marker, and wrote 'Oblivion' in capitals on the shiny white surface. He looked at it, his head to one side, and decided to add a small question mark.

'Sir?'

DC Holmes was hovering in his doorway, looking like she was trying hard not to laugh.

'What is it, Sally?' He usually addressed his team by their last names, but he never called her Holmes, for fear she would start calling him Watson.

'There's a Mr Walsingham to see you, sir. Says he has an appointment.'

Of course, the distraught academic. Collins looked around his office. Better than an interview room? Or worse?

'Give me two minutes. Then show him up here.'

'Will do.'

'Cheers, Sally.'

He did a little futile tidying, shrugged on the jacket of his suit and made another call. He thought he'd better give that list to Sergeant Walter to pursue. Meanwhile, he would get on to his own contact in the world of small-time dealers. Someone who Jim in Narcotics, with any luck, didn't know anything about.

10

On her first morning, after a long lie-in, Simon announced he was taking her for a ride through the park. Not having come near a horse since a brief crush at age eleven, Claire reluctantly agreed to try out the mildest mare in the stables.

'You'll love it,' Simon said confidently, 'We can go along with dad and aunt Esther as far as Drovers' Lane, and leave them to have a proper ride while we go back the easy way.'

'Oh, your father's back, then?'

'Yes, he came home last night. And I think he's pleased you're here,' Simon replied with a grin.

Once she got used to all the things one had to pay attention to when sitting on a horse, Claire had to admit that it *was* lovely. And just wait till she told Julia, her friend would be green with envy – their own stables!

'I suppose most of the surrounding land belonged to the house at one time or another?' she asked Simon's father – calling him Simon as well didn't come easily, and he insisted she should not be formal, so in practice she didn't call him anything much.

'Yes, all the farms and the fields once belonged to the house. Not for years now, of course. Even my grandfather hardly remembers the time when tenants came up to the house at Michaelmas to pay the rent.'

It sounded like he was talking about an impossibly remote past, but of course his grandfather was the spry old gentleman Claire had said hello to only this morning. It always surprised her what people would and would not call a long time ago. To her it seemed amazing that old tenancy customs had persisted to within living memory. It was practically yesterday.

The cottages they were now riding towards had stood there longer than that, though. White-washed prettily, sporting faded hanging baskets, no doubt extensively converted inside, but still, Claire thought, three-hundred years old if a day. Julia and her husband had recently bought something like that, for weekends away from London. Was she any different, wanting to spend her days in that big house behind them? Maybe not.

'Is that the kind of history you are interested in? Social history?' Simon's aunt asked.

'Not exactly. I'm interested in the gendered experience of history, and so also in the social structures that frame those experiences. But of those it is religion which interests me most.'

She realised Simon's father, riding beside her now, was watching her intently. She assumed he was taking her measure, seeing if she was going to fit in. But not in the nothing-but-the-best-for-our-son way Simon Peter had yesterday at dinner. There was something else, a sense that what she answered now might actually be very important.

'So you believe past experiences can be recovered?' he asked abruptly.

'I hope my words have not suggested that,' Claire replied carefully, 'Certainly not in any crude sense. The past is not just the present in a longer dress. But I think we may at least find where past experience differs from present, even if we cannot know exactly what constitutes the difference.'

He nodded. 'A realistic aim.'

'No more than that, Claire? Really?' Simon asked. He seemed disappointed.

She understood. It was often like that with people who weren't professional historians. The kind of history everyone was taught at school gave a deceptively confident front to a mass of questions and intelligent guesswork.

'I'm afraid so. The next time you read a narrative history, try asking 'how do we know that?' at every turn. The answer is usually that we don't, we just assume.'

'Surely historians could not proceed otherwise?' Esther said.

'No, of course they couldn't. I'm not saying it's wrong. Just that I'm one of the askers of questions.'

They had passed the cottages, and here the lane forked. Past the tidy gardens into the open fields beyond, or looping back towards the park.

'We'll let you go here,' Simon told his father, 'I'll give Claire a tour of the park.'

'You know,' Claire said, when she had convinced the placid but stubborn mare that they really were going the other way, 'Usually when I say 'the social structures that frame the gendered experience of history' people go '*what?*' No one in your family has done that yet.'

'Well, that could mean one of two, no, three things.'

'Being?'

'We're all incredibly clever, we were raised too politely to show we're stupid, or we've all secretly been reading up on the subject.'

'And which is it?'

'That's for you to decide. Ready to try a bit of a trot?'

After lunch, Claire meant to settle down in the garden with a book, but instead she found herself wandering through the house. When Simon had said he was going to help his aunt get in the weekly shopping, she had grabbed her book and sunscreen and said, 'You go, I'll just find a quiet corner to work on my tan.' After a pretty dismal summer the weather had turned hot and sunny, and she intended to make the most of it. But on her way to the garden she passed a corridor she hadn't been down yet, and she thought she might as well take the long way around. She felt strangely privileged, to be left alone in a house like this, to wander at will. It was a place of browns and goldens, of deep shadows alternating with blocks of yellow sunlight. The passage led to the long gallery, which she had seen before. Rooms opened off this on one side, while the windows looked down on the open-sided quadrangle which it formed with the two long wings.

Snatches of conversation held her briefly as she passed, bits of music drifting from doors and windows, lingering on the still air.

'All right Titus, just this once.'

...tu rondine ca rundini lu mare...

'I am sure nobody saw me.'

'Oh, come on, Judy, don't be a spoilsport.'

It was a time, when silly bees would speak...

Dreamily, Claire rounded a corner and made her way down the corridor of the east wing. Some voices she recognised, but most were just disembodied fragments, and she rather liked that.

'Have you seen young Simon today?'

'... might have been better with a few peppers.'

'I'll speak to Solly, just in case.'

'Claire, are you lost?'

She snapped out of her reverie and focused on the man standing in front of her. Simon, as near as dammit, only at least twenty years older.

'No, no,' she told Simon's father hurriedly, 'I thought I'd go out by the garden doors at the end of the passage.' She hoped she had remembered right, and there *were* garden doors at the end of the passage. She waved *The Sense of an Ending*, to show she had a serious purpose.

'It's good to have you with us again, Claire. Our Simon is a lucky man.'

'I'm a lucky woman,' she said awkwardly. She felt acutely conscious of the fact that she was dressed only in a skimpily cut top and shorts. It would have been all right in the garden, in a deckchair with her sunglasses on, but here in the shadowy corridor she felt exposed. Not that he was ogling her, or anything, he just looked intently at her face.

'Did you have a good journey from France?' she blurted. She never thought to ask the question this morning. Why did this man make her so uneasy?

'What? Oh yes, fine, fine.'

He walked with her to the end of the passage in silence.

'Do you like it here?' he asked, as she reached the doorway that was her escape into the sunny, outside world. It sounded like a real question, not just politeness.

'Very much.'

Why did everyone ask that question so insistently? she wondered, as she found her deckchair and settled down. Were they really vetting her for the position of daughter-in-law? And did it really matter so much? Yes, she had entertained the fantasy of coming to live in this wonderful house, and it must have shown. But she would think very carefully indeed before she ever gave up her London flat.

For now, this just looked to her like the perfect place for a holiday. Especially in such glorious weather...

'Enjoying yourself?'

She opened her eyes. How long had he been standing there? Not as long as she had been asleep, probably.

'*You* seem to be.'

'You look lovely.' Simon settled boyishly in the grass at her feet and ran a finger down her bare leg. It set off goosebumpy tingles in quite unrelated places.

'Hmm, I could lie here forever.'

'You can, if you want. But I suppose it gets boring after a century or two,' he said.

'You've been here for centuries, haven't you? So tell me some family history,' she asked him, 'There must be lots of it. Did you come over with the conqueror?'

He rested his head against her knee. 'Not quite. And we never did anything spectacular, really.'

'No?' she teased, running her fingers through his hair, 'Not one of your ancestors captured a Spanish galleon for Elizabeth? Or discussed strategy with Wellington before Waterloo?'

'You're winding me up,' he grinned, 'You're always telling me things like that do not make history.'

'You're learning. But I am interested, you know. I'm interested in your family.'

And I think your family is just a bit too interested in me. But that could wait.

11

'Let me get this straight,' the inspector said, 'You think these people were killed because they were historians?'

Put baldly like that, it did sound a bit feeble, Dominic had to admit. He wondered if this was where he got thrown out for wasting police time. But the inspector still looked slightly more curious than furious.

'Not exactly,' Dominic said, 'They were a specific kind of historian.'

Detective Inspector Collins wasn't what he had been expecting. He'd been thinking in terms of the middle-aged, divorced, hard-bitten copper, probably drinking more than he should. In contrast, Collins looked remarkably fresh for someone with a murder on his plate. Also remarkably young. He was certainly younger than Dominic, probably just his side of thirty. He wore a beautiful grey summer suit, but the air of business-like efficiency this exuded was counteracted somewhat by the extreme untidiness of his office. He had carefully pointed Dominic towards a chair with its back to a disturbing set of crime-scene pictures. 'Mr Walsingham? Owen Collins, County CID. Take a seat.'

He had shaken the inspector's hand, introduced himself, taken the proffered seat. Then he had hesitantly launched into his story. Collins had listened patiently, and summed it up pretty efficiently when he reached the end.

'Yes,' Dominic said now, 'They were all historians of the Chapter of St Cloud. And they were all killed before they could publish anything on the order.'

Dominic's search through old newspapers at the city archive that morning had taught him that in Alice Wright's case there had been a suspect, but the man was released due to lack of proof. The name stuck in Dominic's mind, and convinced him that he was right to be here, even if the DI was doubtful. It was the same name as that of the seventeenth century abbot of the chapter. He put this rather weak argument before the inspector.

'It's quite a common name around here, Danvers,' Collins said. He was probably too polite to say 'there's three centuries in between'.

'Look, Mr Walsingham,' he went on, 'I'm prepared to admit that there may be a connection between these murders, it *is* a bit of a coincidence. On the other hand, there may have been a very different motive for each. I'm sure you can see there is little I can do about it now. Twenty-five and sixty years may be yesterday to an historian, but to a simple copper that's just a long time.'

But you're not just a simple copper, are you? Dominic thought, or I would have been shown the door already.

'I thought murder didn't age?' he asked.

'Maybe not, but murderers do.'

Dominic almost said 'this one doesn't', but stopped himself just in time. He could tell Collins was taking this as seriously as his time and training would allow, and he shouldn't push it. 'I'm sure Barry Skinner's family and friends are still alive. Did anyone ever make a connection with the chapter back then?'

The inspector heaved an audible sigh. 'You are right to think that an unsolved murder case is never truly closed. But you must also realise that I have a recent case that needs attention much more urgently. I'll see if I can drag up the Skinner file. That's all I can promise you.'

'Then will you let me know if you are quite sure the chapter had nothing to do with it?' Dominic rose, correctly interpreting this as a dismissal.

'Of course. And Mr Walsingham?' Collins added, as they shook hands again, 'Do be careful. No book is worth its writer's life.'

He felt unexpectedly cheerful when he got home. The interview with the detective had gone better than he had hoped. At least he hadn't been laughed out of court, and Collins looked a reliable sort of chap. Of course he had been right in his parting words, and until now Dominic had fully planned to heed his warning and leave the Chapter of St Cloud for what it was until he was quite sure there was no danger. But now he thought: fuck that! I'm not going to be dissuaded so easily. If the chapter did not want to be investigated, the more reason to do so. Wondering vaguely why he suddenly felt so light-hearted, he changed the solemn church music in his CD player – he would get enough of that tonight – for something folksy and Italian. Maybe it was just that he had had a chance to talk about it all. Made him see things in perspective. He was almost beginning to think it wasn't serious enough to have added to the inspector's workload. But then if he hadn't, he would still be worried about it, so that line of reasoning ate its own tail. Laughing at himself, he popped a pizza in the oven and turned on his computer to check his email.

First he read his mother's weekly missive. She had moved back to the Netherlands after his father died, but she always kept in close touch with both her children. Her email reminded Dominic that he hadn't spoken to Saskia for a while, and he made a note to send his sister a long message soon. There was also an email from Claire

Althorpe saying that she heard he'd moved, and that she was staying in the neighbourhood. Time for a drink, perhaps? He didn't answer that one right away. He never really knew where he was with Claire. He got the feeling she disapproved pretty strongly of the kind of history he wrote. On the other hand, she was great in her field, and she might be helpful on St Cloud's female houses. He realised that with looking so hard for published material, he had rather neglected other sources of information about the chapter. On an impulse, he wrote an email to James Sutherland, asking for the address of the student who had given up his Ph.D. project in favour of teaching. He might have made quite extensive notes. And Dominic wouldn't mind asking him why, exactly, he had not continued his research.

The oven gave a discreet 'ping!' to tell him his pizza was ready, and he realised he was both hungry and tired. It had been a busy day, with his unplanned trip to Oxford and his visit to the station. And there was choir practice still to come.

'A bit unsteady there, Dominic,' Michael Taylor said, 'Are you paying attention? Let's go through it again.'

Deus salutis meæ: et exsultābit lingua mea justítiam tuam... The choir master was right, Dominic's thoughts were elsewhere. No matter how often Taylor told them that 'in here, there's only music', it always took a while before he could concentrate fully on the singing. And he had reason enough to feel distracted.

'*Exsultaaaabit*,' Taylor sang, 'That's a long 'a', gentlemen, please. Right, again from the beginning of the phrase.'

Līberā me de sanguinibus, Deus, Deus salutis meæ...

'When we practice together with St Oda's choir next Saturday, I do not want to have to pay attention to this,' Michael said sternly, 'As I will have enough other things to pay attention to. Let's sing it through one more time, and then it's enough for today.'

Miserere mei, Deus...

'Dominic, wait a moment,' the choir master said, as the others filed out of the quire to go home. 'Are you quite all right? It's not like you to be so absentminded. At least not after the coffee break.'

'Yes, I'm fine,' Dominic tried to reassure him, 'I've run into some trouble with my research, that's all.' And he did feel fine, the music and the church had done their work, as usual.

Taylor looked as if he didn't quite believe it. 'I hope it sorts itself out, then.'

'It will, it probably will.'

It was nice of Michael to be so concerned. The choir master had gone out of his way to make him welcome when he joined three months ago, and Dominic had never been sure whether that was because he was relatively young and therefore a welcome addition to the choir, or because Michael Taylor had another kind of interest in him entirely. He'd kept his distance, as a result. He was a bit ashamed of that now.

While he was walking home Dominic noticed a man crossing the street behind him. He was sure he had seen the same fellow earlier, loitering in the Close. He had noticed him, checked him out, the way you did. And now here he was again. He hoped he hadn't been too obvious, he wasn't looking for that kind of encounter. But as Dominic opened his front door, the man passed behind him without a second glance, and got into a red Vauxhall parked a little further along the street. There was a prominent rental company sticker on the doors. Just a tourist then, who had been having a look at the church. Couldn't fault a man for that. Dominic went in, eager to see if James had answered his email yet.

12

It's happened before, of course. That's what you get when you live a long time, you get to the point where everything has happened before. You get to the point where even acknowledging the fact becomes habitual. You forget that for younger generations, this time round is still new and urgent.

The abbot thought about this as he observed the prior dealing with things. That's what the prior did, and did well. He dealt, he managed, he handled. He made the decisions weaker minds shied away from, and was admired for it. Had it always been thus, from the very beginning? The Rule said that under the abbot there was a prior as second-in-command, the abbot caring for the spiritual needs of the chapter and the prior for the secular. But priors came and went, and the division was not always that clear-cut. Tension between abbot and prior was nothing new, either. So the abbot was not surprised when one of the brothers came to speak to him in private, soon after his conversation with the prior.

'Tell me everything,' he commanded.

'I don't *know* everything,' Brother Stephen complained, 'That is what I wished to talk to you about. Apparently, there is a threat to our secrecy. Sarah says so, but of course *he* will not trust me with it. What's he planning?'

'Are you sure you wish to know?' the abbot asked him.

'No!'

It took the abbot a moment to realise that this was not an answer to his question, but a protest against its implications.

'No, it can't be that bad,' Stephen said, 'Not again. Surely he won't.'

'I am afraid he will, if he believes it necessary.'

Oh, the weasel words of it. No one, hearing this conversation, could tell what, exactly, they suspected the prior of planning. But that was always the way of it. The prior had his responsibility, and it was not theirs.

'We must protect the younger ones,' Stephen said, 'They can't know of this, father.'

'I agree. But let's not be hasty. We may forestall this, if we are careful. We may do some dealing of our own.'

He outlined his plan, so much simpler and milder than the prior's machinations.

They can't know of this! had been that early brother's cry, too, when he learned the secrets of the abbey. Dear Lothar. He had been horrified by where his convictions led him, but yet with the courage to carry them through. He had dissembled before Charlemagne himself, he had been a master of words, never betraying his unbelief. For that was the creed of the Chapter of St Cloud, brought into being by the death of two young princes: *there is no life but this life and we must strive to keep it*. This had been a shocking thought in an age of almost universal belief, they had been heretics before heresy was even thought of. They had been alone so long in this conviction that the abbot still found it strange that these days, most people shared it. Strange, also, that most people instead of a promised life eternal just accepted the inevitability of death. It didn't follow at all, as Lothar had so clearly seen. If this life is all there is, then we must hold onto it above all else, and that had always been the chapter's aim. Heresy and hubris. Such sins they had been, in the eyes of the church. But there was no concept of sin in the Rule of the chapter, though there had always been, and always would be, responsibility. Lothar's words still survived, in their much-copied uncial and later Gothic guises, and now in scholarly editions. He was always cited together with Theodulf and Alcuin, whom he knew and exchanged views with at the emperor's bright court, a scholar among scholars. It was easy to miss what wasn't there: nowhere in his ornate Latin did Lothar refer to the life to come. Already the chapter's thoughts were only for this life, already the abbot's days were long. Lothar died, his brothers died, and that pain was never mitigated by a fantasy of heaven.

13

DC Dasgupta waved a file at him. 'Pathologist's report, sir.'

'Just in time, give it here.'

He was on his way to see his boss, but he quickly leafed through the file to see if there was anything exceptional. He needed to see the DCI in full possession of the facts. But there was little in it of interest. The cause of death was blindingly obvious, and that the victim had been in excellent health was now sadly irrelevant.

'Morning, ma'am,' he said, entering his superior's office.

'Good morning, Collins.' She continued typing for a moment. DCI Flynn was a small, exceptionally neat woman with expensively cut grey hair. Her first name was Bridget, and she was known among her colleagues as 'old Biddy', but never to her face. She wasn't old at all, he put her at forty-five or thereabouts, and Collins always thought they might have been friendly if they hadn't had a slightly prickly work relationship. Bridget Flynn liked order, and she thought her DI's methods unnecessarily chaotic. He could never convince her that, in his head, he had it all sorted. Investigations took a certain shape where the DCI got increasingly impatient at his complete lack of progress, right until the moment when he suddenly collared a suspect. She never believed that he, too, could only explain how he got there afterwards.

'Right, that's done,' she said, 'The Chief Super is on to me again about statistics. You'd think statistics were the be-all and end-all of Her Majesty's police force, to hear him talk.'

'I'm afraid the violent crime stats have gone up by one,' he said.

'As long as the solved murder cases also go up by one,' she said. 'Will they?'

'I hope so.'

'So what have we got?'

He rapidly filled her in on the Whiteside case. 'I've got a strange feeling about this,' he concluded, very glad that Sergeant Walter wasn't there to hear him say it. 'It doesn't fit any picture I've seen before.'

Not that DCI Flynn was inclined to give him much quarter.

'Collins, a long tradition of fictional detectives notwithstanding, we're not paying you to have feelings. This is a criminal investigation. Investigate.'

Yes, Ma'am.

'Ma'am? If I wanted to look at a file from years ago, the mid-eighties, where would I look?'

'Why would you want to do that?'

'Just something that caught my attention.' He had learned by now that she didn't always push it if he refused to answer. She gave him a slightly exasperated look. 'You look it up in the computer, like you would a recent file, note down the number and ask the desk sergeant for the keys to the cellar.'

Walter and Dasgupta were questioning the people on Jim's list, to see if any of them were connected to the victim. Sergeant Pardoe was interviewing neighbours. Holmes was in the Hollow Crown, talking to Whiteside's colleagues. Collins spent the entire afternoon going through the events of last Sunday with the boy's parents, hoping to find a clue, a chink in the story, something that did not fit. They returned to the station one by one, filed their statements, filled in reports.

'The landlord nearly socked me one, when I suggested Sean might have been on the bend,' Sally said.

'He gets violent, does he?' Dasgupta asked.

'I said 'nearly'. Anyway, he didn't pull a gun on me.'

'And *was* he on the bend?'

'I don't think so. He seems to have been a pretty straight bloke.'

'Apart from the drugs.'

'Yeah, but if we locked up every student who got some pills for himself and his friends, we might as well merge the prisons and the universities. Right, that's it for today, I think.' She pushed back her chair and stretched. 'I'm going to catch some sun while it's here. Anyone coming for a drink?'

'Can't,' Pardoe said glumly, 'We're having my sister-in-law over for dinner.' It was clear he would have preferred a pint in a pub.

Sally and Chandra were already on their feet. 'Sir?' she said, 'Are you coming? I think we'd better not make it the Hollow Crown, though.'

'Just a moment, Sally. You grew up here, didn't you? Does the name Danvers mean anything to you?' Collins asked her.

'I've read *Rebecca*, sir.'

'We had a teacher at the comp called Danvers,' Chandra recalled, 'Took me years to figure out why everyone called her 'Mrs' even though she wasn't married.'

'Why do you ask?' Sally wanted to know.

'Oh, just something that came up today. It was a long shot anyway. Enjoy your drinks.'

'You're not joining us?'

It was tempting, but Owen had looked up the number of the Skinner file, and had asked the desk sergeant for the keys to the cellar. 'Some other time,' he said regretfully, 'Got some things to do first.'

The look DC Holmes gave him had a lot in common with that of Bridget Flynn earlier in the day.

What's got into me? he asked himself as he carried the buff-coloured folder up to his desk. Sally was right, he should be out in the sunshine. But he had promised Mr Walsingham he'd have a look at the file, and here it was. He had promised only because there was nothing else he could do – even if there was something in it, it struck him as too outré and nebulous a matter ever to bring to court. No use wasting his time on, so why? Maybe because his detective's mind had noticed just enough oddities to command his attention. It seemed to him absurdly convenient, for example, that they had Barry Skinner's file in the archives here. Alice Wright was killed in nearby Oxford. Danvers was a local name. And the site of the medieval priory of St Bernard, which Mr Walsingham assured him had belonged to the chapter in a way he couldn't quite follow, lay just west of town. It seemed to be a local matter. On the other hand – how many hands did he need for this case? – he had very little experience of murdering monks, so perhaps it was best to keep an open mind. He started reading the file from the top and soon forgot all about sunshine in a familiar routine.

14

Simon was still asleep. He looked like a movie-still, all youthful glow and tangled sheets. Claire had woken early, moved quietly to open the curtains and let the early sunlight in. It looked set to be perfect. She leant against the windowsill, enjoying the sun on her naked shoulders, and looked at Simon. He really could sleep like the dead. Was that something only men did? She would definitely have woken up if someone walked around her bedroom opening windows, not to mention pulling the chain of the noisy lav next-door. And the birds were staging a riot out there. Claire felt like going out. Should she wake him, wait for him? She quickly pulled on a skirt and top, still undecided. Simon made a small snorting sound and turned over, rolling onto his stomach and taking the sheets with him, as if determined even in sleep to give her the best view. She smiled at his unconscious boyishness and went out, closing the door firmly behind her.

She ran lightly down the stairs. There were voices coming from the kitchen, but she ignored them. She wanted to get outside while there was still dew on the grass.

'Also going for a walk?'

She looked around to find Anna, in a summer dress and sandals, selecting a straw boater from the hat stand in the hallway.

'That was the idea. It's such a lovely day.'

'Shall we walk together? Or would you rather be alone? – I shan't mind either way.'

'Oh, let's walk together. You can point out the interesting bits for me. It's just that I didn't want to wake Simon, anyway.'

'Is he still like that? When he was a teenager he sometimes couldn't be roused till after midday.'

They went out by the garden doors of what was grandly called the morning room.

'What was he like, as a child?' Claire asked curiously. Surprisingly, with so many female relatives around, she had as yet been spared the family album.

'Oh, very much like Titus is now. You think they're just boys, doing the things boys do, and then suddenly they come out with something clever and you know they're just adults waiting to happen.'

What an odd way to put it, Claire thought. Did Anna regret having children so young? Were her books a way of living a lost youth? One of her novels was called *Two Is Company* – but she lived in a crowd.

'It goes so fast,' Anna continued, 'Remember that Claire, when you have children of your own. Enjoy every moment. They are gone before you know it.'

She must be thinking of her other son, Claire thought. No one had told her yet what had happened to him.

A set of steps led down from the formal garden into an unexpected multitude of rose bushes. Claire lingered by a Hybrid Tea, wondering if she could ask.

'Anna, why did you marry so young? Don't get me wrong, I'm glad you did, or there would be no Simon for me. But all my friends' parents are older.'

'Because *my* Simon ever so charmingly insisted we should. And we were very much in love. It wasn't as if I had to either. Young Simon was born a whole decorous year after the wedding.'

Claire laughed. 'I understand. And they can be charming, can't they, those Simons?'

'Oh yes. They all have it, this way with people. Even Titus, he's everyone's pet. And Judith has got boys coming out her ears.'

'I can imagine that.'

It occurred to Claire that within the larger family, Simon's parents actually led entirely separate lives. His father had returned from France two days ago, but she had not seen him and Anna together even at dinner. They might have been very much in love twenty-five or more years ago, but she doubted they were still. They walked in silence for a bit. The rose garden smelled wet and sweet now, but there was a hint of something else in the air, something that would turn heavy and rotten in the sunlight. Claire was glad they had come here in the early morning, or she would have found it oppressive.

'Wasn't it strange, becoming part of this family?'

Anna snapped off a blown rose and looked at her, almost conspiratorially. She must know why I'm asking *that*, Claire thought. But then, Simon had made his intentions pretty clear by bringing her here, so what the hell.

'Strange, yes,' Anna replied, 'But also very nice. I came from a large family myself – four girls – but that was very different. I was used to always being Emma-Sophie-Jilly-oh it's you. And here suddenly everyone made a fuss of me. It was different, though, back then. More formal and old-fashioned, like you would expect in a house like that.' She gestured behind her, and a few orange petals drifted away. 'I think maybe I left more of a mark on my kids than Edie did on hers.'

'Looks like you did a good job.'

Anna's mouth curled in a small, almost sad smile.

'If I hadn't seen the way you look at Simon, I'd say you were flattering me.'

'I mean it,' Claire said, 'Not just Simon, you should be proud of your children.'

'Oh, I am. I am.' Anna dropped the wilting bloom and set off again, leading the way through a shadowy trellis. 'So tell me about your family, Claire. Do you have brothers and sisters?'

'Just a younger sister. Francesca. We were never close, but things got better when we grew up. In fact, we get along very well now.'

Claire thought of Gina's prickly relationship with her mother-in-law, of Bryony's formal cordiality towards hers. And here she was talking to Anna almost as she would to Gina or Bry. As if they were friends. They walked back towards the house in comfortable silence.

She was soaking in the bath when a tinny rendition of *O frondens virga* alerted her to a call.

'Hey Claire, it's Bryony.'

'Bry! How are you? You know I'm staying with Simon, right?'

'Yes, yes, I know. I'm fine. Look, about staying with Simon. I wanted to say, I mean, I wanted to ask you something.'

She sounded strangely hesitant, for Bryony.

'What's wrong?'

'Has he told you how old he is?'

So it was about that. 'I haven't asked. Look, I know you and Julia think I'm a bit of a cradle-snatcher, but it's not–'

'He was at school with Luke,' Bryony interrupted, 'You know, Paul's brother. That's why he was at the wedding. They were best mates. Luke's only twenty-one, Claire.'

Oh.

'Fuck.' Claire said quietly.

'Well, *that's* legal,' Bryony said, apparently relieved to have got it off her chest. 'I thought you should know, I mean, if you didn't know already.'

'Yes, yes you're right Bry. Thanks, I suppose. I'll have to think about this.'

'Of course. You'll be all right, Claire.'

It wasn't clear whether that was a question and Claire didn't know what to answer if it was.

15

It was weeks yet before term began, but today Dominic had his first meeting with his colleagues to go over the lecture and tutorial roster, and divide administrative duties. He was looking forward to teaching his courses, but he wondered if there was any teacher, anywhere, who enjoyed the administrative side. While he was putting fresh pencils and his new teacher's diary in his bag, his phone rang. He didn't recognise the number. One of his new colleagues?

'Mr Walsingham? It's DI Collins. We spoke yesterday.'

'Of course.'

'I wondered if we could meet again. I have some information that may interest you.'

Dominic imagined that that was a sentence the DI was more often on the receiving end of. 'Of course,' he said again, 'When do you suggest?'

'I'm meeting someone at two in Costa, on Market Street. Could you be there at three?'

He suppressed another 'of course' and managed, 'I'll be there.'

'Right. I'll see you then.' The inspector rang off without explaining further.

Having to be in the town centre at three would mean ending his meeting with his colleagues tightly on schedule, but that wasn't a bad thing. These meetings always ran on, he was glad to have his excuse to leave on hand. Singing under his breath, he slung his bag over his shoulder and left the house.

He ran into James Sutherland on his way to the faculty office, and of course James wanted to know how his work on St Cloud was coming along. For a moment, Dominic didn't know what to say. James was a fine scholar and a good teacher, but he had no imagination and little interest in the world outside his subject. To tell him of his suspicions about the chapter was out of the question. Dominic could already hear his reply: 'a bit far-fetched, don't you think?'

'It's not coming along as well as I'd hoped,' he said instead, 'I don't wonder that student of yours gave it up. Thanks for giving me the address, by the way.'

'Have you been to the Bibliothèque Nationale yet?' his old teacher asked, 'You know they have Charlemagne's original grant of land to the abbey. 811, if I'm not mistaken.'

'Yes, I know,' Dominic said glumly, 'It's about the only year we do know for sure. And no, I haven't been yet. It's interesting, but it's not going to be of much use.'

'I suppose not. It was the time Lothar of St Cloud was active, though. It could help build up a picture.'

'Do you know anyone who could tell me more about Lothar? I'm afraid the Carolingian renaissance passed me by, rather.'

'There's Helen Woods at Cornell,' James suggested, 'One of the very few people in the world who understand bilingual puns in Frankish and late Latin.'

It didn't exactly strike Dominic as the kind of ability he needed here, but he noted down the name.

Even with an excuse, getting away on time proved difficult, and when he pushed open the door of Costa Coffee it was three exactly and Dominic was slightly out of breath. He spotted the inspector at once, at a table in a corner. It looked like his companion was just leaving. He was a young man dressed in jeans that barely covered his buttocks, giving a generous view of sugar-pink underpants before his tight grey t-shirt began. It wasn't a style Dominic admired, but a boy like that could handle it, he thought, as he lingered just a little so he could hold open the door for him. The boy said 'cheers' and threw him a knowing smile. What was the inspector doing entertaining this apparition to tea?

'Criminal?' he asked, pulling out the chair the boy had just vacated.

'Ah, there you are. You'd be surprised. Or maybe not. He doesn't exactly look innocent, does he?'

Unsure how to interpret this, Dominic tried to get back on a professional footing. Surely a look from that boy shouldn't throw him like this?

'Why did you want to see me?' he asked brusquely.

'I read the file on Barry Skinner, like I said. Took some finding too. Look, will I get you some tea? It's on the taxpayer.'

Dominic offered to go to the counter himself, but Collins wouldn't hear of it. The DI returned a minute later with a pot of tea and a piece of shortbread, which he set down on the table between them. 'Jake – the boy you just saw – insists I buy him these. I think it's because then he doesn't have to eat at all the rest of the week.'

Dominic saw his point. He knew this stuff. Thickly covered with caramel and chocolate, the shortbread was a good way to keep him quiet while the inspector talked.

'The investigation into Skinner's death was a bit of a mess, as far as I can tell,' Collins told him, 'Apparently the police at the time went mob-handed after a roommate who couldn't be tracked down immediately. They pulled him in when found, only to realise that what they'd got was a very upset boyfriend with a firm alibi. Reading between the lines, I think the inspector in charge would have liked to bang him up just for being gay, but he was thirty years late for that. They had nothing else to go on. Skinner had no enemies, no debts, no record. Some cases are like that. I don't think anyone specifically looked at his research, it just says 'history' in the file. So I'm afraid I can give you nothing conclusive there.'

He could easily have said all this on the phone. Surely there was more. Dominic licked his fingers. 'So there's nothing to connect his death to the chapter?'

'Nothing that we know of. So I can't help you with Skinner, unless I go a whole lot deeper. But there was that other thing you mentioned, the suspect in Alice Wright's case. Danvers. You said it was the same name as the – was it seventeenth century? – abbot of the chapter. I asked a colleague in the district to do a little digging for me. He found a picture of the man they arrested over Wright.' He put a print-out of a black-and-white photo on the table. 'And I knew there was a notable Danvers I'd come across myself once, took me a while to figure out. I attended Abbey Hill school in my teens. It was founded as a boys' school early in the nineteenth century by one Barnaby Danvers. And this is a picture of the headmaster in Alfred Poole's time, Samuel of that name.' A second picture joined the first. Dominic moved his napkin out of the way.

'It looks–' he began. The inspector held up a hand. 'Wait, there's more. As I said, the name Danvers is quite common around here. We must have had Flemish textile workers over at some point. So looking for people of that name gets you a whole tribe. But there was another curious case, back in the twenties, the apparent suicide of a 19-year-old woman called Evangeline Danvers. I only know because Sally – one of my DC's – had read about it in a book. She called me last night to tell me she'd remembered. Do your realise you've got half of CID chasing your shadows?'

I do believe he's actually interested, Dominic thought, the attempt at severity didn't quite work.

'Sorry,' he said. And contrition didn't come off very well either. 'But what has this Evangeline got to do with it?'

'This is a picture of her brother. Now you tell me what it means.'

It wasn't completely unexpected, but he couldn't believe it even so. All three pictures showed what was unmistakably the same face. A handsome, serious-looking man, perhaps in his thirties or early forties, with dark hair and sharp cheekbones. Dominic drank his tea. 'Well?' the DI said.

Perhaps it was time to introduce Inspector Collins to one of the wilder myths about the Chapter of St Cloud. 'Inspector, have you ever heard of Nathaniel Cottington?'

Collins raised his eyebrows a little. 'Let's pretend I haven't.' Dominic decided he must be enjoying this.

'He was a clergyman active in the 1650s, who wrote some influential pamphlets against Catholicism, and not to be discriminate about it, various other -isms that weren't straightforwardly Puritan. He wasn't quite John Knox, but close. This was a time not only of religious, but also of many other kinds of fervour, and besides theologians' pamphlets, the printers were turning out those of astrologers and alchemists and even fledgling scientists.

Somehow, and it isn't clear where the rumour started, it got about that the alchemists of the Worshipful Society of Philosophers of St Cloud had managed to produce the elixir of life, and soon this was appearing in print as practically fact. The Society of Philosophers was closely allied to the religious, *Catholic* Chapter of St Cloud, and Nathaniel Cottington felt it incumbent on him to denounce their godless practices. He announced a pamphlet *Against the Monstrous Idolaters of the Order called St Cloud etc. etc.* The title runs on for a page. But it never got any further than that, because Cottington died in a fire in his home shortly after the manuscript had been promised to the printer. All his papers burned with him.'

DI Collins leaned back in his chair and crossed his arms. 'You should be writing novels.'

'The thought had occurred to me, yes. I'm not telling you because I think he was murdered, but because of the rumours surrounding the chapter. Somehow, whether encouraged by the chapter or not, the idea spread that the abbot was immortal. That every generation's abbot was in fact the same man, and had been from the beginning. Alfred Poole mentions it, dismissively. Even Alice Wright paid special attention to the visionary of Paris's thoughts on immortality. Rumours about the abbot apart, eternal life is something that always gets associated with St Cloud. And now you show me three pictures of the same man taken decades apart, all bearing the name of the abbot.'

'You're not seriously suggesting...?'

Dominic wasn't sure what he was suggesting. He needed time to think about this.

'Something needs explaining. You must think so too. Why else did you put so much time into this? I thought you had a murder to investigate.'

'That's easy,' Collins said glibly, 'Because I am as stuck as the poor sod who got Barry Skinner. That's why I had to see Jake, just now. See what the word on the street is.'

'On the street?' Jake hadn't looked especially down-and-out.

'Not literally. Jake is a pricey escort with a side-line in various pills and powders. We have reason to believe our murder victim was a dealer, so I thought Jake might have heard something.'

So that meeting had been professional. 'Isn't he awfully young?'

'Nineteen, he says, and I have no reason to disbelieve him. Look, I shouldn't be talking about the case. What about your immortal abbot?'

'I think–' Dominic began, but he got no further, because the DI's phone interrupted. Collins answered, listened, replied in terse sentences. His words gave nothing away, but his face showed Dominic something was badly wrong.

'I have to go,' he said, snapping his phone shut. 'I'm sorry. Police work.'

Watching him walk away, Dominic wondered what this had been, then.

16

It was a girl this time. Lying in her own blood, just like Whiteside had been, dead of a single shot. Collins stood looking down at her, not blaming DC Dasgupta for walking straight out again. You didn't get used to it, whatever they said. He would be suspicious of anyone who did. Violent deaths, young deaths, they just weren't right.

'Lisa Wilson,' DS Walter said behind him, 'Nineteen years old. Sociology student. Girl upstairs found her. Pardoe is on his way to inform the parents.'

Thank God for small mercies, Collins thought. Pardoe was an old-fashioned sergeant who wouldn't make a hash of that, at least. Two scene of crime people were busy inside the room, and the pathologist had just left, giving permission for the body to be moved. The room was small, and he could smell the blood.

'Any idea of the time?' he asked the DS.

'Sometime this morning seems likely, but you know the pathologist won't say until she's sure.'

'Was she interfered with?' the constable asked from the doorway.

Collins bit back on 'apart from a bullet through her lungs, you mean?'

It was what the journalists would ask, it was what her parents would want to know. The question always got to him. The prurience of it. The suggestion that murder wasn't appalling enough by itself. The way it was never asked when the victim was male. But he was relieved when Walter shook his head.

'Pathologist says unlikely. She's fully dressed and there's no sign of a struggle. Someone just walked in and shot her, then walked out again.'

Walter didn't say it, but Collins knew they were all thinking the same thing. Just like Whiteside. They couldn't know there was a connection, there might not be one, but the resemblance was too great to ignore.

'You've organised door-to-door?'

'Called in uniformed right away. Her flatmates are in the sitting room downstairs, the one who found her and three other girls. Sally's with them.'

'Well, let's go and talk to them.'

He sent the friend who found the body away with Walter and DC Holmes to give her statement, while he talked to the other three himself. He looked around the kitchen at their tear-blotched young faces. 'Ashley, Devi and Selina, have I got that right? I'm very sorry for your loss. We will need to take a statement from each of you separately, but there's no hurry. Right now, I would like you to tell me anything you can about this morning, and anything you can about Lisa. Don't be afraid to mention things that seem silly, or to go over things twice. Anything might be important.'

By some mysterious process Selina was elected spokeswoman, and she told him flatly that they had all been out that morning.

'So Lisa was alone in the house? Did you notice anything strange, before you left? Was Lisa acting like she normally did?'

'Yes, insofar as none of us saw her. She always slept late when she could,' Selina said.

'I saw her last night,' her quieter friend added, 'She was okay. Tired, cheerful. She was looking forward to the party on Thursday.' She started to cry.

Selina put an arm around her. 'Inspector, do we have to talk about this now?'

'If you would. You may recall things now that you won't remember later.'

'I'm all right,' Devi sniffed.

Gradually, with many interruptions, a picture emerged. The other girls had all gone out that morning, to work, to meet friends. They hadn't seen or spoken to Lisa, who they knew not to disturb until late. As far as they could tell there had been nothing strange in her behaviour recently, and she hadn't had strange callers or received any threats she told them of. She was an average student, liked to party, got along with her mates. She was mixed up in nothing dangerous, and her friends vehemently insisted that no one could have wanted to kill her. This was so obviously untrue that he did not comment on it. He was reminded not so much of Sean Whiteside as of the Barry Skinner case, who had been similarly without enemies twenty-five years ago. 'Some cases are like that' he had told Walsingham. He fiercely hoped this one wasn't. He almost asked the girls if the name St Cloud meant anything to them, but desisted. No need to get fanciful, he wasn't that desperate. Yet.

'There's one thing, though,' the girl called Devi said hesitantly.

He stayed silent, waiting.

'Lisa was selling drugs,' she said in a rush, 'Pills. I saw them. People came for them sometimes. She offered me some, but I wouldn't touch them.'

The two other girls were glaring at their friend. They had known, he thought, and hadn't been going to mention it.

'What kind of pills, can you tell me? You won't get into trouble.'

Devi shook her head, but Selina spoke up again. 'All right, I had some. Cool stuff, it was. Lisa was making a mint, but I don't know where she got it, or what it was called. It was something new.'

And finally Ashley opened her mouth. 'It was called Oblivion.'

So there it was, the connection.

17

She seriously considered calling him on his mobile, it would beat charging down the grand staircase while he might at the same time be leisurely climbing the backstairs. But she didn't want to give him advance warning. She found him eventually in a room she had never seen before, a kind of mini-library on the second floor. He was talking to one of his aunts, who got up and left when she saw Claire's face.

'Ah, there you are,' Simon said, as if she hadn't been looking for him all over. 'Enjoy your bath?' He smiled, obviously glad to see her, and she wondered how she could ever have believed this boy was over twenty-five. How stupid she had been!

'Simon, I have to ask you something.' And she wasn't going to let the knowledge that she sounded like a poor actress stop her, either.

'Yes?'

'How old are you?'

He put down the book he was holding. *The Sense of an Ending* again. Hardly auspicious. 'I take it that your asking the question means you already have some idea?'

A boy, yes, but one who could sound middle-aged when he wanted to. Don't get distracted now.

'Well?' she insisted.

'I'm twenty-two.'

'And you didn't tell me. Twenty-two! Some of my students are that age.' She looked at him, so effortlessly fit, not a line on his face. So absurdly young.

'Does it really matter, Claire?' he said calmly, 'And if it does, shouldn't you tell me *your* age? I thought you were younger than your friend Bryony, but you aren't, right?'

Well, yes, she might have given the impression that she was a few years younger than she was, though she hadn't actually lied. A lot of women did, didn't they? But whoever heard of a man pretending to be older than he was?

'I'm thirty-one,' she said reluctantly, 'And I think it does matter, actually. You're only a boy.'

He was wise enough not to deny it. 'I won't always be. Claire, I've never known a girl – a woman – like you before. Will you let this ruin things for us?' He gently touched her cheek. 'I don't care what age you are. I don't think you should care what age I am. It didn't bother us when we didn't know, did it?'

She caught his hand in her own. 'Maybe not.'

It had certainly bothered Bryony and Julia, she thought, even when it had only been a few years. Her friends had been doubtful about Simon from the start. Should she have listened to them? Why hadn't she? Simon was looking at her, patiently, trustingly, waiting for her to say something, to say it was all right. She knew why she had not heeded her friends. This was Simon. He was hers. That was what mattered.

'Si, why didn't you tell me?'

'Because we had to get to this point first,' he said promptly. 'You'd never have gone out with me if you'd known from the start. I had to convince you it was worth it.'

'You *planned* it this way?'

For the first time he looked embarrassed. 'Sort of, yes. Don't get angry now.'

'I'm not. I think.' God, he looked attractive when he blushed. And after all, it was very flattering, that he'd gone to such lengths to get her. That he had put thought into it.

He laughed and leaned forward to kiss her. 'All right?'

She kissed him back. 'Oh, all right. Let's go downstairs.'

Apparently he wasn't entirely reassured, for while they went down together he continued to talk to her earnestly.

'Claire, I know things must seem strange to you here. I know we're a weird family in some ways. But it doesn't matter, it shouldn't matter. All that matters is you and me.'

'I don't think you're strange,' she protested. Where did that suddenly come from?

'You don't know us very well yet.'

'*Now* you've got me worried. Have you all lied about your age?' she joked.

Before he could react to this, his sister came running up the stairs, looking agitated. She passed them without a word.

'Judy? Hey, what's wrong?' Simon shouted after her.

'Nothing,' she called back, without stopping on her way up.

A middle-aged woman came up behind her at a slower pace. 'You young people, always charging about.'

'Do you know what's up with Judith, aunt Dorrie?'

'I think she knew that girl who was killed. She's upset about it. Wouldn't you be?'

'What girl?' Simon and Claire chorused.

'This student who was shot. Lisa something. Judy was at school with her, I think she said.'

'I hadn't heard,' Claire said, 'How terrible. Do they know who did it?'

'Not a clue,' she said almost cheerfully, before continuing on her way up.

'Do I know aunt Dorrie?' Claire asked, when she judged the woman was out of earshot.

'She lives in the porter's lodge with her husband Joe,' Simon explained, 'It's quite possible you haven't been introduced yet. Did you hear what she said? 'you young people' – seems we're all tarred with the same brush.'

Claire wasn't listening. 'That poor girl though. I want to know about her. Let's find a newspaper.'

'I'm doing a book signing in town tomorrow,' Anna announced, 'You remember, Simon? I wondered if you two would like to come along.'

Claire looked up from teach-yourself-Italian. They were sitting in Simon's parents' living room. It was the first time Claire actually saw his parents together, although 'together' did not seem to describe the situation very well.

'Shall we?' Simon asked her, 'You haven't seen the cathedral yet, have you?'

'Do come,' Anna insisted, 'I get so nervous about these public occasions when I've no company. And Simon can show you the town while I'm doing my authorly duty.'

'That sounds fine,' Claire said, 'I'd like to see the cathedral, and I wouldn't mind seeing a few shops.' A thought struck her. 'Would Judith like to come too? It might take her mind of...'

Anna shook her head. 'Judith has other plans tomorrow. I asked.'

'Are you coming, dad?' Simon said.

'What?' Simon senior looked up from his newspaper.

'To town tomorrow? You could give Claire your cathedral tour. Dad knows all about church buildings, more than I do,' he said to her.

'I think I'd better not,' his father said, 'We have a meeting of the board of directors tomorrow. About the boy who died.'

'That boy who was killed, what was his name? He was one of your scholarship students?' Anna asked.

'Is it really too much trouble to remember their names, Anna? He was called Sean Whiteside. So sad.'

There was an uncomfortable silence.

'How did you learn about church architecture?' Claire asked brightly.

'At my grandfather's knee,' he said, with a friendly smile in her direction. 'You must have noticed we are not an especially religious family. We gather at the breakfast table on Sundays, not in church. But we've always had a proper respect for our Christian heritage. I remember my grandfather showing me the grave of an ancestor of ours. I remember being a little boy in a big church and being... awed, I think I should call it. And in a building like that we all remain small, even when we grow up.'

'I'm curious to see it.'

Claire didn't like to admit it, but the vast spaces of medieval cathedrals did not move her much. She tried, sometimes, to clothe them in the colours they would have known when in their proper use, to see the people for whom that building had been the centre of existence. But it didn't work. All that Babel-like striving, all that heavy stone bearing down, she could not like it. Simon senior was so obviously fond of the building that she had meant not to show her dislike, but he must have seen something in her face.

'Of course, it's not to everyone's taste,' he said matter-of-factly, getting up. 'Enjoy yourselves tomorrow. Goodnight, now.'

That night, when Simon cozied up to her, she allowed him to hold her, but no more.

'You're not smarting about the age thing, are you?' he whispered into her hair.

'No.' She tucked his hand under her thigh to show him she wasn't keeping her distance. 'I'm just thoughtful, that's all.'

'Hm. I like thoughtful. What are you being thoughtful about?'

Claire reckoned that to say 'your father' would be a wrong move at this point, and tried hard to come up with something else she could be plausibly thinking of. She finally settled for 'your mother'.

'Why?' he asked.

'Is she happy, Simon? She and your father don't seem... close.' What she had really been pondering was the way Anna was so much easier to get along with, so easy to talk to, but also, maybe, just a little shallow? While she felt that Simon's reticent father saw through her without her having to say much at all.

'Simon?' she said into the silence.

'I'm thinking about what you said. They're not couple-close anymore, no. But they are part of the same family. And I think they understand each other very well.'

This answer brought so many new things to be thoughtful about that Claire settled her head against Simon's shoulder and pretended to fall asleep. Every time she saw Anna and Simon senior, or Edie and Simon Peter, she saw possible futures. Now she was getting to know them, she wasn't quite so sure she wanted to be 'part of the same family'. She wondered if Simon would ever want to live away from this house. Did he love her enough for that?

18

While walking back through the Close, Dominic asked himself what he had been going to say to the inspector before they were interrupted. He hadn't been sure even when he opened his mouth to say it. There was something very odd going on. He didn't doubt now that it was the chapter who had effectively silenced his predecessors, but he did not understand why. Given that in an age of religious freedom the order itself no longer needed to be kept secret, what was it they were protecting? There was little in his research that suggested anything controversial or dangerous. In fact, the chapter's history was exemplary, even if the seventeenth century abbot had, in his opinion, been a few arches short of a cloister. So if there was a secret, it had been well kept indeed. He had no idea what it could be. He certainly didn't believe it was the secret of eternal life, though he had hinted at it to provoke a reaction from the DI. He wondered if Wright or Poole had known, if Barry Skinner had come across something. He wondered if he dug deep enough would he find it? And was the chapter of today still so protective of its secrets? And inevitably, unthinkably, he wondered: would they try to kill him?

Too preoccupied to pay attention to his surroundings, he didn't notice anything wrong when he came home. He put his bag down by his desk and got himself a drink, still wondering about the chapter. It was only when he went into the kitchen again to see about food that he saw that the pane next to the door was broken. There was a tiny balcony outside, with the fire escape attached to it. Easy enough to get onto from the garden. The door wasn't locked, and he was pretty sure it had been when he left. He looked around – what was missing? The spare cash he kept stuck in a mug when he didn't want to carry too much on his person. Must have been the first thing they'd seen. It hadn't been very much, as far as he could recall. He walked around the flat, checking shelves and drawers. All the larger electronic stuff was still there, and his netbook had been safely in his bag. Nothing taken from the bedroom either, his cufflinks, Blake's ring which he no longer wore, all there. Only the iPod he never used was gone.

'Odd sort of burglar you've had here. Tidy,' the uniformed constable said, having looked at the broken pane and dusted the door handle for prints. 'And there was nothing taken except the cash and the music player?'

Dominic could tell this wasn't really important enough for him. 'Nothing else. The cash was maybe forty pounds. Why bother to break in for something like that? They could have taken more.'

'Probably a kid doing it for a dare,' the policeman shrugged. 'I'll have the prints checked, but I have to warn you that the chance of catching the perpetrator is very small. This was probably a one-off, the big boys would definitely have taken your television and PC.'

'I see. Well, thank you for coming.'

'You'd better have a secure lock put on that kitchen door, something they can't open even when they reach through the pane. No sense in inviting them in.'

'Yes, yes. I'll speak to the landlady. Thank you.'

He had had enough of the police for one day. He called on Mrs Withers downstairs, who owned the house, to tell her what had happened, and telephoned a glazier to have the pane replaced. He stuck a bit of cardboard over it for the time being. He wondered if he should feel more upset. But he supposed that as break-ins went, this was pretty painless. The policeman was right, they had been tidy, and they hadn't actually taken anything he would miss. He sat down in front of the television he still miraculously owned to watch the news.

The town had made the national news, somewhere towards the end of the programme. Another murder. Dominic suddenly paid more attention. So that was why the inspector was called away so abruptly. A girl had been shot. They showed a photo of her looking happy, and a brief sequence of the street where she had lived, the house where she was killed, police vans parked in front. There were no suspects, the newsreader said solemnly, and the police would be grateful for any information the public could provide. There was a phone number.

Dominic turned off the television. He couldn't imagine it, he did not want to imagine it. Just one shot and then you were gone. You probably wouldn't even know it. The girl had been found by one of her flatmates, they'd said. Poor girl.

Dominic wondered who would miss him, if the Chapter of St Cloud decided they wanted him out of the way. Who would find him? His mother would worry if he didn't email or phone for more than a week, his colleagues would miss him if he didn't turn up for a meeting, but there was no one he saw every day, not until term started. And who would miss him when he was gone? His mother again, of course. Saskia. Blake? His old friends in Canterbury who had promised to stay in touch? The master of the cathedral choir? Did he really have so few friends?

Dominic didn't want to be alone right now. He did not really believe he was in immediate danger, but that hardly seemed to matter. He was in danger from his own thoughts. He wanted to talk to someone, but he could imagine how alarmed his mother or sister would be if he called them now, with a tale like this. He decided he had better go out. Take a walk, clear his thoughts. He went to his desk to pick up his mobile and his keys. Only then did he see what else was missing. Had he put it down somewhere else? Put it in his bag, maybe? He knew he hadn't, but he checked anyway. This made him in even more of a hurry to get out of the house. He walked fast, too fast, not slowing down until he reached the cathedral. He couldn't go in at this time of night, but he walked over the grass to lean against the cool stone of a buttress. He didn't believe it. He couldn't believe it. But as the night and the stone calmed him down, he realised there was someone he could call now.

He answered on the second ring. 'Mr Walsingham, how can I help you?'

The DI sounded curt and businesslike. Did he regret giving Dominic his phone number?

'I've had a break-in today,' he said, 'They smashed in a window and just walked in.'

'A burglary at your house? Have you contacted uniformed?' Collins said, still sounding impatient. Maybe he shouldn't have called.

'Yes, of course I did. They didn't seem very interested. I just wanted to tell you, they took the notebook. The book I kept of my St Cloud research. I think the chapter have found me.'

19

Dominic felt better after speaking to the inspector and he slept all right, eventually. Collins had been reassuringly down-to-earth. And now, in the light of day, it seemed to him that there was one very simple solution. He could forget all about the chapter. He could tell his colleagues there was nothing in it, that he was concentrating on some other subject now, he could forget he had ever owned that notebook. He could send the chapter a very clear signal that he would no longer be in their way. He would do that, he thought, yes he would do that. He could call Inspector Collins again, for the last time, and tell him to forget about it too. It was all years ago, it didn't matter. He should just let it go. Dominic ate his cornflakes and asked himself who he thought he was fooling. He could do all that, and it wouldn't change a thing. He would try to convince the world that he would be leaving the chapter alone, and if they believed it, so much the better. But he had both curiosity and a conscience, and he could stop neither from working. He wanted to know what the chapter's secret was, and he wanted to know where they got the gall to bump off innocent historians at the drop of a hat. He suspected that if he told DI Collins to back off, this last point would be most forcibly put to him. If he didn't want to find out, he shouldn't have involved the police. The simple solution only looked simple from the outside. With any luck, that was from where the chapter would be seeing it. If they could hide, so could he.

With the distraction of the burglary and the missing notebook, he hadn't really taken the time to think about the things Collins had told him yesterday afternoon. He took out the file and looked again at the photographs the inspector had found. Was this the immortal abbot of the chapter, the man who had Alfred Poole and Alice Wright murdered? If he ever found the abbot of the Chapter of St Cloud, would he be looking at this face? He stared at the picture of Isaac Danvers, the one whose sister had committed suicide. Or maybe not. He had the feeling he had heard her name before, read it somewhere. Evangeline Danvers... he tried to recall where he could have seen the name of a bright young thing lately. Maybe that book Saskia left behind the last time she was here? It was still there, on the shelf. He was always looking through other people's books, he was sure he had read bits of *The Letters of Beatrice 'Baby' Cavendish: 1921-1951*. Let's see, it had to be somewhere before 1927. This woman, whoever she was, had written and received a lot of letters. Asquith, Harmondsworth, Churchill, other Cavendishes... And there it was: 'letter from Evangeline Danvers to Baby Cavendish, 15 April 1926'. He read it through quickly. There was a lot of chatter about balls and parties and mutual friends, but also a more serious and almost bitter note about Evangeline's family.

> *I feel sorry for poor Isaac, everyone is always talking about finding the right girl for him, and in truth I do not think he wants a girl at all and – oh! I shouldn't have written that, but Baby, you know what I mean, my uncle's word is law in this family, and it is beyond bearing sometimes. The saint reigns as if this was still the dark ages.*

He hadn't spotted that when he first read it, though he now recalled the Isaac who didn't want a girl at all. But he hadn't been looking for references to the chapter the first time, and that, in a letter from a Danvers, it must certainly be. Had Evangeline been too free with her references to 'the saint'? He copied the relevant bit of the letter and put it in the folder with the photographs and the article about Skinner. He missed his notebook. Maybe he should buy a new one.

The usually quiet bookstore on Woolweaver Street was full of women, all of them carrying paperbacks with icing-pink or sky-blue covers. Dominic worked his way through the throng towards the information desk, where a student of his was working.

'Hello Rashida, what's going on?'

'Oh, hello Mr Walsingham. Laura Garnett's signing today. Quite a good turn-out, don't you think?'

'Should I know Laura Garnett?'

'You don't know the author of *Wishful Thinking*?' she exclaimed in mock-horror, 'Well, between you and me, I don't think you're missing much. But she's very popular.'

'So I see.'

He watched a clutch of young girls giggling their way to the desk where Ms Garnett was signing and smiling and having her photograph taken. The author looked towards him for a moment, as if she was very surprised indeed to see a man in her vicinity. She smiled, and he gave her a polite nod.

'Did you hear about Lisa?' Rashida asked, 'I didn't know her myself, but it's so close, isn't it? I keep thinking, she must have come in here, I must have seen her at the students' union, things like that. She was only nineteen.'

'Yes, it's very sad. And for the parents...'

'Is there anything particular you were looking for?' she asked after a small pause.

'No, I just came to quietly browse. I wasn't expecting such a crowd.'

'The first floor's deserted,' she promised him.

What he was looking for, had he been inclined to tell the truth, was some easy reading that would distract him from thoughts of the chapter. He looked through the shelves of new fiction, reading back covers, picking up several titles he had forgotten he had intended to buy. It was remarkable how many books started from incredibly sad premises. No wonder Laura Garnett and her like were so popular. He turned doubtfully towards the crime section. A nice police procedural, perhaps? With plenty of unlikely characters and the criminal safely caught in the end. The DI would probably tell him it did not work like that. But he wasn't here, was he? There was a new book by Reginald Hill. That would do. He went downstairs and selected a cheap notebook from the stationary department, as unlike his first one as could be.

He had planned to get in his shopping this afternoon, but with more books than intended in his plastic carrier, he decided to drop them off home first. That meant going past the cathedral and *that* meant going in. The sun was blazing through the clerestory windows, and he stood in the crossing looking upwards until he was dizzy.

'Dominic! Over here, Dominic!'

He closed his eyes for a moment until the world stopped moving, and tried to focus on the woman waving from the south transept.

'Claire! How nice to see you here. Are you doing the tour?'

'I was, but I escaped. My boyfriend's around here too, somewhere, he's quite mad about churches. So how *are* you?'

'I'm fine, I'm fine. I live here, now. But you knew that, of course, you emailed. Are you staying here with friends?'

'No, Simon – my boyfriend – and his family live in the old bishop's palace south of town. Do you know it?'

'Of course. Bishop's grave is in the second bay on the north side, if I'm not mistaken. I mean of the one who built the palace. I had no idea it was still a private residence.'

'It's quite spectacular. But tell me about you. Are you still on that order old James came up with? What was it again, St Loup?'

'St Cloud. Yes, I mean, no, not really. I decided there was nothing in it after all.' He had almost forgotten this morning's resolution already.

'Hm, yes, I suppose it's been done. So what's next?'

He tried to evade the question. 'I don't know yet. I think I'll wait and see what happens when I start teaching again in September. Have you been up in the gallery yet?'

She shook her head. 'No, I haven't. To tell you the truth, I'm only waiting till Simon has looked at whatever he wanted to see. I don't really care for all this Gothic grandeur.'

'I see. I love it, of course. It's better when it is quieter, though. You should come to evensong sometime, I'm in the choir.'

'Maybe we will,' she said, but he could tell it was only from politeness. 'Ah, there's Simon, waving. You should come up to the house and meet him. Send me an e anytime.' She walked off towards the south entrance.

She could have perfectly well called Simon over and introduced them there and then, Dominic thought irritably. Claire always got on his nerves. The way she dismissed things that were important to other people – 'I suppose it's been done', really!

20

Really! Dominic wasn't very good at small talk, Claire thought. Always talking about *things*, as if people weren't important. She had forgotten he was dotty about church architecture as well. He'd looked quite put out when she rejected his suggestion to go up to gallery. Was it her destiny to be surrounded by men who worshipped Gothic buildings? She wondered vaguely if more men than women liked Gothic churches – if it was a phallic thing, and how you would go about finding out.

'Who was that guy you were talking to?' Simon asked.

'Dominic? He's a colleague. I mean in the distant sense of 'another medieval historian'. He teaches at the university here.'

Simon looked back towards the church. 'I see. Do you know him well?'

She shrugged, 'We're more rivals than friends, I suppose. You're not being jealous, are you? Just because I was talking to another bloke?'

'Would you like me to be?' he suggested, slipping his arm around her waist.

'No, not really,' she told him, 'Anyway, there'd be no point in being jealous of Dominic,' she added, as they walked down Market Street.

'I won't be, then. Hey look, it's Uncle Bennett. Uncle Bennett!' Simon waved. 'He didn't see us.'

They found a table in the Newmarket in front of a small Italian café.

'Simon, you see the man every day of your life. Maybe for once he'd like to walk around town without being surrounded by family.' I suppose that's what they call 'projection' she thought – but they really are everywhere!

'I suppose so. Two cappuccinos, please,' Simon said to the waitress. 'I'm always tempted to ask for *cappuccini*,' he added to Claire.

'Best refrain,' she advised him. 'Si, about your family – could you draw me a tree? Because now I've adjusted your age, the rest get shaken up a bit too. Uncle Bennett just now, he's your *great*-uncle, right? Despite the fact that he looks no older than my dad.'

Within moments, Simon was happily drawing on the table's paper placemat. Claire drank her cappuccino and looked at his busy sketch. She had the feeling she kept coming up against something, something to do with Simon's family. She thought at first that it was what he called 'the age thing', but it wasn't. There was something else, which she, rightly or wrongly, associated with the distant relationship between Anna and Simon senior. Something about the big happy family that didn't ring true.

Simon looked at his handiwork. 'It's only a rough version,' he said, 'Do you think they'll let me have another placemat so I can do one in my best writing?'

'Yes, you've had to squeeze a bit to get Abigail in, I see.'

Simon jumped, and Claire laughed. She had noticed Anna coming up silently behind her son.

'Anna, sit down. All done signing? Can we order you something?'

'I'll have a latte, I think. So, have you been enjoying yourselves?'

That evening, Claire was sitting at the desk in her room, looking at the untidy family tree Simon had made for her.

She was feeling unsure of her own judgement, and she didn't like that at all. When they had been sitting there in the sun, this afternoon, in their little chairs in the market, it had all felt natural and fine. She hadn't noticed any of the regret she had previously sensed – imagined? – in Anna, and Simon had been so funny and carefree. What could possibly be wrong? Her finger traced the line from old Toby down to Simon, and she imagined that line running on, adding another Simon at the bottom, and maybe a girl, a Laura, or a Catherine, after her mother.

There was the bloody phone again. She should really turn it off. Gina this time.

'Claire, I wanted to talk to you. I've spoken to Bry, but–'

'Gina, I wish you and Bry would just fuck off about this, all right? Simon's just Simon, and I love him.' Christ, she felt snappish. Maybe it was just that her period was due.

'I heard that!' Simon called from the bathroom. She stuck out her tongue at him. 'And I saw that, too!'

'He's with you right now, isn't he?' Gina asked, 'Look, I actually wanted to say... if it feels right, go for it, Claire. You don't know how lucky you are.'

'Oh,' Claire said, feeling suddenly deflated, 'Thanks, Geen. Are you all right?' She didn't sound it.

'Not really,' Gina said, 'I'm seeing someone.'

'You mean someone who's not Daniel?'

'Of course that's what I bloody mean. I'm confused, Claire. I thought me and Dan were forever. But I love– this other guy. And he's older than me, since you ask.'

'Gina's having an affair,' Claire explained to Simon after she rang off.

'Is that... usual?' he asked, 'The way you talk about it, it's almost like those books mum writes.'

'To my knowledge, it's the first time she's done something like this, and she's pretty cut up about it,' Claire said sharply. But she could see this wasn't about Gina, for him. It was about the two of them.

'I want us to be faithful, Claire,' he said seriously, 'I can't imagine wanting anyone but you.'

No, she thought, you can't now. But in ten years' time I'll be practically your mother's age, and you'll still be young. I can only hope you will remember this day, in ten years' time.

'Look, we're not Gina and Daniel and we are certainly not like the characters in your mother's books. We're us, we can be whatever we like.'

'I hope so.'

And suddenly she'd had enough. 'Simon, I wish you would tell me what's the matter! You keep hinting at something, but you never come out with it. What's the dirty secret?'

He looked at her for a long time without saying anything. Finally, almost inaudibly, he said, 'I wish I knew.'

21

The historian's pencilled scribbles were hard on his old eyes. There were pages and pages of facts and queries that were, on the whole, familiar to the abbot. He had seen these things before, not quite in their present form, but enough to give him a strong sense of déjà vu. But déjà vu was when you only felt something had happened before, wasn't it? And he knew in this case it was history repeating. First time as tragedy, second as farce, he thought. What would it be the fifth? Postmodern drama? Or maybe it was time for history not to repeat. Maybe things need not always be as they had always been. He smiled at the thought of voicing this heresy to his brothers and sisters. The chapter was forever, he knew that as well as any of them.

The notebook had been divided into neat sections. One for Clodoald and the early history of the abbey; one for the burgeoning Cistercian chapter; one for the seventeenth-century crypto-Catholics; and one headed 'the Chapter today'. This last section was short on citations and rich in question marks. The few lay communities and priories of the chapter that had survived did not go by the name of St Cloud anymore, and the abbot was pleased to see that the historian hadn't got very far there. He could imagine Walsingham's frustration, as addresses were scratched out and titles of books marked 'useless'. He almost began to believe they were not in danger at all. How he longed to tell the chapter that there was nothing to worry about.

That even this small theft had been unnecessary. But then, towards the back of the book, where Walsingham had jotted down odd thoughts and reminders, something made him pause. There was a neatly written half-page about grandmother Clothilde, which read like fiction. Under this was drawn a straight line, as if to say 'no more'. Below it was a short list:

Poole
Wright
Skinner

and then, more faintly, with a doubtful question mark:

Cottington?

The abbot gently closed the book, certain now that Dominic Walsingham knew more than he should.

The secret they had always had to protect was called heresy for a long time, finding its way out only subtly, in the queries of St Cloud's theologians. In the twelfth century they had found a welcome hiding place under the wings of the reforming Cistercians, and soon there were daughter houses with very little idea of what the great abbey taught its own. To confess to heresy meant death, and death was what every chapter member sought to evade. Not for nothing was Thomas's book called 'De *Vita Sancta*'. Like Lothar before him, the great scholastic confined his writing to the holiness of this life, and sought no other. For him and his fellows, secrecy became ingrained, as much part of the creed as 'this life is all there is'. But times changed, beliefs faded and mutated. What was secret now was what they had done to keep their secrets in the past. What was secret now was the silencing of threats to an older secret, repeating until the crimes in between stood in the way of revealing what was nowadays laughably normal. What would have sent Thomas to the stake wouldn't cause a blink in this century. So you don't believe in life after death? Doesn't that make murder even worse?

The great misunderstanding. From the very beginning, members of the chapter had dismissed the idea that anything continued beyond the body. But that only made more urgent the belief in life eternal. The abbot was old now and he was, but slowly, beginning to see that living forever might not always be for the best. The prior was still young, and his zealous devotion to the chapter was equalled only by his passionate belief that immortal life was possible and desirable. And he did not gladly suffer those who stood in the way of this end.

22

Dominic went through the north door and out into the Close. There was a car parked at the far end, which was strange, and certainly not legal. The driver was in his seat, studying a large map. Dominic started walking towards it. Maybe he could give directions? But before he got very close, a figure stepped free of the cool shadow of a buttress. 'Mr Walsingham?'

Dominic looked sideways to find the inspector's young informant falling into step.

'You are Jake, right?' He suppressed an added 'what do you want?'

'Mr Walsingham, I need to talk to you.'

'I don't think–' Dominic began.

'Please, I have to, it's important.' Jake looked at him pleadingly from under his black fringe.

Dominic gestured at a bench. 'Well, I've time now. Talk away.' He couldn't imagine what the boy wanted with him. Did he look like a potential client for his services?

But Jake shook his head, and stepped back closer to the walls. 'Not here! Can you meet me tomorrow night? At Bitters?'

'Look, I have to know what this is about first. You're a complete stranger.'

'When did that ever stop anyone? Anyway, you know the inspector.' He lowered his voice, 'It's about St Cloud, all right? Don't tell anyone you're seeing me. Tomorrow in the club at half ten.'

'Tomorrow at half ten,' Dominic repeated dutifully.

'Right. Later.' Jake slouched nonchalantly off, hands in the impossibly low pockets of his jeans.

Dominic watched him go, admiring the view while contemplating this odd exchange. He would go and meet Jake tomorrow, if only out of curiosity. He couldn't imagine what the boy could know about St Cloud, but neither could he understand why the chapter would be used as bait for anything else. Or was the chapter using Jake as bait for something else? That was a disquieting thought. The idea that Jake himself was somehow involved with the chapter he dismissed out of hand. It was hard to imagine anyone more worldly.

The illegally parked car was still there, the driver's map still unfolded all over the steering wheel. Dominic bent down close to the open window. 'Excuse me, can I help you, sir? You are not allowed to park here, you know.'

'Oh, yes, I did think it was blessedly empty. I seem to have got turned around somewhere. How do I get to Infirmary Road?'

'Oh, that's easy. If you leave the Close on the south side – that's the other side of the church, you take the first right from Market Street...'

He looked familiar, and yet Dominic was sure he had never seen this man before. He recognised the rental company of the car, though. It was the same as that of the man he'd seen in his own street two days ago. That one had been young, this one was middle-aged. If he hadn't known he was being pursued by a quietly fanatic religious order Dominic would have considered himself quite paranoid.

'Thank you so much,' the driver said, 'Good afternoon.'

'DI Collins? Sorry for bothering you again. How is the murder investigation coming along?'

'I assume you mean the official one? Frustrating. Please tell me you're calling with some useful information.'

'Not really. I wanted to ask you something. This boy Jake–'

'What about him?' the DI said sharply. A bit too protective there? Dominic wondered.

'I met him today. That is to say, I almost had the idea he was lying in wait for me. He says he needs to talk to me. About St Cloud.'

Dominic doodled a stick figure while the other side remained silent. 'Inspector?'

'That's... strange. How would he know about St Cloud?'

'He knew my name, too. You didn't tell him?'

'No, we had other things to talk about,' the DI said, 'So are you going to see him?'

'I'm meeting him tomorrow at Bitters. Not really my scene, but I suppose it is his. Are you sure you didn't mention St Cloud to him?'

'No, why should I?'

'You talked to me about him, why shouldn't you talk to him about me? But I suppose I'll just have to wait and hear what Jake has to say, then. Is he– is he likely to want money for information?'

'You can tell him he'll have my eternal gratitude if he tells you all he knows. Seriously, though, if he wants to talk to you so urgently, he'll say what he wants to say, money or no.'

'He was pretty emphatic that no one should know about our meeting,' Dominic recalled.

'I think it's safe to assume I'm outside that prohibition.'

'Inspector, how do you know Jake, anyway? What do you really know about him?'

'You meet all kinds, in this line of work,' Collins said vaguely, 'He's not an utter druggie, and actually quite well-behaved when he drops the fake low-life front. But I've no idea where he comes from. I don't even know his last name. Look, will you call me when you've seen him? I don't want Jake to get into trouble.'

Yes, I noticed that. 'Will do. Oh, and there was something else...'

He told Collins about Evangeline's letter.

'We'll make a detective of you yet. So the family *is* connected to the chapter. That means the current crop shouldn't be too hard to find.'

'I suppose you have access to the electoral register, that kind of thing?' Dominic said hopefully.

'So do you. This isn't an official investigation. Which reminds me, I have one to run. I'll talk to you later.'

After a visit to the supermarket as planned, Dominic sat down and thought about the family connected with the chapter. Danvers, originally *d'Anvers*, meaning 'from Antwerp'. And like Collins had said, there were a lot of Flemish weavers here in the sixteenth century, and people probably weren't *very* precise about where these came from. Which meant that the white pages listed too many Danverses to be useful, and he knew the chapter didn't have its number listed publicly. He had to approach this problem from another direction, starting from the names he knew. Samuel, Isaac and Tobias Danvers. He would try genealogical websites, he thought. Didn't everyone go looking for their ancestors, these days? He made himself a cup of tea and set to work. He soon found the problem with this line of reasoning, though. Working back from a given person through their fathers and mothers gave you a neat tree, but following down through their descendants got you lost in a thicket. And it was full of dead branches, too. Eventually he found an Isaac Danvers, born 1907, with sisters called Evangeline, Benedicta and Thomasina. That had to be the right family, given the girls' names. Isaac had apparently been fixed up with a wife and produced three offspring of his own, but there the facts ran out. He had noticed that before, information about generations still living was usually omitted. At least, he thought, if Isaac was born in 1907, he couldn't be the same person as Samuel or Tobias Danvers. But his pleasure at this rational thought dimmed somewhat when he couldn't find a year of death for Isaac anywhere. He didn't understand the relationship between the Danverses and the abbots – or abbot. Evangeline's letter implied that it was her uncle who was head of the family, so maybe the abbacy passed from uncle to nephew. That was a pattern he was familiar with from the middle ages, when one dynasty often wielded both clerical and temporal power in their home region. Inspired by this idea, Dominic looked for signs of worldly power in the local Danvers families. He was pretty sure they would be found in the neighbourhood. Isaac Danvers was listed as born in the town, and Abbey Hill school was on its outskirts. There was a solicitor called Danvers, a C of E pastor, a freelance IT consultant – hardly the corridors of power. And of course they were unlikely to all be from the same branch. An army chaplain, a neurosurgeon, a schoolteacher, a pharmaceutical company based west of town, founded by one Solomon Danvers in 1969. That brought him up short. The company was called Cloud Laboratories. Its logo showed a stylised silver cumulus formation, but Dominic was past believing in coincidences.

He resisted the impulse to inform DI Collins about this find at once. It was getting late, anyway. Tomorrow morning he would see what else he could turn up.

23

In the Chapterhouse, the brother he had set to watching the historian dutifully reported the day's activities.

'I followed Mr Walsingham, just like I was told. He left his house at one-fifteen, and visited the bookshop and the cathedral. He was inside both for a long time. I think he noticed me, though. He was kind enough to give me directions.'

'One of the others can take over,' the prior said, 'So there was nothing in particular you noticed?' There must have been, he thought, the man was shuffling his feet like a schoolboy.

'I did, father,' he answered reluctantly.

'Well?'

'After leaving the church, Walsingham spoke to a young man. I think they agreed on a meeting. I could not hear very well, but I saw who it was.'

'Who?'

'It was the runaway.'

The prior was silent for a long time. When he spoke again, the brother flinched, as if he expected him to be angry. Really, time was when they were made of sterner stuff.

'There may be an innocent explanation,' he said, 'Or not so innocent. You know the runaway's profession?'

The brother nodded, a look of distaste on his face.

'Well, then. They may never even speak about us. But ask one of the others to keep watch over the runaway, just to be sure. Not Lucas, though. Ask Rachel, or Austin. I think they will know where to find him.'

Officially, their runaway brother did not exist anymore. He had another name, another life. He was out in the world, and no longer of the chapter. But there was a bit of the chapter in him, and it could not be allowed to reach Dominic Walsingham.

'Have we been careless, father? About the runaway?'

'The runaway made his choice, brother. It is not for us to judge,' the prior said sternly. 'Now, I'll make sure this Walsingham chap is warned off. He does not strike me as the type who'll take needless risks.'

He was a little surprised that further warnings were even necessary. A pity the historian was so tenacious. Maybe he simply hadn't realised yet he was playing with fire. In that case, it had to be brought home to him what the chapter could do. What was it again? Tomorrow at Bitters at half past ten. Right. One for Rachel and her sister.

24

'I don't think you are telling me everything, are you, Selina?'

From the moment he had first spoken to her he had had the idea that Miss Brinkmann was keeping something from him. That nonsense about not knowing what the drug was called – even old grannies knew about Oblivion.

She looked away. 'It's difficult.'

'Are you afraid you will get into trouble over the drugs? I'm investigating a murder, you know. A few pills here and there are not CID's concern.'

'All right, then. But please don't tell anyone else.'

'Only what is relevant to the inquiry.' That was a sizeable loophole, anyway. He waited patiently while Lisa Wilson's flatmate chose her words. The shy girl in mourning act might have worked on Walter or Pardoe – she was pretty enough for it – but for his money Selina Brinkmann's behaviour was too calculated to be convincing.

'Yes, I knew about the drugs,' she said slowly, looking at him from behind the veil of her long dark hair. 'Everyone was at that game, I didn't see the harm. But Lisa was taking it too far. She didn't take them herself, you know, just sold the pills at a good profit.'

'You thought the drug trade was about having fun at parties? Of course she made a profit. You didn't actually like Lisa much, did you?'

She sat up straight, flicking her hair violently away from her face. Not so pretty now.

'What do you mean?'

'Exactly what I'm saying. It must be hard, with everyone singing her praises right now. But it doesn't matter what you say about her here. You can't hurt the dead.'

'No. She was okay, I suppose, but we weren't really mates.'

If he had been hoping for a deadly rivalry, this wasn't it. Back to the case.

'Do you know who supplied Lisa with Oblivion?'

'That's obvious, isn't it? I thought you knew.'

Of course, when she told him, it was obvious.

'The woman next-door noticed a middle-aged man in a dark blue parka ringing the bell, at around eleven, she thought,' DC Dasgupta reported, 'The Taylors living across the road also noticed someone, they said an elderly man in a grey trench coat.'

'So all we know for sure is that it wasn't a girl in an orange hoodie,' Collins said moodily. He felt they were grasping at straws. They had already interviewed Lisa's colleagues at the office where she was temping, her friends from the health club, her parents, her brother and sister, as well as, again, her flatmates. Now they were reviewing the results of the door-to-door enquiries.

'There may have been two different men,' Walter said, 'Mrs Taylor couldn't be certain of the time.'

'Whatever, it gets us nowhere. What about that list Jim sent us? Any connection with the victims?'

The DS shrugged, 'Pretty useless. They're still not sure where most of the Oblivion comes from, but by the time it reached our boy and girl, that connection would have been lost anyway. There's one guy called Howard who usually deals to students, who thinks he might have sold them some stuff. There's CCTV coverage from the Newmarket Bar showing he was there at the time of the first murder. Second alibi isn't so good, though.'

'Did he have a motive? Non-payment?' the DC put in.

'He hardly remembered Whiteside and he seemed pretty shaken about Lisa,' Walter said, 'Might be an act, but I don't think so. And if the big fish start killing the little fish, they'd soon be out of a livelihood. I don't see it.'

Collins didn't either. It was beginning to look like this was a professional job, a large gang warning off the smaller fry by taking a few out at random. And if that was what it was, the killers were going to be very hard to find. They would be experts, and they wouldn't have a motive, but a contract. Even if they found the person who pulled the trigger, they might never find who told them to do it. He hated this kind of case. If it made sense to have a kind of murder you disliked more than another, he hated the coolness and finality of contract-killing. The human mess of domestic dramas and crimes of passion were heart-breaking, but at least they happened because people felt things, felt them, in most cases, too strongly. But here there was no feeling at all, no violence, no struggle, just an end. A dead end.

He kept thinking of those earlier murders, the one of Barry Skinner especially. Somehow, the two cases were getting mixed up in his mind. Although he reminded himself that Skinner had been a blunt instrument job, not a gunshot, the situations were uncomfortably similar – he'd thought at one point that he would have to arrest Selina, she looked guilty as hell. But when she finally came out with whatever she was withholding, it was nothing every time, schoolgirl stuff.

There was also this strange development of Jake wanting to talk about St Cloud just after they had spoken about Whiteside. He might have told him that he was meeting a man called Walsingham, but he certainly had not mentioned the chapter. When he tried to reach Jake on his mobile the boy wasn't picking up. He never did, he would call back in his own good time. Collins had even checked out Walsingham's record – he didn't have one – and had probed a little to find if he a had an alibi. It didn't make sense, and he couldn't find any indication that the historian had even known the victims, but somehow, somewhere, he felt there had to be a connection. It got so bad he caught himself being suspicious of one of Lisa's temporary employers just because the man was called Danvers. Nothing to do with it, he told himself sternly, nothing to do with it at all.

'Jim's sent us a whole bunch of stuff about Oblivion,' Walter told him, 'Down to the company who first made it. I can't imagine what he thinks we'll do with it. Maybe do his job for him.' He shoved a file in Collins's direction.

'I'll have a look at it,' he said without enthusiasm, 'You never know, I might learn something.'

'You might,' Walter said, managing to put a lot of disbelief in that short phrase. 'Well, back to work. I'll check on Whiteside's neighbours, see if they remember a man in a grey or blue trench coat or parka. Coming, Holmes?'

'Coming. Sir?'

Collins looked up from the file as she halted in the doorway.

'Yes?'

'Is it going to happen again?'

He shook his head. 'Maybe, Sally, I don't know. But it's up to us to find them first, okay?'

The thought had occurred to him, of course. In fact, it wouldn't go away, and he looked through Jim's file without really seeing anything. Were all the small dealers in danger now? Selina Brinkmann, who was definitely farther in than she admitted? The dealer Walter had found? Jake?

Please God, not Jake. He *would* find them first. He sat up straight and finally focused on what was glaring at him from the page.

25

'Sir? Could I talk to you for a moment, please?'

Claire knew it was too formal a way of addressing him, but she wanted him to know this was important.

'Of course,' Simon senior said, 'Do sit down. Would you like something to drink?'

'Oh no, please don't bother.' Please don't let me lose momentum now. 'I'm worried about Simon,' she went on hurriedly. 'He's being... mysterious. I asked him if there was anything wrong, and he said he wasn't sure, and he would tell me tomorrow, or the day after. What's going on?'

'I see. And he has given you no indication what this is about?'

'It's something to do with his family, your family. It's as if he does not know himself – or just won't say.'

His father's face was anything but reassuring. She had come to him because she thought of him as trustworthy. She realised now that that judgement was not based on anything more than the fact that he appeared to like her.

'Claire, I'm sorry, but I cannot tell you any more. If Simon has said that he will tell you, he will. Be patient.'

'But do you know what it is about?'

'I– I am not sure,' he said, not meeting her eyes.

She kept looking at him. 'Yes, you are. You don't lie well.'

'Claire, listen. When Simon tells you, remember two things. One is that I share his concern. The other is that whatever the family does, Simon is not his family.'

Was that all he could say?

'I see. And can you tell me another thing?' she asked, 'Can you tell me why I don't just pack my bags and leave? Nothing is straightforward here, is it? Not even Simon. I was stupid to expect a straightforward answer from either of you.'

To her horror, she found she was close to tears. Why was she being so emotional recently?

'You could take him with you,' Simon senior said quietly.

'What?'

'When you pack your bags and leave. You could take him with you.'

She got up. 'And how likely is that?'

She resisted the impulse to slam the door behind her and walked out with her dignity – just – intact.

Simon himself had been just as vague. 'I'm not sure what's wrong. I will tell you, I promise. I just have to check a few things.' That's what he said after her outburst yesterday evening. And she had hardly seen him since. He had got up earlier than she had, for a wonder, and by the time she arrived at the breakfast table he was gone. Looking for him, she had been side-tracked by aunt Rhoda into a discussion about redecorating the music room. When she'd extracted herself from this, Bethany told her Simon had gone into town. He kept his telephone turned off. At this point Claire had decided she needed to talk to *someone*, and thought of Simon senior. It had hardly proved a resounding success. If anything, she was more worried now than she had been before.

Not really knowing where to go after she left his room, Claire found herself in the library, which was usually empty at this time of day. Right, she thought, I'm an intelligent woman, trained to think rationally. So let's do just that. She picked up a notepad from a desk and selected a pen. Then she proceeded to make a list of all the possible things that could have made Simon so worried and evasive. Let's see. He could be married already, she supposed, although at his age it seemed unlikely. Maybe he was *engaged* to someone else. But he'd said it was about the family, hadn't he? Maybe he had found he wasn't his father's child. That would be upsetting for him. Claire thought back to her interview with Simon senior and had to admit that that was even more improbable – the likeness between them was remarkable. But maybe Simon was his grandfather's child? It might be a sordid little secret like that. She put it down on her list. What else? It could be that the family did not approve of her. The way they stuck together, they might feel that Simon hadn't made a very good choice in her, an older woman. But if that was the case, they were very good at hiding it. She might not get along with each and every one of them, but only his sisters had shown signs of clannish disapproval. Never mind, it was a possibility, and down it went. Of course, she might be wrong in thinking it had anything to do with her and Simon at all. Were members of his family involved in something criminal, perhaps? Fraud? Espionage? This was getting increasingly far-fetched, and she could see it was a bit comic, her sitting there making a list of all the bits of melodrama her boyfriend might spring on her. But it worked, too. When – if – Simon chose to tell her, she thought now, she wouldn't be upset, she would be understanding. After all, how bad could it be? If he was not involved himself, it would not affect them. He had to learn to think of himself as himself, not as part of his family. That was what his father had been getting at, she realised.

'Hello Claire. Studying your Italian?'

Tiny, white-haired aunt Abby – somewhere from the very top of the family tree – came walking slowly into the room.

'Hello,' Claire smiled at her, 'Not exactly.' She folded her notes and put the sheet in the pocket of her skirt. Better not let anyone find that!

'I like to sit here and read,' aunt Abby said. 'Not those books,' she added, nodding at the leather-bound volumes covering the walls, 'I have my own.' She held up a yellowed orange paperback. *A Natural Curiosity*. 'At some point you stop reading new books,' she continued, 'You stop reading the reviews in the paper and just return to the stories you always loved. And to be honest, I don't understand women these days, this 'chick-lit'. In my day, we wanted examples, we wanted strong, intelligent women to show us that we owned the world as much as men did. Women like her.' She waved the paperback again. 'And now... I read one of Anna's books. Forget what it was called. It's just weak little woman stuff with a mouth on it. And those books the girls read – teenage mush with vampires in!' She shuddered theatrically. 'Do you read books like that? You're an intelligent woman.'

'Sometimes. I mean, I've read Anna's books, I don't like vampires. It's not that bad. I don't think women take romantic stories that seriously.'

'By that you either mean you hope they don't, or just that *you* don't. Stories tell people how to be. That's what they're for,' Abby said with great conviction.

'Do you think so?'

'I know so. That's what I always taught my girls. It's not just about what the author intended, or what he put in subconsciously, or whatever interpretation was fashionable at the time. It's about what stories tell us about us.'

She wasn't just an old woman confused by new fashions, Claire realised. Abby had been thinking about this for a long time.

'Abby, can I ask you something? Do you regret staying here? Did you never want to live somewhere else? It sounds to me you could have had a university career.'

'I could have, I suppose. But I came back after I got my degree at Oxford,' Abby said, 'It seemed the natural thing to do. I taught at a nearby school, I had a home here. And as you may have noticed, one never lacks for intelligent company in this house.'

'Aunt Abby…'

'There are people old enough to be your parents who call me aunt Abby,' the old woman interrupted, 'I've had a long time to think about it. One thing this family lives by: you can't do things over again. I chose to stay here, it is useless to regret it. That does not mean I would like a girl like you to make the same choice now.'

'You could still choose differently.'

'I am seventy-nine years old, my dear. Where would I go? Whatever was good for me at your age, at my age, this is many times better than any nursing home.'

Claire had to concede the point. 'So you do not think I should come and live here, then?'

'Did I say that? I think you should make your own choices. And it will be you who makes them, not young Simon.' She opened her book, signalling that that was final.

'Thank you,' Claire said quietly, before she left the room.

26

Judith of Paris had always been a bit of an embarrassment to the chapter. She was the abbess of St Cloud's most prestigious daughter house, a king's niece who had embraced the life of the convent with fervour. Her visions were written down by one of her sisters and already often copied in her lifetime, and the good and the great of the age sought her guidance. But to an order whose bent had always been rigorously rational, her mystical approach was suspect, and the greater her standing in the eyes of the world, the greater the distance between her and the abbot who should have been her spiritual father. In his lighter moments, the abbot thought it was probably better that the secret of eternal life had remained hidden from Judith. He had not been sorry when her writings fell into disregard in the later, reforming centuries, and he had thought them safely buried there. When her work was rediscovered in the middle of the twentieth century the interest was at first purely academic, but with that odd new mysticism that took hold of a later generation, Judith became once again popular. There were sisters of a certain age who regularly quoted her and found great wisdom in what was, in the abbot's opinion, manifest twaddle. The striving for oneness with the divine came too close for his liking to negating responsibility for one's own life, and the love for that life became lost in a vague, ineffectual benevolence. He did not often find himself in agreement with the prior, these days, but in this they saw eye to eye. Judith was a bad influence.

Nonetheless, when her works were theorised and deconstructed, he found himself interested. However unconventional the order might have been in a religious sense, they had always lived within the constraints of their time. It helped when you saw Judith's visions as the only way open to an intelligent woman to exercise power, it made better sense of her world. He was glad those centuries lay behind them. They were much healthier now, as a community of men and women of all ages. They still had the internal struggles of all closed communities, though, and not everyone was as free as they liked in the exercising of their power. Including the abbot himself. He had tried to reason with the prior, to have the man at least tell him what he was planning to do about the troublesome historian. But the prior just told him not to worry, and treated him as if his opinion was of no consequence. It wasn't that he was old and considered past it; Brother Stephen, in the vigour of his youth, got the same treatment. There were those in the chapter who were trusted by the prior, and those who were not. It was but poor consolation to the abbot that among his confidants were as many women as men.

27

Dominic tried to reconstruct the contents of his stolen notebook, but what he wrote in the new one was turning out quite different. Questions that had seemed no more than mildly intriguing when seen in the context of the long history of the chapter now suddenly became relevant. The fact that Simeon, abbot from 1188 to 1214, had been surnamed d'Anvers, for example, had always seemed to Dominic a coincidence not worth remarking on. But now the name Danvers was suddenly important, and he found himself wondering if the connection could really go back all those years. A pity that the first d'Anvers had been of obscure origins, it would be impossible to trace his family.

He was surprised by the ringing of the front door bell. He frowned at the clock, knowing he wasn't expecting anyone.

'Hello,' DI Collins said when he opened the door, 'Sorry for bothering you like this. I hope I haven't arrived at an inconvenient time?'

'No, no. Do come in.'

'Nice place you've got here,' Collins said approvingly when they had arrived in the living room. 'I would have called, but there's something I'd like to see your reaction to.'

'I'm curious. Can I get you a drink?'

'A soft drink would be nice, I'm still on duty.'

Wondering what brought the inspector here, Dominic got them both glasses of cranberry juice. He found himself quite pleased that Collins was visiting. Surely it meant that he was taking the case seriously.

'Thanks,' the DI said, seating himself in an armchair, 'Look, I'm going to tell you a lot of things that might seem irrelevant, so bear with me, please. A question, first. Have you heard of Oblivion?'

'That's the new drug all the kids are on, isn't it? I think my ex wrote an article about it. Some kind of pills?'

'Not all the kids, thankfully, but yes. Oblivion first hit the market about a year ago, and it became popular very quickly. It was a drug that got pulled out in the human trial stages because of dangerous side effects, but a batch was stolen and sold, and of course by now some other enterprising spirit has analysed it and started producing more. It comes in capsules, and one of those dissolving slowly gives a gentle, easy high. But take too much or too quickly, and you lose consciousness, and in nine out of ten cases, the loss of consciousness is associated with memory loss. An unfortunate combination from a policeman's point of view. It tastes sweet, it's easy to dissolve in someone's drink, and they won't even remember what happened later.'

'Nasty.'

'Yes. And dangerous. Even two capsules in combination with alcohol may be fatal.'

Dominic sipped his juice. 'Wasn't there...'

'A girl who died? That's why everyone knows about Oblivion. Naomi Miller, seventeen years old, a nice middle-class girl who was pissed out of her mind and agreed to try something new.'

'I remember. We sang at her funeral, with the choir. Those parents... He looked so small, huddled in his coat even though it was a warm day, and she with no expression on her face at all. Completely empty.' He didn't really want to think about that. It had been such a dreadful, irredeemably sad occasion.

Collins looked suddenly animated. 'So that's where I've seen you before!'

Dominic smiled. 'And I thought you were having a brilliant professional insight.'

'Nothing like that. Just that I was also at the service.' Collins shook his head. 'People never know how close things like that are until they hit. You see it all the time in my job. I don't just mean death. Parents who are convinced that *their* son would never touch drugs. Parents who think *their* daughter makes all that money by waitressing. And the kids themselves – no idea how dangerously they live. Take Jake, for example. I swear that boy thinks he's immortal. And unlike Naomi, he's in the demographic most likely to die violently.'

'You do care about that boy, don't you?'

This elicited a small smile. He really was a good-looking man, Dominic couldn't help noticing.

'I think you've got the wrong end of the stick about me and Jake. But yes, I do care what happens to him.'

Oh dear, Dominic thought, this is where it turns out he's as straight as a line and feeling broody because his wife is pregnant.

'I'm not saying he never tried it on,' Collins continued, with an almost helpless shrug, 'And well, you've seen him. But like you said, he's awfully young. Not my style.'

'Okay. We're getting away from the point, aren't we?' Dominic said hurriedly, 'You were telling me about Oblivion.'

'Right. Both our murder victims, Sean Whiteside and Lisa Wilson, were selling Oblivion in a small way. Just to friends and fellow students, they weren't what you and I would call dealers. But the drug is the only thing we have that connects them. That's why I started looking into it. Oblivion was first designed as a kind of rejuvenating or life-prolonging medicine, if I've understood things right, and the company that produced it–'

'Cloud Laboratories,' Dominic said with a sense of great inevitability.

'Don't go spoiling my grand revelation, now. So much for observing your reaction. Yes, Cloud Laboratories, founded by one Solomon Danvers. How do *you* now about them?'

'I don't, really. I just came across the company yesterday, looking for Danverses – Cloud, Danvers, you can see why it drew my attention. And you'd only be telling *me* all this if it had something to do with the chapter.'

'The business was founded in 1969 and Solomon Danvers is still company director. As far as I can ascertain, the company doesn't actually develop medicines against specific complaints, but its sole aim is looking for substances that halt or reverse senescence. It must be privately funded in some way, as it doesn't compete for contracts with the bigger pharmaceuticals. My colleagues in the drug squad even think they may have leaked the Oblivion deliberately, as a nice, quiet earner.'

'That makes sense, rejuvenating drugs. A modern version of the elixir of life, it's what you would expect, from the chapter,' Dominic said.

'That's what I wanted to ask you about. What do you know about the chapter, now? If it turns out they are involved, where do I look for them?'

'That's difficult. It's not as if they have a website and a contact address. Look, this sounds strange, but before all this I was beginning to wonder whether the chapter actually still existed. According to Alice Wright there were still several religious houses affiliated with them. But that was sixty years ago. I tried to arrange an interview at one of those houses about a month ago. Have you ever tried to get into a community of enclosed nuns? I bet even a policeman would find that difficult.'

'I've no doubt,' Collins said, 'And the connection with the Danvers family? They are English, and probably from around here.'

'I don't understand that at all. The connection may be financial, one of patronage. Or the abbots may usually have come from the family, passing the office from uncle to nephew. But it would be remarkable for either of those connections to have lasted so long. Actually, the whole chapter having lasted so long is a bit unlikely.'

He was aware that they both refrained from referring to the idea that the abbot had been the same person all that time. He really didn't want to go there. And he was distracted by the time.

'I'm sorry, but I'll have to go soon. It's evensong tonight.' He had an idea. 'Could you walk with me to the cathedral? There's something I'd like to show you there.'

'Of course. Right now?'

'I'll just change into my neat chorister-clothes. Won't be a moment.'

He left the DI alone in the living room. Would a detective resist the temptation to have a quick look through his stuff? He always got stuck in people's bookcases himself. But when he returned Collins was still in his chair, looking through the letters of Beatrice Cavendish.

'Ready?'

'Ready.'

'Inspector?' he said, as they walked down St Mary's Lane towards the Close.

'Please call me Owen. And it's Dominic, right?'

'Of course, of course. Owen.' But the question he wanted to ask he wanted to ask of the Detective Inspector. 'Do you think they may actually try to kill me? Should I be... cautious?'

'I know it is hard to imagine. But people do kill others for what may seem to you and me very inadequate reasons. Some people just lack that inner seventh commandment. I think it is important that we find the chapter soon, to let them know the game is up, the secret's out. I think it's unlikely they would kill simply out of revenge.'

'But the secret isn't out,' Dominic protested, 'I've still no idea what it is they are hiding, apart from their involvement in earlier murders. But it needs to have started somewhere.'

'What's the chapter's religious position? Fundamentalist?'

'You know, I can't even tell you that. I suppose they are still Roman Catholic, the house in the Netherlands associated with them certainly is, but the Vatican does not recognise the order, I checked. Throughout their history they seem to have been in line with the more enlightened ideas of their times, but where that would put them now I have no idea.'

'Curiouser and curiouser. So how do they recruit?'

'I think they select promising members of other organisations and approach them personally. But it's all speculation.'

They had arrived at the north-east side of the choir, and Dominic led the inspector the long way around to the front entrance. He trailed a hand over a buttress as they rounded the protruding chapterhouse off the south transept. 'Should you be working on this? I know I asked you to, but...'

'You mean shouldn't I be in hot pursuit of a mad gunman?'

'I suppose that's what I mean, yes.'

'Yes, I should be, and I can't make this other thing official without having a lot more to go on. But I don't like the idea that someone may be planning another murder on my patch. Or that they got away with it earlier, either.' Collins looked at the repeating windows of the long nave. 'It's bloody big, isn't it? I've lived here half my life, but I don't think I ever really look at it. I only see it at weddings and funerals.'

Dominic laughed, but Collins soon turned serious again. 'To get back to your original question: I think they will only make an attempt on your life when you become a real threat. You say you don't know their secret, and if they have your notebook, they know that as well. If you show no signs of finding out more, they will probably leave you alone.'

'I find it hard to leave the chapter alone,' Dominic said.

They were in the central portal now, a last judgement over their heads. The inspector looked at him sideways as they stepped inside. 'Don't go courting trouble now. Let's see what I can do, first.'

Dominic led the way to an elaborately sculpted side chapel. 'It's the grave of Bishop Danvers, who held the see from 1604 to 1631. I would never have spotted it myself, but look at his coat of arms. It's that of the see – the three croziers – quartered with his own, a device of two crossed nails. It's an odd choice of blazon, you'd think. But they are canting arms, a kind of visual pun. The French word for nail is *clou*, and St Cloud is the patron saint of nail makers, because they sound so similar.'

'So the nails are a reference to the chapter?'

'Nails in heraldry usually refer to those of the cross, but in this case I don't think so.'

'They're quite hard to make out,' the DI said, bending close to the tomb, 'Who pointed it out to you?'

'The choir master. But he didn't connect it with the chapter, that was me. He just thought the nails a strange device.'

'He must have looked pretty closely even to spot that.'

'He knows this building inside out. There's so much to look at here, I think I'll never get tired of it.'

They walked slowly down the aisle, Dominic occasionally pointing out something he liked especially, like the lopsided vaulting of the easternmost bay.

'I suppose there's a lot of weight bearing down on it,' Collins said, following the line of the crooked ribs with his eyes, 'The whole thing must have subsided several feet over the years. They sure knew how to build.'

'Up to a point,' Dominic said, also looking up at the ribs, 'But you have to remember that there's a kind of natural selection going on. The badly built ones have all collapsed.'

'You do know how to take the mystery out of it.' He smiled at Dominic. 'Do you always do that?'

'Do what?'

The DI nodded at Dominic's hand, resting on the pier behind him. 'Touch it?'

'Why, yes, I do, at least once every time I'm here.' He turned around a little so he could feel the ridged stone against his back. Collins put his own hand on the pier, testing it, just above Dominic's shoulder.

'I'm not sure why I do it. To tell myself it's still really there I suppose or...oh.'

He tailed off as Collins leaned in to kiss him. He finally let go of the cold stone to rest both his hands on Owen's warm back, pulling him closer so he was locked tightly between the man and the pillar.

'Mm,' Owen mumbled, reluctantly disengaging, 'You have singing to do.'

'You could stay and listen.' Please don't let go.

'No, I had planned to get back to the station for a bit.' He did let go.

'Of course. I'll be in touch when I've talked to Jake, okay?'

'Okay.' He touched his lips very lightly to Dominic's cheek. 'I'll see you.'

Dominic watched him go, full of purpose, his jacket slung over his shoulder. He looked back and raised his hand in salute before stealing out through the devil's door.

'Dominic?'

He turned to find Michael Taylor beaming at him. 'It's ten to seven.'

'Coming.'

28

'I don't know what the matter is Claire, truly. But something's wrong. Dad is worried about something, and grandfather is looking even more severe than usual. There's some sort of crisis going on.'

'So just ask them,' Claire said practically.

'You think I haven't tried? They just mutter something about 'it's business, nothing to worry about'.'

'So maybe you shouldn't.'

'Look, I'm old enough to be told, even if it's nothing. They've never acted like this before.'

'I don't think you're telling me everything,' she said, scrutinising his face, 'Are you?'

'How can I when I don't know anything myself?'

'You can't even make a guess?'

He looked uncomfortable. She was sure he knew more than he was letting on, whatever it was.

'Tell me, Simon. You want me to be part of this family, you can't keep things from me.'

'Promise me you won't talk about this to anyone.'

'How can I promise that if I have no idea what it's about?'

'It's not that bad. Promise.'

'All right, I promise.' She felt as if they were children swearing a pact, it didn't feel real.

'I think it may have something to do with my cousin Adam's business,' he told her.

'Which is?'

'Manufacturing and selling drugs.'

Claire thought of the list she had made. Not so silly after all.

'I take it you do not mean patent medicine? You mean drugs as in substance abuse.'

He nodded. 'Pills.'

'And you all know about it?'

He nodded unhappily.

'And no one has thought of going to the police?'

'Of course not! It's not as if it's really our business. And he doesn't live here, we don't have much to do with him. But he's family.'

Of course, she thought, he's family, that should excuse everything.

'So what do you think is going on?'

'I really have no idea. I just think it must have something to do with the drugs because it's the only remotely worrying thing I can think of.'

She was tempted to pull the list from her skirt pocket and give him some ideas. In fact, why didn't she? 'It could be anything, you know,' she said, 'Your great-grandfather may be ill, your parents may be divorcing.'

He shook his head emphatically, 'They would have told me.'

'Well, it doesn't help sitting here speculating,' she said, 'What can we do to find out what's going on? Who knows? Who'll talk?'

He looked unhappy, but she felt impatient with him. Did he think it would all just go away?

'You know, I spoke to your father while you were agonising over whether to tell me. He wouldn't say anything, of course, but he did give the impression he was concerned about something. And he is certainly concerned about you.'

'Why should he be concerned about me? I'm fine.'

'I don't know, he's *your* father. But I think you're right when you say something is wrong. So let's see what we can do to make it right. You can tell me exactly about this drugs business, for starters.'

In a way, she felt relieved. Just a cousin running a dodgy trade, nothing to do with her. It could have been much worse.

'Are you coming to town with me on Sunday, Claire? You can help me shop for party clothes – it's my twentieth birthday in two weeks.'

'Oh, I'd love to Bethany, but I'm not sure I'll still be here by then.'

'Until when were you thinking of staying?' Esther asked.

'I'd been planning to get back to London on Sunday. Why, am I due for housework duties?'

'No, it's just that we're having a dinner party on Tuesday, for this year's scholarship students. I thought it would be nice for them to have an accomplished academic present. And of course we'd love to have you here a little longer.'

'Oh, do stay, *cara*,' Simon pleaded.

She would have been pleased, but she suspected he simply did not want to be left alone with the mystery of his family. But she agreed readily enough. She, too, wanted to get to the bottom of that mystery, and spending more time with Simon was hardly a chore.

'Good,' Bethany said, 'Then we can go shopping after all.'

'Does Bethany know what's going on?' she asked Simon when his aunt and cousin had left, 'She doesn't appear very worried.'

But Simon was thinking of something else. 'The scholarship students. Remember what dad said? Sean Whiteside was one of them.'

'Yes, and? I don't see what that has got to do with anything.'

'Just, maybe that's what dad is upset about. Things like that tend to hit him hard. Maybe it's nothing to do with the family at all.'

'Simon, that doesn't explain your grandfather's behaviour very well, does it? I think you're backtracking. Anyway, I'm going to talk to your father.'

She followed Simon's aunt up the stairs, maybe Esther would know where Simon senior was.

'Esther! Please, wait a minute.' Why was she in such a hurry?

His aunt finally turned around on the next flight. 'I am not Esther.'

Of course, now she came to a halt a few treads below the woman, Claire knew it wasn't Esther. This one was younger and less kind. What was her name again? Hannah? Dinah? Something biblical, at any rate.

'Oh, I'm so sorry.' Though why she should come over all apologetic she didn't know. Surely the sisters knew well enough they looked alike. 'I was looking for Simon senior. I mean,' she corrected, realising that only she called him that, 'My Simon's dad.'

'Well, I'm not him either,' the aunt said, with a crinkling around her eyes, 'But I think you'll find him upstairs with my father.'

She's not so strict after all, Claire thought, whatever her name is.

'Thank you.'

They continued to climb the stairs together.

'Are you enjoying your time here, Claire?'

Only two days ago she could have answered that question honestly. Now she was suspicious of the very reasons for asking it.

'I love the house,' she said, 'And you've made me very welcome here. But it is very different from what I am used to.'

'I daresay it is. What did you want to talk to my brother about?'

She thought quickly. 'Just to ask him about the scholarships. Esther just invited me to the dinner on Tuesday, you know. I'd like to know more.'

If lying was this easy, how could you ever expect people to tell the truth?

29

'Enough!' the prior said sternly. Brother Stephen was trying his patience with his awkward questions. 'Mr Walsingham will be dealt with as those of his kind have always been dealt with.'

'You can't,' Stephen protested, 'Do you think we're still living in the middle ages? You won't get away with it. Not this time.'

'Don't you worry about me. It will all come out right.'

'I'll go to the police,' Stephen said defiantly.

'You know that is an empty threat, my son.'

The prior had always been disappointed in Stephen. He simply did not have the resolution to carry things through. In the end, his own stronger will would prevail, it always had. They both knew no word of this would ever reach the police. If the chapter failed, Stephen had more to lose than most of them.

'How can you? How can you stand there, so convinced that you are right, planning someone's death?' The prior could see there were tears in the brother's eyes. Such weakness.

'It may never come to that,' he said, attempting to placate, 'You are well aware that that is always the last measure, and not undertaken lightly. I will not put our brothers and sisters in unnecessary danger. I hope you know that, my son.'

'I find it hard to believe.'

But there was no more Stephen could say. His bluff had been called, now he just looked defeated.

'It will not matter in the long run, you know,' the prior told him, 'A year, a decade from now, this will be forgotten, and the chapter will still be as it always was.'

'Not as it always was. We've not always had blood on our hands.'

'Are you forgetting? This order was born in blood. Two died, that one should live, and live forever. Do not deny your heritage.'

'My heritage, maybe, but not my responsibility.'

'No. Mine. Don't interfere.'

'I cannot bear it.'

'You have no choice. Your brothers and sisters bear it. You can take your responsibility or run away from it, as some have done. But you will not breathe a word of this, either way.'

'You're very sure of that.'

'I will *make* sure of that.'

Unlike Brother Stephen's, the prior's threat carried force. This conversation would not be forgotten.

30

It was the first of September. He had known that already in a general way, but the date on the noticeboard announcing today's music made him suddenly conscious of the fact. It was September, and in less than a week it would be St Cloud's day. In former times all the abbots and priors of the order would have gathered in a general chapter on September seven, just like the annual meeting of the Cistercians one week later. There was a good chance they still did. Would it be possible to find out where they met? It would bring all the important people of the chapter together in one place. Dominic had a brief vision of himself infiltrating the meeting, making a grand entrance and crying 'the secret's out!'. Except, of course, that it wasn't. But maybe tonight would bring a timely revelation. In about two hours he would be talking to Jake in a popular club.

He decided that the black shirt he wore for services would do well enough for Bitters, if he changed into jeans to go with it, undid the top button and rolled up the sleeves. There was a strange interval where he wandered about the flat, waiting until it was time to leave. It had been years since he had been in a place like that, all dancing and loud music. It wasn't his scene, he had said, and even putting it like that felt strange on his lips. But he found he liked the thought of going out of a night. He confronted the idea that he had allowed himself to get perhaps a tiny bit stuffy. No need to go frequenting clubs, but why didn't he go out for a drink sometimes, or go to a concert or a film? Because he didn't really have friends here – or did he not have friends because he never went out? Whatever, something could be done about it. He wondered if they gave Inspector Collins time off to go gallivanting about town. And why was he still thinking of him as 'Inspector Collins'? *Owen.* He had kissed the man in church, he was allowed to use his given name. It was strange, he had plenty to worry about, but he was feeling all pleased and jumpy with that kiss. Dominic resolved to ask Owen out when he spoke to him again, arrange a proper date. There was that Brazilian film he wanted to see, he had half-heartedly told himself he would buy the DVD when it came out. What nonsense! He would check when it was playing and they could go and see it together. Content with his decision, Dominic set out for the club at a smart pace, not caring he was much too early.

It wasn't time for the partying crowd yet, and the interior of the club looked rather desperate and dingy to Dominic's eyes. Later, full of people and coloured lights, the music turned up even more, it would, he knew, take on a magic of its own. Now he found a banquette with a view of the entrance and watched twos and threes of people trickling in. He felt conspicuous, all on his own. There was a group that might be an office party, and another that was clearly the start of a hen night. There were a few couples at the bar. Everyone seemed to have something to shout at their neighbour. Three girls got up and swayed onto the dance floor, self-consciously pretty. Dominic watched them, a sweating glass of iced tea in his hand. More people came in, and the music changed character, becoming faster and louder. Two nervous young men claimed the end of his banquette, not looking at him. It was already ten minutes past the time Jake said he would be there. Finally Dominic saw him, coming in on his own. He scanned the room as if he owned the place, until his eyes came to rest on Dominic. He waved and started to thread a way through the crowd. It seemed to Dominic he had to hug, kiss or wave at every person between the door and where he was seated. So much for telling no one.

'Hey!' he finally shouted by Dominic's ear, 'Glad you're here. Let's go downstairs. What can I get you to drink? I'm having a rum and coke.'

'Just a coke for me,' Dominic said. He felt an urgent need to keep his head. 'Is it quieter downstairs?'

Jake shrugged beautifully. 'I hope so. Just find a table at the back, I'll be down in a moment.'

Downstairs proved as crowded as upstairs, but there were no bright, pulsing lights here. It was smokier, more intimate. He took a table as instructed and waited – again – for Jake.

'Do you come here often?' he asked, when the boy arrived with their drinks. He had the feeling it might take a while to get to the point of their conversation.

'Fairly,' Jake said, taking a healthy pull on his drink, 'It's better than the Newmarket Bar.'

'It doesn't look like the best place to talk,' Dominic offered. They still had to shout to make themselves heard.

'Yeah, but no one will be surprised to see me talking to a strange guy in a place like this. It's all part of the pattern.' He drank again. 'Look, I wanted to, I mean I–' He closed his eyes for a moment, and Dominic could see him take a deep breath.

'What did you want to tell me, Jake?' he asked gently.

The boy looked at him as if for the first time. 'Yes,' he said vaguely. 'About the chapter. I–' He suddenly set his glass down, too hard, upon the table.

'Are you all right?'

'Yes. No. I feel...'

Without further warning, Jake slid down from his chair and onto the dirty floor.

'Jake! Dominic scraped back his own chair and knelt beside him, upsetting their drinks. 'Jake!'

He did not respond, but he was breathing, short, steady breaths, and the wetness on his hands was just Coca Cola. His eyes were closed, and he did not react when Dominic shook him gently by the shoulder. Dominic scrabbled in his pocket for his phone. A curious circle began to form around their table.

'I'm a medical student,' a brisk young woman said, also hunkering down by Jake and feeling for a pulse. 'Did he take anything?'

'Ambulance,' Dominic said into his phone, 'Bitters, on Woolweaver Street. Yes. He's unconscious.'

'Heartbeat steady but slow,' the medical student said, and Dominic repeated.

'What did he take?' she asked again.

'I don't know,' Dominic said, putting his phone back in his pocket, 'He'd just arrived. He only had a drink. Will he be all right?'

'Sure,' she said, 'People pass out here all the time. Though not usually so completely.'

The other spectators drifted off again, when it emerged that there were not going to be spectacular attempts at resuscitation. After a while that seemed long to Dominic but was perhaps five or ten minutes, the neon-yellow vests of two ambulance men appeared in the crowd, followed by that of two police officers. Who called the police? Dominic wondered, as he started to tell the ambulance personnel what had happened. Jake was put on a stretcher and carried out. But when Dominic tried to follow, one of the constables held him back. 'We would like to talk to you, sir,' he said, leaning in close to make himself heard.

'I want to make sure he's all right,' Dominic protested.

'He's in good hands,' the other policeman said, 'Now.'

The odd emphasis carried no meaning for Dominic. Nor did the words the constable shouted at him over the music.

'... right to remain silent...may harm your defence...given in evidence...'

'You are detained under suspicion of introducing a harmful substance into the victim's drink without his knowledge or consent,' the custody officer said, after entering his personal details in a file, 'Do you wish to inform anyone of your arrest?'

Dominic looked at the officer, stunned by his speedy transfer into a police cell. Who was he going to worry with this news at midnight?

'That can wait until the morning,' he said. 'What happens now?'

'You will be interviewed by a detective tomorrow, who will decide if you will be released or need to remain in custody.'

'But I didn't...'

'You may have a solicitor present, if you wish.'

He understood he would learn no more tonight. The custody officer escorted him to a cell, locked the door and left him there.

31

The chapter had faced enemies of all kinds through the centuries, but Nathaniel Cottington had just been a fool, an obnoxious fool. He was the worst kind of reformer, one whose zeal far outstripped his understanding. His pamphlets made up in polemic for what they lacked in subtlety of thought. There were many like him, but only Cottington had blundered so close to the truth, shouting about sorcery and the devil. Of course people believed him, read his ranting manifestoes, were convinced that philosophical experiment and enquiry were black arts. In the abbot's long experience, it was much easier to convince people of codswallop like that than to have a reasoned argument with them. So. When Cottington mentioned the chapter by name, and threatened to expose its 'heathen practices', something had to be done.

It had been easy, really. Cottington had a study full of books and papers, cheap broadsheets, quires of foolscap. It had been easy for Brother Jonas to lure him outside with a 'message of some importance', while Brother Balthasar climbed in through the study window. Cottington wrote by the light of a lamp, and there was a small fire burning in the grate. The lamp was smashed, the oil poured over the table, the flame caught at the paper. Balthasar pulled a brand from the hearth with a set of tongs and dropped it on the strewn floor. On the desk a bible burned merrily. He only had to throw open the door to the hall to create a draught, and climb back out of the window, his work done.

When Cottington, still talking to Brother Jonas at the front door, smelled the smoke, he ran back into the house to save his books. He was not seen again on this earth.

Cottington's death had not been intended, although no one had discounted the possibility that setting fire to his house would lead to his demise. His poisonous papers were burned, and with them, for a time, the threat that the chapter's alchemical experiments would be exposed and, inevitably, condemned. The Worshipful Society of Philosophers of St Cloud were, like all alchemists, looking for the secret of eternal life. But they did not hold with astrology and mystical symbolism. The society, with the then prior of the chapter at its head, sought the secret in a spirit of reasoned experiment. The prior corresponded with Hooke and Boyle, and had been invited to read a paper at the Royal Society. To the ignorant, it all seemed equally ungodly. Cutting up animals, looking through strange glasses at little many-legged demons, boiling up hissing and spitting concoctions in strangely shaped vessels: where would it all lead?

It led, of course, by a long and tortuous route, to modern science, which had finally brought them to the point where they could recover the lost secret mentioned by Lothar in his treatise on the resurrection of the body. Brother Solomon always kept the prior up to date with the latest discoveries in the laboratory, and the prior assured the abbot there would be a breakthrough in the next two or three years. They were so close, he said, it was important that the chapter's work was not interrupted, especially now. To the abbot a few years more or less were hardly important, and there had never been anything very special about 'now'.

'What has he done?'

'You know he will not tell me,' Brother Stephen said testily, and for a moment the abbot was reminded of the surly novice he had been. 'But I am sure Rachel has hacked into his email and university accounts. She likes a challenge like that.'

'Already we are breaking the law.'

'Breaking his windows made sure of that.'

'I had hoped that would be discouragement enough.' He wondered if the prior had found out about that little escapade yet.

'I do not think– that is, I've no way of telling, of course, but I think this Walsingham doesn't take it very seriously. It is a bit unthinkable, isn't it? Even I don't quite believe the prior will take that final step.'

'He will. I have doubted it of others, but not him. He will do whatever he thinks necessary.'

'Don't you ever think we'd better go to the police with this?'

'And lose everything we've got? Everything we've built, over centuries?'

'I know. We couldn't.'

'And what could they prove if we did? He will have hidden his traces well. He'll deny it. Accidents, minor crimes. But it will rend the chapter in two.'

'I know.'

Oh, this discussion has been held before, too. The abbot knew he was old, but he never felt it so much as at times like these, when the same old arguments ran their worn-out course, and the same old conclusions were always safely reached. And he never felt so helpless as in the face of men like Brother Stephen, who looked to him for guidance and found none.

32

'Sir?'

'Inspector Collins, sir.'

'Sir!'

Everyone wanted to talk to him at once when he came in in the mornings. He knew this could be undermined by being the first to arrive, but he didn't have the knack. Half eight was early enough for him. Now he looked at the people who had followed him into his office, bringing anxious faces and bulging files, and, bless Sergeant Pardoe's kind heart, a cup of coffee.

'All right, let's take it in order of arrival,' he said, as he settled behind his desk. 'Dasgupta?'

'I have the results of the interviews with Whiteside's neighbours, sir. One of the men on the other floor of the flat recalled a visitor on the day of the murder. A man in a dark three-quarter length coat. Not exceptionally tall or short, couldn't be sure about his age, but maybe sixty or so.'

'I see.' Parka or trench coat? He could see Sally and Chandra were pleased, they thought they were one step away from having a suspect. But there wasn't anything very remarkable about a dark three-quarter length coat, unless it was that someone chose to wear it in this weather.

'Well done,' he said, 'Long shot, but try the description out on Lisa's flatmates, see if they remember someone like that visiting at other times.'

'I will, sir.' Chandra left.

Collins opened his email. Another one from DCI Flynn? Did she think he worked in his sleep?

'Pardoe?'

'I've seen the ballistics report, sir. Whiteside and Wilson were definitely shot with the same gun.'

'Thank you. At least that means we don't need to look for two killers at once.' He'd nearly said 'three'.

'Odd, though,' the sergeant added.

'What, Pardoe?'

'It's a sporting weapon, a gun-club thing. Not the kind of weapon you would expect a contract-killer to carry.'

'No, it's not. Something to keep in mind, that.'

The sergeant left.

'Sally, you're next,' Collins said, drinking his coffee and trying to decide whether he could risk ignoring the DCI's message.

'Remember that gentleman who came to see you last Monday, sir? Mr Walsingham?'

Was that only last Monday? 'Of course, what about him?' He wondered if Sally had picked up on his interest in the historian. If so, she'd been quicker on the uptake than he had himself. He hadn't known he was going to kiss Dominic until he'd actually done it.

'He's here again. I mean, he's in custody.'

'He's *what*?'

'Detained on suspicion of causing bodily harm, sir. Apparently he put something in some boy's drink in the club last night.'

He stared at her. Did she mean Jake? 'What happened? How is he?'

'I've heard the victim has already discharged himself from hospital. DS Walter is on the case, he'll be interviewing Mr Walsingham soon. Um. Apparently Mr Walsingham wanted you to be the person who was informed of his arrest. Are you all right, sir?'

'Yes. Thanks, Sally.'

He didn't understand. He didn't believe it, not Dominic. But that's what they all thought, wasn't it? To hell with that, it didn't make sense. But apparently someone had wanted to hurt Jake – why? He picked up the phone to call Walter, then decided against it. He wanted to talk to him face to face.

'Sir?'

'What is it now?' he asked irritably, before he saw Sergeant Pardoe's expression. 'Not another one?'

'Afraid so, sir. Body found this morning.'

Everything else receded into the background. 'Right, I'm on my way. Tell Sergeant Walter– oh no, he's busy, isn't he? Call Sally and Chandra back, then.'

'Do we know who he is?'

'Not sure yet, but probably who it says on the door,' the uniformed constable told him, trying to sound casual about it. It was probably his first dead body.

It was different this time. The body had been discovered in an office when the cleaner let herself in that morning. It was one of those buildings where small businesses rented office space, and the cleaning lady came from an agency and did not know who her employer was. The name on the door was 'Charles Howard, IT consultant', which didn't tell him much. Practically everyone called themselves an IT consultant these days. The name did ring a bell, though. Hadn't Walter mentioned a dealer called Charlie Howard? All this went through his head as he stood looking at the body, killed by a single shot, just like the others. A fly was buzzing around, making an odd counterpoint with the whirr of a computer fan. Had he been working when he was shot? Did that mean he had lain here since yesterday afternoon? Sally swatted the fly against the almost empty desk. 'Oh Christ, I shouldn't have,' she said at once.

'We'll let the SOCO boys know the handprint with the crushed bluebottle in the middle is yours,' Collins told her.

He walked to the window. The street below was quiet, there wouldn't be many nosy neighbours to interview here. There were offices, a childcare centre, a high-end furniture store on the corner where the street met the main shopping area.

'Are the owners of the other offices in here?' he asked Pardoe.

'No, we had the place sealed off before they started to arrive. We have some rather upset individuals outside wanting access to their workspace.'

He had vaguely noticed some people on the pavement when he came in, but had just thought the press had arrived exceptionally early. 'Set up some tables in the lobby downstairs and start interviewing them,' he told Holmes and Dasgupta, 'And make a list of those who aren't here so we can talk to them later. Pardoe, we'll do the next of kin.'

'Mrs Howard, I am afraid we have some bad news for you.' Mothers were the worst. They had always already imagined how bad it would be. All you came to do was confirm their worst fears, and break their hearts in the process. He wasn't surprised when the pleasant-looking woman who came to the door immediately said, 'Is it Charlie?'

'May we come in?' It wouldn't do to blurt it all out on the doorstep.

'Of course, do come in. Would you like some coffee?' Brightly, as if she could stave off the inevitable.

'No, thank you. Let's sit down. Mrs Howard, is your husband here?'

'He's in the garden. Ed! Ed, come in here for a moment!' she cried down the kitchen. Her husband joined them.

'Mr Howard, DI Collins and DS Pardoe, county CID. We're here about your son.'

'What has he done?' Howard said, pulling off his gardening gloves to shake their hands.

'I'm afraid Charles was found dead this morning in his office. We are treating his death as suspicious.'

No one said anything for a moment. Mrs Howard stared at him, motionless.

'Charlie?' Howard said, 'He's dead?'

'I am very sorry for your loss. Is there someone we can contact to be with you right now?'

'What happened?' Mrs Howard said, ignoring his question.

'Your son was shot in his office. The cleaning lady found him this morning.'

'And you are sure it's Charlie?' Hoping against hope that it was all a mistake.

'He had his ID with him, so there really is no doubt. We do have to formally identify him, though, if one of you feels up to that.'

'I want to see him,' Howard said forcefully.

'Of course, sir. As soon as the body has been removed from the scene of crime.'

'It was murder, then?' his wife asked softly, 'He did not kill himself?'

'That is highly unlikely. Do you have reason to believe he would do such a thing?'

'No, not at all. I just, I can't believe anyone would want to kill our Charlie.' She finally started to cry.

'Now, Mary now,' Howard said helplessly, putting his arm around her.

'We will have to take both your statements later,' Sergeant Pardoe said, 'For now, we would like to leave you in good hands. Is there someone we can contact for you? We can also arrange for you to talk to a professional later.'

Mr Howard said he would call his sister, and that further people would not be helpful right now. Collins always felt most intrusive at this point. As if it wasn't enough to inflict this kind of grief on people, he had to ask them to listen to a lot of tedious but necessary information about arrangements and interviews and warn them about the press. He did not think they took much of it in.

'We will return later to take your statements,' he concluded, 'Today or tomorrow, whenever suits you. Please call if you have any questions.'

'I always knew he would be in trouble,' Mrs Howard said through her tears, contradicting herself somewhat, 'It was the drugs, wasn't it? Like those other two in the paper?'

'It is too early to say, Mrs Howard. We will let you know as soon as we know more.'

33

'I never touched his drink,' Dominic repeated for the third time.

'*Someone* put a powerful anaesthetic in it, Mr Walsingham. Why were you meeting him?'

Sergeant Walter had a habit of switching tracks like that. It would have caught Dominic off guard is he had had any guard left to be caught off.

'He said he had some information about a religious order I was researching.' God, but that sounded improbable. He didn't blame Walter for looking incredulous.

'Given the boy's profession and your choice of venue, I consider that unlikely, but never mind. Tell me again what happened from the moment he arrived at the club.'

Dominic went through the whole thing again. 'He got the drinks on his own,' he concluded, 'I have no idea what happened between the bar and our table. He was gone a long time, he seemed to know everyone.'

Something was bothering him. Why was Walter so sure it was him who put the Oblivion – he was assuming that was what it was – in Jake's drink? How had they even known that he hadn't just fainted naturally?

Walter answered this pretty definitively with his own next question. 'We have information that someone of your description was seen stirring something into a glass at your table. We take accusations like these very seriously,

Mr Walsingham. You may recall a similar incident that turned out fatal.'

'Look, it doesn't make sense, what you are suggesting,' he protested, 'You think I wanted Jake unconscious or misjudged the dose or something. Presumably you think I wanted him for sex, but if so, I could just as easily have paid for it. I am assuming drugs like that don't come cheap either.'

'Some men like their victims helpless, Mr Walsingham. Did you find Jake attractive?'

Jesus, who would want to be a policeman? Always thinking the worst of people. The constable sitting in on the interview was looking properly disgusted.

He tried for nonchalance. 'He was good-looking, but a bit young for my taste.' And where had he heard that before?

Walter went off on a tangent again. 'How did you meet?'

Now there was a problem, and he knew that whatever he said, Walter would think he was lying. He could only be vague and hope for the best.

'Someone I know told him about the research I was doing. He accosted me in the Close, saying he wanted to talk to me.' To cover the embarrassment of this, he went on to the attack. 'So who told you I put something in his drink? And do you have anything approaching *proof* that I did?'

'I ask the questions here, sir, if you don't mind.'

There was a knock on the door of the interview room.

'Interview suspended at 09:35,' DS Walter told the recording equipment.

A second constable entered the room. 'Sir, we have got a CCTV tape from the club. It shows the victim at the bar, talking for a time to two young women. It's grainy, but it looks like one of them handles his drink at one point.'

'I see. Does Mr Walsingham show up on the tape?'

'Not that I can see. And since our anonymous tip-off was a woman... bit of deliberate misdirection there, I think.'

Dominic heaved a sigh of relief at the disappointed look on Walter's face.

He was released quickly afterwards, with apologies and assurances that he would be contacted if there were any more questions. He had rarely felt so happy just walking through town, even in yesterday's clothes, which smelled of sweat and cigarette smoke. He headed for the cathedral, but then decided that going home really had priority right now. He wanted a shower and his own place around him. His interview with DS Walter had shaken him more than he could have predicted. He had not really been afraid they could frame him for something he had in the end quite evidently not done, but the sergeant's insistent suspicion had got to him. Did Owen conduct interviews like that, always assuming the worst? He had been stupid about DI Collins, he realised now. They had known each other for four days, had kissed once. He didn't really know anything about him. He had inquired if the inspector was at work, and asked that nice DC Holmes to tell him he was there. What had he been expecting – immediate rescue? When the custody officer brought him to the interview room, Collins had walked past without even looking in his direction. It was probably just an embarrassment to him, this ill-advised association with a suspect. Especially one who was thought to have drugged a boy he clearly cared about.

As he turned into St Mary's Lane, he wondered how Jake was doing. The DC had said he was out of hospital, so presumably he was okay. Dominic regretted that he had no means to contact him.

'There he is!'

Two lads he hadn't been paying attention to suddenly got up from next-door's garden wall and blocked his path.

'They let you go then, didn't they?' one asked. He was young, barely twenty, tall and thin, not much to look at.

'What do you want?'

'We want you to leave our mate alone, mate,' the other said, taking a step closer. He was shorter than his friend, but looked stronger.

'You mean Jake?' Dominic said incredulously.

The first man pushed him in the chest. 'Don't play ignorant. We're here to teach you a lesson.'

'I had nothing to do with it!' Dominic protested, stepping back. That was a mistake. It brought him with his legs against the low wall of Mrs Withers' front garden, and one more push sent him sailing backwards over it. He landed awkwardly in a flower bed, and his assailants were over the wall and after him before he could get to his feet. Tall and willowy stood on his hand, while short and brawny aimed his foot at Dominic's kneecap. When the next kick connected with his temple, Dominic stopped trying to defend himself and just curled into a protective ball while his attackers continued to use him as a punchbag.

'Take that, you bastard.'

'Get up and fight, why don't you?'

'Enough of that!' another, authoritative voice interfered, 'I'm calling the police right now.'

As suddenly as they had appeared, Dominic's assailants stopped what they were doing and fled. A neatly manicured hand reached over the garden wall to help him up.

'I would have set off in pursuit, but that wouldn't be wise at my age. Are you all right?'

'Just bruised, I think,' Dominic said dizzily, brushing earth from his clothes.

'They weren't trying to kill you,' his rescuer said, 'But you got a good kicking. Would you like me to drive you to A&E?'

He was a man of about sixty, in a three piece suit that made no concessions at all to the weather. He looked distinguished and completely unruffled. 'Danvers,' he said, shaking Dominic's dirty hand, while Dominic not quite truthfully protested that he felt fine.

The name cleared an instant pathway in his brain.

'Mr Danvers, thank you so much, I don't know what I would have done if you hadn't come along,' he said, suddenly coherent. 'But you are right, they weren't trying to kill me, no need to bother a doctor. Would you like to come in for a moment, have a cup of coffee? Least I could do.'

'No, no, I'll have to be on my way. I hope those bruises soon heal, Mr Walsingham.' And with that he walked off, a perfectly composed gentleman on a quiet street, as if there never had been any violence.

Dominic walked up the stairs and went into his flat. He locked the door behind him, and then stood leaning against it, the back of his head touching the wood, taking very deep breaths.

I should call the police, he kept telling himself, as he made tea, had a shower, studied his bruises in the mirror. I should call the police, I was attacked in the street, people should not get away with that. But he did nothing. He could tell DS Walter – he did not want to think about talking to Collins – what those two boys had said, in effect telling him that other people did believe he had drugged Jake. He could also tell him that a conveniently passing Danvers had come to his rescue, though presumably Walter would not see anything significant in that name. The rescue had almost been more peculiar than the assault. Why had those boys fled as soon as a silver-haired gentleman approached? They had been young and strong enough to take him on as well, Danvers had been a small man, and forty years older than they were. But as soon as he had spoken they hadn't struck another blow, they'd just run. And Dominic thought he might have been bumbling a bit, in the aftermath, but he was sure as hell he had not told Danvers his name. The unpleasant thought presented itself that it had been Danvers who set those lads upon him in the first place, the references to Jake just an excuse. And he was not going to try and explain that to Sergeant Walter.

As he sat drinking his tea, trying to regain a form of composure, it occurred to him what he really wanted to do. He did not want to give up, not even pretend to. But he did not have to play by the chapter's rules either. He still did not know their secret, but there were also a few things about him he hoped the chapter did not know. He turned on his computer and went online. There were quite a lot of things to arrange and find out, if he wanted to put his plan into practice soon, and he got so busy that a few times he forgot he ached in a dozen places. He wrote a letter to James Sutherland's former student, asking for information. Sending an email might have been easier, but he didn't. For all he knew the chapter might be reading his email. He had no idea how that worked, but he knew it was possible. He also dashed off a reply to Claire Althorpe, suggesting lunch next week. She might be able to help, too.

Having a plan and something to do was good, but he still startled at perfectly normal sounds, and he found himself looking out of the window too often. How long had that car been there? He wished the pane in the kitchen had been repaired, and that the door had a stronger lock. Sleep was not going to come easy tonight. It had been a hot day again, and the air was heavy and oppressive.

When the bell rang at half past eight he almost jumped out of his skin.

34

'Simon, I've been thinking,' Claire said, folding up her evening paper, 'These murders the whole town is in uproar about, isn't that what's got everyone worried? I mean, it says here the victims were all small-time drug dealers. Your cousin may be in danger.'

'Could be,' Simon said doubtfully, 'Although there must be a lot of those around, surely? And Adam's not– I mean, it's not as if he hangs around on street corners or in the bars or anything. I think he's got people for that.'

She disliked the casual way he said that. 'People who are getting killed,' she reminded him.

'Do they really think these people were murdered because of the drugs?'

'It's apparently what connects them. Or maybe it's just a way the police have of saying that they're stumped.'

'Can I see?'

Claire handed over the paper. Something about the article was troubling her. 'Can you read me the bit about the chronology again?' she asked him.

'Sure. Let's see. August 28: Sean Whiteside is shot inside the family home. August 30: Lisa Wilson is found dead by a roommate. September 1–'

'No, no, that's it. That's it right there. Simon, do you remember when we met your aunt Dorrie on the stairs, and she said Judith was upset about the murder? I'm sure that was the very same day the girl was killed. It wasn't on the news till much later, only that night. So how could they know?'

'Are you sure?'

'I know, it was the day before your mother did the book signing.'

'I doesn't mean anything,' Simon said, 'Judy knew Lisa, someone must have called to tell her.'

'They were at school together, not that close.'

'Look, there are so many ways she could have heard. Email. Twitter.'

'I sincerely hope people do not tweet about their murdered friends,' Claire said, thinking she sounded old and grumpy.

But Simon wasn't paying attention to that. 'I don't like what you're suggesting, it's preposterous. You can't be saying my auntie or my sister goes around shooting people dead.'

'I wasn't saying that. But it's as good a reason as any for behaving mysteriously,' Claire replied. She couldn't believe it herself even so.

'Judith hasn't been behaving mysteriously.'

'No? I think your sisters are always behaving as if they have mighty secrets to share.'

'They're teenage girls, what do you expect?'

This was coming perilously close to a row.

'All right, forget about it. It may mean nothing, anyway.'

She thought he didn't want to talk about it anymore, but half an hour later he was back, still carrying the newspaper.

'I thought you were going for a ride with Bethany this evening?'

'I changed my mind. Look, I think you're right that it's these murders everyone is worried about. But maybe it's not because of my cousin Adam.' He unfolded the newspaper on her desk. 'Sean Whiteside. My father knew him, he won the scholarship two years ago. Lisa Wilson. She was with a temping agency, she worked in my uncle's office at some point. And Charles Howard, he was a colleague of Luke's.'

'You mean your friend, Paul's brother Luke?'

'No, I mean our Luke, who lives here. Well, sort of. Not that he's ever in. But what I mean is, all the victims had something to do with the family.'

'Yes, but Simon, only tenuously. And you're a large family, I bet together you know nearly the whole town.'

They had switched roles, with Simon suggesting connections Claire thought improbable. But it wouldn't let her go. There had to be something they were overlooking. Something useful someone could tell them. She resolved to talk to Simon's father again. She had the idea he had been steadily avoiding her, and that suggested there was something he wasn't saying.

What he did say, when she tracked him down in the stables, was anything but reassuring. He wouldn't really look at her while he was putting away his horse's tack, just answered her question evasively.

'I think it's better you don't know. Can you trust me on this? It's better for Simon if he isn't involved. And for you.'

'That's not fair, you know. He's old enough to make his own choice in that, you cannot keep it from him.'

'I'm not keeping it from him, I hardly know more than he does. I just know it can only damage him.'

'Is it to do with the murders?' she asked boldly. He turned away, fussing with the bridle. He looked so much like Simon, the same helpless boy in twenty years' time.

'Can't you leave, Claire? Take Simon home with you, have nothing to do with all this.'

'I just promised I'd stay on for the dinner party on Tuesday.' I promised Simon I'd stay.

'Never mind about that,' he said, 'It doesn't matter. Your loyalty doesn't have to be to this family.'

'I know, but I can't. I can't just walk away,' she told him.

'You're a brave woman.'

But it wasn't that. She was more cowardly than he thought. What kept her there was the certain knowledge that if she left, Simon would not be coming with her.

35

When Alfred Poole published his *History of the Monastic Orders*, and made clear his intentions to make St Cloud his next object of study, the abbot had remembered Nathaniel Cottington, and prepared for the worst. He had pondered ways to dissuade the clergyman from his purpose, and had worked hard to unearth anything that might be used to blackmail Poole. Unfortunately, Alfred was a man of impeccable morals. They had just set in train a complex plan to blacken his reputation when he was robbed in the street and left for dead. Brother Bartholomew, who had been following him at the time, set off in pursuit of the miscreants, but to no avail. It was a pity, a good man cut off that way in his prime, but the abbot had heaved a quiet sigh of relief. It wasn't often that problems like that went away of their own accord. They certainly wouldn't this time. The abbot paced the long corridors of the Chapterhouse, thinking, thinking.

How he loved this house. It was where they had ended up after the troubles, it had been their safe haven for centuries now. The thought of leaving it was unthinkable. The house held memories, and reminded him of the other buildings where they had been safe, secluded. Things weren't like that anymore, of course. Seclusion was neither practicable nor necessary these days, and he looked with wonder at the few religious houses that were still enclosed. Secrecy was another matter. It was hard-wired, part of his being, part of their being. There was secrecy even within the chapter, as he had been forcibly reminded these past few days. It should not matter, every member of the chapter was accountable for their own actions, and as long as they acted in good conscience, the abbot had nothing to do with it. But he was worried now. He thought of Nathaniel Cottington, choking on the smoke of his own burning papers, of Alfred Poole dying on the wet cobbles. Not that, no, not that. He would talk to the prior again, convince him there were other ways.

He was glad there was the general chapter meeting coming up soon, it was only five days until then. Even the more distant members would attend, and there might be cooler heads among them who would take a rational view of the situation, who might prevail on the prior to think twice. In the past, the general chapter had been a grand occasion, with other abbots and priors from far and wide gathered in the great abbey on the Seine, and later at St Bernard's Priory. Time was when they had to speak Latin because they did not understand each other's tongues. Nowadays those who gathered in the Chapterhouse did not need to travel far, and every member of the order was welcome. There weren't that many of them left now, and the chapter was not their entire life as it was for earlier generations. Yes, these secular folk might show the prior that his singular concern was not the right way anymore. If it ever was.

36

'I've come to apologise.' It was DI Collins, neatly suited as ever, carrying a bottle of wine. 'May I come in?'

'Of course,' Dominic said, taking the chain off the door. He wasn't sure what to think of this. 'What are you apologising for?'

'The appalling behaviour of Walter in keeping you so long, mostly. And for not dropping in on you this morning. As you may have heard, something else interfered.'

He hadn't heard yet. 'Another murder?'

'Another murder,' Collins said with a sigh, 'A known dealer this time. But I'm not here about that. Are you all right?'

'Of course,' Dominic said, and immediately thought that that must be obviously untrue. He accepted the bottle of wine.

'Then what's this?' Collins asked, touching his fingers gently to Dominic's temple.

'Nothing,' he shrugged away the hand, 'A bit of bother on my way home.'

The inspector looked at him much as DS Walter had done that morning, disbelief plain on his face. 'Are you going to tell me?'

Dominic gave in. 'Would you like a glass of wine?'

'Since you're offering.' Collins sat in the same armchair as last time.

'How's Jake?' Dominic asked, prevaricating, 'You do believe I had nothing to do with that, don't you?'

'Jake's fine. He called this afternoon. Doesn't remember much about what happened, though.'

'But–'

'I know it wasn't you, Dominic. But after that tip-off they had no choice but to arrest you. And Walter may be obnoxious, but he's a good cop, he wouldn't hold anyone without good cause.'

'So do you know who it was, then?'

'You heard about the girls on the CCTV tape? We're looking for them. But Jake says he doesn't remember talking to any girls, which *could* be true, given the nature of Oblivion.'

'You don't believe him?' Dominic asked, surprised.

'He says to forget about the whole thing. He may be protecting someone, or he may just not care. I've no idea what he knows, or even about what, and he's refusing to give a statement.'

'That's strange.'

'It's Jake,' Collins shrugged, 'Things happen on his terms or not at all. He'd be an arrogant little fucker if he didn't charm the hell out of most people. Why are we talking about him and not about you? Who roughed you up?'

Dominic told him what had happened that afternoon, including the gentleman called Danvers.

Collins frowned at him. 'You should have come straight back to the station. Assault is a serious crime, Dominic.'

'Is that all you can say? Whatever happened to 'Christ, I'm sorry, how are you feeling now?"

'I would have said that if you'd turned up at the station all bloody and beaten,' he said. 'It's just that you're not making my job any easier you know, first Jake and now you, refusing to make a complaint.'

'I didn't because I don't think they were friends of Jake at all. I think it was Danvers who sent them in the first place, I think it was a warning. And I'm heeding it. I suppose that's what Jake is doing, too.'

He poured them both another glass of wine. It was excellent. He didn't want to talk about this, really, he was sick of it. Did Collins have to look at everything professionally? He'd hoped for a bit of sympathy, but like this morning, he was disappointed.

'It would be useless making a complaint, anyway,' he said, 'Like with the burglary – they'll never get caught.'

'You've not much confidence in us.'

Didn't he? It was a question he'd never really given thought before, he just assumed the police did their jobs. He was pretty sure Owen Collins was conscientious about it. But the last few days hadn't given him much reason to be confident.

'I spent the night in the cells while a murderer was free to go about his business,' he said.

'That's not quite fair, I think,' Collins said sharply, 'But I'll make allowances for your condition.'

'You make me sound like a pregnant woman. What condition?'

Collins got up and plumped down next to him on the settee. 'Dominic, you had a date with a boy you don't know from Adam, you saw him faint dead away, were arrested before you could get to grips with that, spent the night in custody, were interviewed by a right bastard – you didn't hear me say that – and when you were released you were attacked by two yobs who may have been sent by the chapter. And now you've got a visitor of whom you don't know why he's here. I'd have been very surprised to find you all calm and collected.'

'Oh.' Dominic stared at him. 'Why *are* you here?' he asked.

'Because I thought you might like someone to talk to, after what happened. Because you asked for me this morning and I wasn't there.' He touched the bruise on Dominic's temple again, and it was almost a caress. Sympathy after all.

'Thanks,' Dominic said. 'You're right, I'm all in a state. It's brought it home to me somehow, what happened to Jake, more than the break-in did. They're serious about this. They're serious about wanting me out of the way.'

'Jake didn't get the chance to tell you anything?'

'Just that it was about the chapter. Then he went out like a light.'

Collins shook his head. 'I really don't see what he's got to do with it.'

'I suppose he, um, gets to meet a lot of different people. He may have heard something from a client.'

'The randy monk confiding in the kind-hearted prostitute? I only wish real people were so free with their secrets.'

The flat was lit by a flash of lightning, thunder following almost at once. Dominic didn't really want to talk about Jake right now.

'Hark at that,' he said, 'I suppose we had it coming for days.'

Another stab of lightning, and then he could hear the rain beginning to clatter down. Collins got up to look out of the window. 'Yes, it was high time. You do know you're being watched, don't you? That car's been there all evening, and the driver's not going anywhere.'

'I know.' He came to stand behind Collins, looking at the rain streaming down. Another crack of thunder split the air.

Collins half-turned, his shoulder brushing Dominic's. 'You know I'm not just here to talk. Will your bruises allow this?'

He slid his arm around Dominic's back, gently pulling him in for a kiss. Dominic forgot all about his bruises. Of course this was what he wanted, what he had wanted all the time.

'We're being watched,' he said, pulling away a little, looking out again.

'Exactly,' Owen said, 'So now they know you have police protection tonight.'

'You're staying, then?' he asked, with a quick, sideways glance.

'You wouldn't send a man home in this?'

37

Walsingham's entanglement with the police detective was unfortunate. The prior couldn't understand how the relationship had escaped his watchers. If he had known, he would never have allowed Brother Austin to employ his thugs on the historian. He had been counting on Walsingham to be frightened into silence by the encounter, but he suspected that the arrival of the boyfriend in blue had put paid to that. It was unfortunate, too, that presumably the name Danvers was now known to the police. This complicated things. It would be much harder to tackle Walsingham with Collins hanging around like a loyal watchdog. He would have to find a way to call the inspector off. Possibly Brother Austin could help him again, he was proving extremely resourceful.

The prior was beginning to feel hurried. It wasn't long until the general chapter, and he wanted this business out of the way before then. He didn't have the patience for long explanations and argument, this new passion for democracy. It was time to act decisively. He would have Collins removed, make sure Walsingham never mentioned the chapter to anyone again.

There was a quick knock on the door, and Sister Rachel entered, carrying her laptop. 'Look what I found,' she said, 'I knew reading his emails would pay off.'

'Well done,' he said, as he read the short message from the railway company. It looked like Walsingham, far from giving up, had decided to broaden the horizons of his research. The prior saw the possibilities at once, they could hardly be bettered. 'I'm going to call Solomon. And do you know which of the sisters will be free for a short trip to France, tomorrow or the day after?'

'I could go,' she said eagerly, 'What do you want me to do?'

He considered the option for a moment, but he knew she was too young for that responsibility. 'No. One of the senior sisters should go. And I'm afraid Mr Walsingham would be immune to your charms, my dear.'

He dialled a number he knew by heart.

'Solomon? It's me. I need your help. No, something stronger this time, sure to be lethal. Yes? Thanks. Yes, I'll send Lucas to pick it up. Tell me, have you had any trouble with the police recently? People asking questions? Oh, good. Well, be careful. No, it's fine, fine. Everything under control. We'll see you at the general chapter, won't we? Thank you, brother. Until then.'

38

Dominic woke to a warm hug from behind.

'Ouch,' he said pleasantly.

'Sorry.' Owen shifted his grip to spare his bruised ribs. He nuzzled Dominic's shoulder. 'And sorry to wake you up so early, but I have to go.'

'Hm. What time is it?' he asked, burrowing into the embrace.

'Half six.'

'Half six?' he yawned, 'On a Saturday? They do work you hard.' So this hug wasn't a prelude to sex, then. Shame.

'I'm not going straight to the station. I want to stop by my place to get clean clothes and stuff. You can stay and sleep in.'

A kiss on his cheek and a sudden shift as Owen's weight left the mattress. The sound of the lavatory flushing, a rustle of clothes, the thud-*click!* of the front door and Dominic was alone, feeling oddly bereft. But he was glad Owen hadn't slipped off without waking him, and his early departure saved Dominic explaining why he himself had to be up and about at seven. He ate his breakfast standing up while packing his bag. He had meant to do it last night, but other things interfered. Now he quickly threw together the basics. He snatched up the print-outs with travel information, made sure he had his new notebook and the St Cloud folder. He wrote a note for Mrs Withers to say that he would be away for a few days and pushed it through her letterbox. He slung his bag over his shoulder and walked down to the Close. The church wasn't open yet, and he contented himself with a friendly pat on the transept wall, trying to suppress the melodramatic feeling that he might be doing this for the last time. He quickly walked on to catch the 8:02 to London. He was in plenty of time, and he watched from the window as the man who followed him bought a ticket and boarded another coach. Oh well, he hadn't expected to shake them off at once. It was another one again from the lost driver and the young bloke who he'd thought had been cruising him, but he did look familiar. Of course, he did not know how long they had been keeping an eye on him, he might have seen him around before in the library or the church. His heart was beating high in his chest, and he was glad when the train moved off. His whole plan depended on the chapter not being able to predict exactly where he was going, but this first stage was a familiar journey he might make any day. It was when he got to St Pancras that things would get critical. He kept his mobile turned off, he did not want anyone being able to trace him. The papers had been full of a phone-hacking scandal recently, apparently no conversation was safe.

He had left very little check-in time at the Eurostar terminal, knowing from experience that you didn't need as long as the company advised. He was counting on it not being enough time to purchase a ticket for the same train. At best, his pursuer would be on the next train out, and he would have lost him in Brussels. When the train set off, a little on the late side, Dominic felt the safest he had in days – with the possible exception of last night.

He used his time in the long tunnels well. He wrote emails to both Saskia and Blake, telling them what he had found out about the earlier murders and giving them DI

Collins's phone number in case anything happened to him. He didn't send the messages yet, though. That would have to wait until he could make sure it was secure. He still couldn't shake the feeling that this was overdoing it, but he told himself better safe than sorry. It felt odd giving Blake the number of a man he – fancied? had fallen for? rather liked? – but of course he didn't mention that in his message. By the time they were speeding through France, he was typing out everything he knew about the chapter in a master file. He was struck again by how little it really was. If you left out the things he had learned only from Poole's speculations or Wright's research, what was left was sketchy indeed. Perhaps today he would finally learn more.

Four hours later he was walking through one of his favourite cities, confident that he must have shaken off anyone tailing him, if not in London or Brussels, then when changing trains at The Hague. Certainly there hadn't been anyone resembling his earlier followers on the half-empty sprinter train that took him to Haarlem. Now he made a bit of a detour to have a quick look at St Bavo's church before taking one of the narrow, cobbled side streets. Through a brick gate grown with ivy he arrived in a quiet square. The neutral plaque next to the door said '*Sint Clothilde Abdij*'. He rang the bell. It was hard to believe such a peaceful place existed in the middle of a busy town.

An older woman in a white habit and black veil came to the door.

'*Goedemiddag*, I have an appointment with Mother Clarissa. Dominic Walsingham. I emailed yesterday? I'm afraid I'm a bit early.'

'Of course. I'm Sister Bernardine. Please come through.'

39

It was a good thing Collins had a reason to feel cheerful, because the team meeting early that morning was as dispiriting as ever. The problem, he thought, and not for the first time, was that they weren't really a team. He got along with them well enough individually, he even respected Walter's experience sufficiently to take him seriously, but during these meetings he mostly felt impatient. They all waited for the others to say something first. He hoped Holmes and Dasgupta did it out of respect for their elders, they were bright enough otherwise. Stephen Pardoe wasn't a great one for ideas at the best of times. Walter just sat and waited, with a 'you're the inspector here' look on his face. Bridget Flynn always talked to him as if he ran investigations entirely on his own, which didn't help matters either. The result was that he did most of the talking himself, and found it harder and harder to sound convincing. It wouldn't bother him so much if there weren't lives at stake.

'Three murders,' he said, 'I need hardly remind you that it's only a matter of time before there's a fourth. It's up to us – and I hope you are taking this in – it's up to us to make sure that doesn't happen. No one else is going to solve this. We are.'

He quickly outlined again the precious little they knew. 'We cannot discount the possibility of a contract killer, but these people were all small fry in the drugs trade, and the choice of weapon – a sporting gun – makes it unlikely. Which means we are dealing with a lone nutter here.'

'Lovely. So it could be anyone.'

'Thank you for that encouraging contribution, Chandra.' Oh dear. Getting sarcastic now. Bad for motivation. 'No, not just anyone. The victims weren't chosen randomly.'

'Do we know that for sure?' Sally said. 'I mean, I don't want to rain on our only lead, but couldn't the Oblivion be a coincidence? They were all young people, and from what I hear the Newmarket Bar is awash with the stuff.'

'They didn't just use it, though. They sold it. And we know Whiteside got his from Charlie Howard,' Walter said.

'Oh? I didn't know that.'

'There's something new every time you talk to Selina Brinkmann, we should have her on the force,' Owen said, 'But never mind that. As you rightly say, Sally, it is our only lead. And that means we have to be alert for unlikely people seeking out dealers. Jim in Narcotics is keeping an eye out for irregularities. But that's not as easy as it sounds. Never mind the Newmarket Bar, the whole town's awash.'

'Surely that's overstating the case?' Pardoe said ponderously.

'Not as much as I'd like. We're apparently having more trouble with Oblivion here than anywhere except London.'

'Which means more possible targets.'

'Yes. So we'd better get to work. Pardoe, I want you to talk to Howard's family again, especially his mother. It struck me he was being unusually open with her about where he got his money from, he may have told her if he had any strange customers recently. Walter, I want to know everything Miss Brinkmann knows, pull her in if necessary. Holmes and Dasgupta –'

He paused. They were both looking at him expectantly, hoping he had some exciting assignment for them.

'I want you out there tonight being as plainclothes as you can, asking any likely suspect where a person would get their party drugs these days. Bitters, the Newmarket, the Hollow Crown, do them all.'

'But didn't we get that list?' Chandra asked.

'Look, if Jim in Narcotics needs drugs, he arrests a gang. That's very little to do with Sean and Lisa's world. And it is in their world that we need to look for our killer.'

'Okay. What do we do until then, sir?'

'Paperwork.'

'And what are *you* going to do?' Walter asked pointedly, after they had left behind Holmes and Dasgupta with a pile of witness statements to file.

'I'm going to talk to a solicitor.'

'Inspector, sit down, what can I do for you? Is it about poor Lisa?'

Lisa? Oh, she had worked in this office for a while.

'No, it is not about that. Mr Danvers, I would like to ask you a few questions about what happened on St Mary's Lane last Friday. You witnessed two young men attacking another and interfered, is that right?'

'That's right. So they send Detective Inspectors after a couple of unruly youths, now, do they?' Danvers asked, with perfectly arched eyebrows. The unspoken accusation – shouldn't you be catching a murderer? – hung in the air between them.

'Wouldn't usually,' he said, with what he hoped came across as a boyish shrug, 'But Mr Walsingham happens to be a friend of mine.'

'I see.'

Yes, you bloody well do, don't you? Owen thought. 'Could you tell me what happened yesterday afternoon?'

He did, very precisely. The solicitor would have made a wonderful witness, if Collins had believed a word he said.

'So the lads just ran away? That's strange.'

'I did threaten to call the police.'

'But you didn't. Why?'

'Mr Walsingham insisted he was fine.'

'How did you know that was his name?'

'Why, we introduced ourselves, of course. What would you have done in the circumstances? Inspector, with all due respect, but shouldn't you be asking me about those thugs who attacked your friend? It can hardly be relevant what we spoke about afterwards.'

'Very well, what can you tell me about 'those thugs'?'

'I didn't get a very good look at them I must say, they ran away rather quickly. I had the impression one was considerably taller than the other. They were dressed in jeans I think, and T-shirts. Naturally my concern was more for Mr Walsingham at that moment, although now I wish I'd paid more attention. Did he make a complaint? He appeared rather keen to forget about the whole thing, I should say.'

'We take assault very seriously, Mr Danvers.'

'Ah, so he hasn't made a complaint. And does your Chief Inspector know you are out on a limb, Mr Collins?'

'You do not think Mr Walsingham's assailants should be apprehended?'

'Of course, of course. But you must understand I take the law's point of view on this. No complaint, no crime. And no reason for you to concern yourself with me, Inspector Collins. Let me ask my secretary to show you out.'

'Tell me something,' he asked the secretary, 'Does Mr Danvers usually work on a Saturday?'

'He does, sometimes, when there is a matter he wants to attend to personally. I don't mind, I get paid overtime.'

Yes, or a matter he doesn't want his partners to know about, Collins thought. Maybe I'm not the only one who's out on a limb here.

As she walked him down the stairs, Collins asked her whether she had known Lisa Wilson.

'Oh yes, I knew her,' she said dismissively, 'I told that woman Holmes all about it. Why do you keep asking? You know it was the drugs right? It's only to be expected when you get involved with that kind of thing.'

That was one way of looking at it.

'You'd be amazed how many people who are 'involved with that kind of thing' live to a great age. And it doesn't get us very far catching her killer.'

'That's your job.'

Somehow, Collins felt they were glad to see the back of him at Taylor, Danvers & Weir. And he had to admit it had been a pretty useless exercise. He would use it as an excuse to call Dominic and then stop wasting police time and concentrate on the murder case.

Two hours onwards nothing remained of his cheerful mood. Dominic's phone kept diverting straight to voicemail. Walter reported that Selina was nowhere to be found – was that suspicious or just normal student behaviour, staying with her parents for the weekend? Pardoe returned gloomy-faced from his interview with Mrs Howard, complaining he was getting too old for this job. DCI Flynn called to say she wanted an update on the case before she went home, and he had nothing new to tell her.

Maybe he should go home as well. It was just that during an investigation, home was the last place he wanted to be. Should he try texting Dominic or was that too much?

40

The abbey of St Clothilde had been founded in Haarlem in 1242 by a daughter of the Count of Holland, who granted the land to be settled by nuns from the mother house in Antwerp, and joined the community herself when she was widowed. It was one of the two convents Dominic had found which had an unbroken line of filiation leading back to the original *Abbaye de St Cloud*. The other was a house of strict Trappistines in France where he had been firmly told he was not welcome. But St Clothilde's sisters were very different, and quite used to historians visiting their extensive library.

'We had a young Gregorian scholar here only last week, wanting to look at our missals,' Sister Bernardine said, as she led him to the Mother Superior's office, 'But it is our own history you are interested in, isn't it? That is unusual. The monastic life is not, I think, fashionable.'

'You should talk to my colleague Claire,' Dominic said, 'She knows all about the fashionableness or otherwise of the monastic life.'

The first thing he did, after he had been introduced to Mother Clarissa, was ask the use of the landline. He called his mother, asked her the password to her email account and used it to send the messages to Blake and Saskia. He made sure he kept the reason for this request quite vague, implying trouble with his own account. He did not want to worry her. That was also the reason he hadn't gone to stay with her in Utrecht; the bruise on his face and scratches on his arms looked more painful than they felt. Instead, he had arranged beforehand to stay the night at St Clothilde's – the French Trappistines would have been horrified – and to have a look at the archives tomorrow. They made him welcome, these kind, quiet women, most of them elderly. The abbey might be called after St Cloud's grandmother, but he could not imagine there was anything about the chapter which impinged on their ordered, contemplative life. He ate a silent meal in the refectory, and afterwards Sister Bernardine led him to a simple room, where she left him to his own devices. He checked his mother's email account, knowing this was over-eager after only two hours, and then decided to have an early night.

He felt quite sheltered, lying in his cool, narrow bed. Almost as safe as he had felt last night with Owen. It had been too hot to sleep all bunched up together, but it had been so comforting to feel him there. He wondered, now, what he wanted from Owen. Was he just clinging to the only person who could help him? Or was there more to this, would there still be something when the trouble with the chapter was over? It was useless speculating, but he liked the prospect, and he knew he liked more about Owen than what he needed him for now and, not to put too fine a point on it, his body. Though that was a definite plus... what a thing to be contemplating in a convent cell! His thoughts drifted apart, and soon enough he was asleep.

'I would like to look at the founding charters, and any correspondence with the mother house in the early centuries,' Dominic explained, 'I'm looking for references to the Chapter of St Cloud especially.'

'It would certainly have to be the early centuries for that,' Mother Clarissa said, 'We've been plain Cistercians since before the reformation.'

'There is no contact with the chapter at all then?'

'I wouldn't even have known what you meant by that, if I hadn't been here twenty-five years ago. You are not the first to be interested in these matters,' she said, while Sister Jacobje carefully placed the *Oorkondenboek* on a lectern, 'There was a woman who came, years ago, I was still a novice. Such a nice lady, asking these very same questions about the Chapter of St Cloud. I had never heard of it, back then.'

'A woman came?' he asked, surprised. He would have expected Barry Skinner, or even James Sutherland.

'Yes, but what was she called? Her first name I remember: Benedicta, so unusual. But what was her surname?'

'Benedicta Danvers?' That seemed even more unlikely.

'Yes! Do you know her? But no, she couldn't be alive yet. I remember I thought her quite old at the time.'

'No, I don't know her, but I've heard of her. She would be in her nineties now, I suppose, if she were still alive. But why would she be here?'

'Why are *you* here?' the abbess asked. He had the feeling she was used to asking questions in that pointed way, and used to getting straight answers.

'Because of this,' he said, indicating the handwritten register, knowing he wasn't being honest enough.

'Most historians are more interested in the originals,' she said. 'Of course, they aren't complete.'

'Are you sure of that?'

She looked surprised. 'Yes, I am sure. There are items in the registers that aren't in the books of charters. That's not so strange. Things get lost, through the centuries.'

You're the historian here, was the implication, you should know that.

'Interesting. Well, I think I have everything I need here. Thank you so much.'

'I'll leave you to your work. Call Sister Jacobje if there is anything else.'

It took longer than he thought, and he felt hurried, knowing there was another train to catch that afternoon. He had never really got the hang of the cursive script used in medieval charters, though he could read the Latin well enough. The seventeenth century copies were easier on the eye, but he was here exactly because he did not think he could rely on them. After three hours of painstaking comparison, he could say with confidence that what he sought could not be found at St Clothilde's. He was glad, in a way. He liked this place, it was a relief to know that the chapter's reach stopped outside its walls.

Dominic continued putting bits of information together on the Thalys to Paris. He had known he could count on Blake to find things out for him, he wasn't a journalist for nothing. His ex had sent him an article he had written a few years ago, about the search for life-prolonging medicines. He had attached his own notes, and a few links to useful websites. A quick look told Dominic that Cloud Laboratories featured prominently. Saskia had been slower coming up with information, but her search for Evangeline Danvers and her family included some interesting snippets. There were other letters, and a rare photograph of a girl with that blandly handsome look women favoured at the time. He emailed back to tell Saskia there was a small chance Evangeline's younger sister was still alive: could she find her?

41

Poor Evangeline. If regret had ever had a place in his life, it would be for her. That crisis had not been handled well. She was killed impulsively, and the effort to make it look like suicide had only just been convincing. It was only because the bobbies were too much in awe of the family to suspect them that Joseph and Isaac walked free. It had been all so unnecessary, a simple threat, blackmail possibly, and Evangeline would have lived to be ninety. And how much damage could she have done, really, with the chatter of an excitable girl in a time when women were not listened to? He hoped the prior had learned from that history. Suspicions, divisions, blunders within the chapter could be as dangerous as outside threats. Looking back over eighty years, he could see that that time marked the beginning of their decline. Girls like Evangeline didn't take their elders that seriously, and although she had paid dearly for it, the times had been with her. The customs of the order had started to look increasingly antiquated to her generation. The chapter no longer attracted new members, affiliated houses closed or drifted away. Soon they had only their own novices to teach. They became more closely knit in the years that followed, and more jealous of their secrets than was necessary. The prior was raised in that spirit, with the creed of the chapter the anachronistic centre of his life. And in the world that only encompassed the order, his own small world in which he had lived for so long, the abbot had seen too late what that could lead to.

Nostalgia was dangerous, it had coloured their judgement too long. There was no returning to the old order, not even the prior, a true chip of the old block, could achieve that. If they wanted to survive, they would have to change, like they had so often changed in the past. They could take on a new habit, forge a new chapter. The abbot knew that that was Brother Stephen's hope. But he felt too old himself to wish for a new start. Couldn't they just let it be, let it die? He had drifted so far from the creed now, giving voice to that thought. If not for the prior and his devoted followers, the chapter would be gone already.

42

'There's a pistol missing from the gun room.'

Her position on blood sports being to ignore them, Claire hadn't even set foot in the gun room yet.

'How do you know?' she asked Simon.

'How do you mean 'how do I know'? It's one of my grandfather's guns, it's always in its cabinet, and now it isn't.'

'So how long has it been gone?'

'I'm not sure. I think it was still there the day Titus and Ezra were allowed to play with the suit of armour, that was on Monday last week.'

The suit of armour. But of course.

'So what are you saying?'

She could see him take a deep breath.

'I think we got it the wrong way around. Maybe Adam isn't in danger at all. Maybe it's his rivals who are getting killed.'

'And you think...?'

'I don't want to think!' he almost shouted, 'But what else can it be? What else is so bad that we have to be protected from it, Claire?'

He had a point. But she just couldn't get her head around the practicalities.'Does your cousin have such a hold over the family that he could force them into– into murder?'

'He must have. And, I don't know, we may profit from Adam's trade more than grandfather ever told me. It costs a lot to keep up a house like this, you know.'

She was distracted for a moment by how little he knew of his family's financial affairs. It was always 'something to do with property', or 'I'm not sure what he does, exactly'. Was Simon just a bit unworldly, or were they deliberately keeping him ignorant? The latter, if his father's words were anything to go by.

'All right,' she said, 'Let's think about this rationally. What do we know for sure, what do we only suspect? And are you quite certain that gun hasn't just been taken by some bored cousin to take pot-shots at the statues in the garden?'

'Grandfather is very strict about who gets to take out a gun.'

They sat on opposite sides of the table in the library, just as they had last week when she had been trying to learn Italian. But this time the dictionary stayed closed, and they kept speaking in low voices and throwing cautious glances at the door.

'We can start by just discounting everyone with an alibi,' Claire decided, 'When Sean was killed, your father was in France, right?'

He looked relieved at that. 'Yes, and Bennett and Maisie were still on holiday. I was here all day, and so was mum.'

They worked through all the residents one by one.

'Aunt Abby hardly ever leaves the house, and, let's face it, she's not a likely killer, is she? And great-grandfather has that tremor in his hands, he couldn't possibly shoot anyone.'

Claire had her doubts about that, but she let it go. It still left plenty of family members without an alibi.

They repeated the process for the murder of Lisa Wilson on the thirtieth, and Charles Howard on the first.

'Didn't we see Bennett in town around that time?' she asked.

'No, that was mother's book signing the day before.'

'Of course. And I know Rhoda was here that afternoon, she kept me talking for ages.' She thought she'd better not mention that Simon himself had disappeared for half that day. 'And I'm sure Esther was here most of the time. And then the only one left without any alibi is...' she ticked off the list.

'...Luke,' he said.

'You said he was hardly ever in, he could have been anywhere, right?'

'He knows how to handle a gun, he's a good marksman.'

She tried to find a face for Luke. Was he the smarmy cousin who thought her bags needed carrying and her doors opening? 'But would he be capable of killing someone?' she asked sceptically.

Simon did not seem to find this as unthinkable as she did. 'If grandfather told him to, yes.'

That she found even more unthinkable. 'He would because someone else told him to?'

'If it was for the family.'

'But–' The door opened, and they fell silent at once.

'No need to look so scared, it's only me,' Bethany said cheerfully, 'Claire, are you ready to go?'

As they wandered down Woolweaver Street, Claire asked about the gun room.

'I hate that place,' Bethany replied, 'The family haven't hunted for years, we should redecorate. Of course, the boys just love the suit of armour.'

'Oh, so the guns aren't used anymore?'

'Some of my cousins shoot at the range. I'm sure I saw Luke take out grandfather's pistol only this week. I don't see the fun of standing there spitting bullets at a target, do you?'

Claire didn't think Simon's cousin was aware of the implications of what she said. That, or she was being very clever – you couldn't tell, with this family.

If only she could have shaken off the suspicion that constantly accompanied her, it would have been lovely, shopping with Bethany, all girls together. Claire realised she hadn't spoken to Gina or Bryony for days, hadn't been answering emails. It was as if the world had shrunk to the house and its inhabitants, a tiny universe with its own laws. It really wasn't healthy. But if she called Bryony now, what could she tell her? The matter of Simon's age, which had seemed momentous a week ago, now appeared to her laughably insignificant. She had no news she wished to share with anyone except Simon and she couldn't imagine ever speaking to her friends about her boyfriend's criminal family in the same way they had made light of the sect that claimed Julia's ex. They had to get out of this, and soon.

'You do know there is only one thing we can do now, don't you?' she said to Simon after dinner that night. 'Only one thing we can do, before it happens again.'

'I can't give up my family to the police,' he said, shaking his head.

'You'd be surprised. And even if *you* can't, I can.'

'You wouldn't! Without me?'

'Of course I would, if that's what it comes to. Simon, people's lives are at stake here, can't you see that? That's more important than your family.'

'Claire, if your sister was implicated in a murder, what would you do?'

The idea of Francesca killing anyone was ridiculous. 'I'd go to the police!'

'No you wouldn't. Not until you were sure. What if she turned out to be innocent? That would sour everything between you. I'm not going to the police until I know for sure who has done what.'

'Is that a risk you want to take? Think about this carefully, Simon. Is that a risk you want to take?'

43

Even police detectives got spare time once in a while, but Owen Collins was spending his free Sunday in a way that felt suspiciously like work, interviewing the surviving partner of a murder victim.

'Thank you for seeing me at such short notice,' he said, as his friendly, fiftyish host poured him a cup of Earl Grey. 'I do realise it is a long time ago, Mr Wood, and I am sorry if I bring back bad memories, but something has come to light connecting the death of Mr Skinner twenty-five years ago with two earlier murders. I'd be grateful for anything you can tell me.'

'I think I told you – well, not you personally, of course, you must have been a child – but I told the police back then everything I could think of, several times. What could I possibly add now?'

'What do you know about the Chapter of St Cloud?'

He looked surprised. 'The chapter? It was Barry's subject, of course. It was always chapter this, chapter that. I'm afraid I didn't always listen very closely,' Daniel Wood said disarmingly, 'And Barry would treat it as a bit of a joke himself. He used to say that any history of the chapter was cursed: for every fact you found, two others would disappear.'

'Was Barry in touch with any members of the chapter that you are aware?'

'I don't think so. Inspector, are you suggesting a monastic order had something to do with Barry's death?'

'I am afraid so. Two earlier historians of the chapter were also killed – before they could publish.'

'Forgive me, Mr Collins, but that sounds like fiction to me.'

And that sounded to Owen like something Bridget Flynn would say.

'I know, and so it did to me when I first heard it suggested. But someone killed Barry, and someone poisoned Alice Wright, and the little we know points at the chapter.'

'I never found his thesis,' Wood said thoughtfully, 'He'd typed out most of it by then, I always wondered where it went, his parents didn't have it. I suppose... But do you have any proof that the chapter was behind this?'

'That is what I'm looking for. Do you know whether Barry knew anyone called Danvers?'

To his surprise Wood laughed. 'You do bring back memories, Inspector! Of course, Roddy Danvers who worked in the library. We both knew her. I think she had a bit of a crush on Barry, to tell you the truth, she was always chatting to him, never gave *me* a second look. Old-fashioned kind of girl. This was the time everyone had peroxide explosions on their heads, and she wore her hair in a bun.'

'I think the nature of her interest may have been a little different.'

'You mean she belonged to the chapter? She was spying on him?'

'I think it's likely.'

Daniel Wood shook his head. 'I find it quite hard to believe. But if the police are taking it seriously...'

Collins let that one go unanswered.

'Why now though, Inspector? Why come after this twenty-five years on?'

He should have given a measured account of the events that brought him here, but what he said instead was, 'Because I couldn't bear what happened to you.'

Realising that that was too strong, he quickly filled the silence that followed with explanations. 'There is another historian of the chapter at work now, and the chapter hasn't changed, on the contrary. I really don't want him to die.'

'I see. This isn't just work for you, is it?' Wood said, looking at him inquiringly. 'You know, it's strange. After a while I learned to think of Barry's death as something like an act of God, something I couldn't help and couldn't explain. And now you come and tell me this. You may still catch his killer! I truly don't know what to think.'

'We'll inform you, of course, if it comes to that.'

'Thank you. And I do hope your friend is all right, Inspector. Will you let me know that as well?' Wood walked him to the front door, but he waited a moment before opening it. 'You know what the worst thing was, after he died? Not being still alive while he was gone. Not missing him, though that was terrible. The worst thing was that helplessness. Knowing there is nothing you can do. Nothing at all.'

Monday morning saw Collins back at his desk again, trying hard to concentrate and see the case as a whole. The three murders – he had to make a conscious effort not to think 'the *first* three' – had happened at two-day intervals. He'd been holding his breath all through Saturday waiting for the call, but nothing had happened since they found Charlie Howard. Maybe this was it, then. Three deaths, bad enough, and all he had to do was find a suspect. He had the reports from Holmes and Dasgupta, who had made good use of their night out. He had been right, there was someone outside the usual demographic looking for Oblivion. Several people had noticed him, an unfortunately nondescript male of middle years. Despite himself, Collins looked at his whiteboard. Connected with dotted lines to all three victims was the word 'trench coat'. It bothered him. They were assuming the same stranger had come knocking on all three doors, and assuming that he was the same man who had been accosting people in the bars looking for the drug, but the descriptions only fitted because of their generic vagueness. He brought the statements up on screen, went through them again.

'A man, middle-aged, I would say, with his coat around him. It was blue, I think. Yes, dark blue. He rang the bell at number 61, but I didn't see if they opened the door, I was getting the shopping in. I don't think I saw him before or since. I certainly didn't know him.'

They were all like that, well-intended but useless.

'Sir?' It was Walter, looking irritatingly smug.

'Yes?'

'Old Biddy wants to see you. In her office. Now.'

'Please, take a seat.'

He sat. DCI Flynn wasn't usually so formal.

'Do you know why you are here?' she asked him.

'If it's not about the case, then no.'

'Let's hope that's a good sign. Right, where to start? I spoke to the Chief Superintendent today. He wanted me to – unofficially as yet – inquire into your conduct as a police officer. A serious allegation has been made that you are having an improper, a sexual, relationship with a police informant and possible suspect. The complaint comes from a friend of the Super's, a solicitor who is apparently acquainted with, and prepared to act for, the boy. I'm not sure whether they think the boy's underage, but that was implied.'

Collins stared at his superior officer. When her words did not become miraculously unspoken, he said the first thing that came into his head.

'This solicitor, is he called Danvers?'

Bridget Flynn briefly closed her eyes. 'Owen, whatever it is you haven't told me yet, it had better sound convincing to the Chief Superintendent.'

'Right.' He told himself to keep this simple and businesslike. 'One. Jake is not an officially registered informant and he is certainly not a suspect in a case. Two. He is nineteen years old and if he and I were to have an 'improper relationship' we would be entirely within the law. Three. We haven't.'

That didn't come out as cool as he would have liked. And he fervently hoped that what he was saying was actually true. He'd taken the boy's word for it when he told him his age, and he'd taken his word for it when he assured him he didn't deal in anything more serious than the odd party drug. Certainly anyone who had seen them together might have misconstrued their relationship. Jake had kissed him once, a clumsy boy-kiss miles removed from his professional persona.

'I see,' DCI Flynn said. 'So there *is* a boy. What I do not understand is why the Chief Super's friend thinks I should concern myself with him. Although, really Owen, nineteen is a bit young. And they lie about their age, you know.'

'There's nothing in it, truly.' Except that I'm meeting him for lunch.

'All the same, you'd better stay away from him. At least keep things strictly professional if you happen to meet. *Something* must have set off this solicitor.'

He was on firmer ground there.

'I think I know what. Austin Danvers knows Jake, he believes Jake will tell me something he wants to keep under wraps. After he was drugged at Bitters someone sent two men to beat up the suspect, I'm sure that was Danvers.'

That must be one of the least elucidating sentences he'd ever uttered.

'Again, please. You think this Danvers was drugged at Bitters?'

'No. The boy with Oblivion in his drink the other day, that was Jake. And the man who actually *didn't* drug him got beaten up for it later. And I think Danvers was behind that.'

Of course, then she asked the inevitable question.

'Why?'

Very briefly, Collins explained about the historians' murders, stressing that no complaint had been made, it wasn't official.

'I wish it was, then I could take this further,' he concluded, knowing that Bridget would tell him what everyone told him sooner or later, that he should be making progress with that other, more urgent murder case.

'It's none of my business what you investigate in your spare time,' she added, when she had told him exactly that, 'Of course I wish Mr Walsingham no harm, and it might explain why Danvers contacted us about you. All the same, do be careful about your professional conduct. Don't get too cosy with your Jake. Mud sticks.'

'I'll be careful,' he promised. He took a deep breath. 'Bridget?'

'Yes?'

'I *am* sort of involved with Mr Walsingham. I thought you should know. You know, in case someone starts complaining about that.' Again, he hoped that what he was saying was in fact true.

She gave him her oldest mother-of-a-teenage-son look. 'What age is he?'

'Thirties.'

'Then you have my blessing. Now go and catch a murderer.'

He put Sally to work matching the descriptions of trench coat with those she and Chandra had collected on Saturday night, and then, feeling like a schoolboy playing truant, Collins went out to meet Jake. Despite the DCI's warning, he wasn't going to stand him up, he wanted to see for himself that the boy was all right after his brush with Oblivion. And he wanted to ask Jake about Selina Brinkmann. He still hadn't given up hope that she was somehow involved, and it was just the kind of thing he needed Jake for. Then after that he was seeing a Ms Althorpe, who said she had vital information about the three murders. He could only hope that that would prove useful. He thought of the last time a helpful member of the public had appeared in his office with a similar claim. Dominic still wasn't answering his calls. Maybe he'd better stop trying.

44

After another night in a strange bed – in a perfectly decent hotel this time – Dominic took the *métro* to the Bibliothèque Nationale bright and early.

He waited patiently for the charter to be fetched out of whatever protective atmosphere they kept it in. They had hundreds of these charters in here, and the library assistant clearly didn't see the point of bringing out the original when Dominic could have easily purchased a scan. But look at the original he would. If that was the right word, he thought, as he studied the discoloured parchment by which the emperor granted all the land between the church of Nogent and the watermill to the abbey of St Cloud. 811, James had said, and that being the forty-second year of Charlemagne's reign, so did the charter. To a layman it just looked old, and where manuscripts were concerned he wasn't much better than a layman. But he did know a lot of monasteries had been creative with 'copying' early grants of land to their houses, and he carried with him a list of the tell-tale signs of forgery compiled by a helpful colleague. He wasn't really surprised anymore when he found he could tick off nearly the whole list. Anachronistic phrasing, seal no longer attached, wrong handwriting for the region... it was a classic example. By now he would have been more surprised to find anything about the Chapter of St Cloud that was actually genuine. The master file on his netbook was shrinking instead of growing. He would have liked to visit Nogent, nowadays called *St Cloud*, but he knew there was nothing left of the original abbey, and he had to get back to England.

He stopped by the gift shop on his way out to buy some postcards, and decided he might as well have something to drink in the attached bistro. He didn't need to be at the Gare du Nord until two.

'You are English, aren't you?' the lady behind him in the queue asked, while he stood wondering whether the tea would be palatable, 'One can always tell. You should try the hot chocolate, they do that wonderfully over here.'

'*Un chocolat chaud, s'il vous plaît,*' he ordered, 'For you as well? *Deux chocolats chauds.*'

He struggled a bit with his tray and the bag that kept slipping off his shoulder.

'Look, let me get that for you, you just bring your bags. We'll get a table by the window – or, really, am I intruding? Just say if you'd rather be alone.'

'No, no, it's fine.'

He found a table by the window while she got them napkins and teaspoons. 'I'm Dorcas Mattingly, by the way.'

'Dominic Walsingham.'

'Nice to meet you, Mr Walsingham. Are you here for work?'

'Yes, I'm an historian, I had to look at some manuscripts. And you?'

'No, I'm just sight-seeing. My husband's at the Centre Pompidou right now, but anything later than 1900 or so is wasted on me. Give me old books any day.'

He stirred his hot chocolate. Something was bothering him about this conversation. She was a woman not unlike his own mother, with that same confident middle-class demeanour. A perfectly friendly woman, who was just happy to meet a fellow Brit on foreign soil. So why didn't he quite believe her when she told him about visiting Notre Dame? ('Magnificent, of course, but the crowds!')

'Have you been to Amiens? It's one of my favourites.' He could talk about cathedrals in his sleep, it was easy enough to keep the conversation going while he tried to figure out what was wrong. He raised his drink to his lips, but only blew on it. Hot was the right word. Mrs Mattingly's chattered on. She reminded him, he decided, of the woman he'd met in the library last week, who had been just as uninvitedly friendly. Talking to strange men.

'Is it? I'll see if I can persuade Joe to make a detour. Have you seen–? Oh, there in the corner,' she exclaimed, 'I've been keeping an eye out for the ladies. Do excuse me.'

As soon as she had gone Dominic carefully tipped over his full glass with his elbow. He had soaked up most of the resulting mess with his napkin before a waiter arrived with a cloth. While he wiped the table, Dominic put the sodden napkin in the dinky plastic carrier they had put his postcards in and placed it in the front compartment of his bag. He would just have to hope his luggage wasn't searched at customs, he'd have a hard time explaining that. The waiter brought him another hot chocolate, which he drank at his leisure, not at all surprised that Dorcas Mattingly failed to reappear. It *was* lovely.

45

Alice Wright had attracted his attention when her book about Judith of Paris appeared. Wright had argued, a bit ahead of her time, that Judith's visions had been ignored for so long because she was a woman, not because they were considered unorthodox at the time. Although that was probably true in a general way, the abbot thought that a visionary male would hardly have been more welcome in an order were rigorous thought had always been honoured above all else. He would have liked to argue about that with Wright, she struck him as an intelligent, clear-headed woman. But he was inside the chapter and she was without, and events conspired to make that meeting impossible. He did not know exactly what had happened on the night of her murder. Was that the point where it started, where his authority began to wane? Isaac had been prior back then, but it had been Sister Thomasina who really ran the show. He suspected it was her decision to send young Brother Zachary to Alice Wright's rooms with the arsenic and a likely cover-story, he only heard about it after it happened. That was the first time he had been tempted to end it all, to go to the authorities with his story. But he didn't, of course not, the chapter came before everything. The police did question him, in fact, Wright's neighbour had seen and recognised him when he had come to visit her. She had been out, nothing had come of it, except that he was briefly detained as a murder suspect. He hadn't breathed a word of what he knew, and sometimes he thought he should have. An odd feeling, that, it was unlike any of them to mourn lost opportunities. The prior would see it as a weakness, but the abbot knew that if you never question you never learn. He hoped that he had learned from past mistakes. He hoped he had learned enough not to make them again, but it was hard to break a habit of centuries.

46

'So we know he had the means and the opportunity to commit these crimes,' Claire finished her story.

She was beginning to consider the detective inspector's reactions very peculiar. He had looked intently at Simon when they were introduced, and then wonderingly at her. Throughout the interview, she felt he was only half listening to what she said, and he was constantly watching her boyfriend. She knew Simon was well worth the looking at, of course, but it didn't exactly strike her as professional behaviour. It heartened her, though, that Simon had decided to come with her after all. Despite her brave words, she wouldn't have liked to tell the story on her own, especially not to this sceptical detective.

'So you think he shot these three people at your grandfather's instigation?' he asked, summing up her account.

He simply doesn't believe me! she thought indignantly. Probably doesn't like it when other people do his work for him.

'Are you taking this seriously, Inspector?'

'I am, Ms Althorpe,' Collins said, 'But you must realise this is a serious accusation you are making. I cannot just go and arrest your – brother-in-law, is he? – because you don't like the cut of his coat. You say he had the opportunity and the means to commit these murders – though I confess myself somewhat confused as to the motive – but like everyone else he is innocent until proven guilty. We will need to establish his whereabouts at the time of the shootings, compare this gun he has with the murder weapon, that sort of thing. And that is not something we like to inflict on innocent members of the public if we can avoid it.'

'But we've established that he doesn't have alibis for the times of the murders.'

'No, what you have established is that he wasn't at home, no more.'

'There's lives at stake here!' she reminded him angrily, 'He may kill again. Do you want to have that on your conscience?'

'I'm well aware of it, Ms Althorpe. I assure you I'm doing all I can to make certain it does not happen again.' Apparently she'd touched a nerve.

'Then why won't you believe me?'

'I think I do know some things about this case which you don't. And what I am trying to decide is whether you genuinely believe this theory about the three murders, or if this is just a clever piece of obfuscation. You have been very quiet,' he said to Simon, 'What do you think?'

'This is ridiculous,' Claire fumed, 'What would we be trying to 'obfuscate', Inspector? Would we be here if we had anything to hide ourselves?'

'Would you? Tell me, please, Mr Danvers, are you quite sure this has nothing to do with anything else your family are involved in?'

'You'll have to tell him about Adam, you know,' Claire told him, thinking that the inspector wasn't lying when he said he knew more about this case than she did.

Simon explained about his cousin and the drugs. It struck her that he made it sound much more sophisticated than she had thought it was. Not a few pills here and there, but a proper lab with a steady output – and income.

'Interesting,' Collins said, 'My colleagues in Narcotics will have to look into this. But I think you know that wasn't what I meant, don't you Mr Danvers?'

Why the odd emphasis on Simon's name? Claire wondered. And why was Simon looking so embarrassed now?

'I think we've told you all we know, Inspector,' he said, 'It's up to you what you choose to do with it.'

'Hold on a minute,' Claire protested, 'I want to know for sure you'll do at least *something* with it.'

'Come on, Claire, you can see this is leading nowhere.' Simon pushed back his chair.

'We will look into it, Ms Althorpe,' DI Collins said, 'Thank you for your visit. And if there is anything more either of you can tell us, don't hesitate to get in touch.'

'Well, thanks for being such a help,' Claire told Simon, as they walked out of the police station. She didn't know who she was angrier with, Simon or the inspector. What a useless conversation! And what could they do now, keep an eye on cousin Lucas to see if he went out armed? She knew that should be a job for the police, but the police had been more interested in keeping an eye on her boyfriend. And those strange questions... as if the inspector had known something about Simon and his family that she didn't. She looked at him, walking beside her quietly, apparently relieved that that was over. Did he really think it would stop here? And what had he kept from her?

47

Early in the afternoon, the prior received a short text message from Sister Dorcas.

Done. On my way home now.

Of course he didn't know whether she had been successful, and it might be a while yet before he could be sure. He supposed this was the kind of occasion when religious people prayed. He would have to occupy his time otherwise. Whether Dorcas's mission had been successful or not, there were other loose ends to tie up. Despite his superior's admonition, Detective Inspector Collins continued to keep in touch with the runaway, and he had not been removed from the investigation. A little evidence would help, there. Brother Austin had not been idle, he would send him to the station at once.

The runaway himself had apparently not been scared at all by his unintended stay in hospital. Foolhardiness like that would have been punished severely if he had still been in the chapter, and he would pay for it now. The prior knew exactly how and by whom the punishment would be meted out.

'You sent for me, father?'

'Brother Lucas, I have a job for you. Do you have the gun?'

'Of course, father. Just like you said.'

He had always found Lucas most loyal, and he was the only one who he could trust to follow his instructions to the letter, and not start thinking for himself. That was the trouble with all these intelligent people, they tended to think they knew better, and didn't always do as they were told. With this one, his only fear was that he would baulk at the job itself, but he need not have worried there. In fact, Lucas looked disconcertingly excited at the prospect.

'Have you understood me?' the prior said, 'One shot, exactly as I say. And if there is any hint, the slightest hint, that you are watched, or that he is not alone, you come away. There will be other times.'

'Of course, father. Tonight?'

'Tonight.'

48

To Dominic's relief there were no more encounters with friendly strangers on the way home. All this travelling was giving him a headache, but the day wasn't over yet. He went straight from the train to the police station.

'I'm sorry sir, DI Collins isn't here. Can I take a message?'

The only thing he hadn't counted on was Owen not being at work. Stupid. Of course he was out doing whatever it was detectives did.

'Is DC Holmes in?'

'I'll check for you, sir.' The desk sergeant was beginning to look fed up with this visitor who wouldn't plainly state his business. 'Sally? Gentleman to see you. Won't say what it's about.'

He was glad when Ms Holmes appeared and took him away from the desk sergeant's glower.

'DC Holmes? I do realise this is a bit irregular, but it's vital DI Collins gets this as soon as possible. Could you put it on his desk?' He proffered the envelope containing the plastic-wrapped napkin.

'I doubt there'd be room,' she said, taking it. He didn't blame her for looking suspicious. Taking packages from strangers couldn't come naturally in a police station. There could be anything in there from a bulky love letter to a tiny bomb.

'Look, remember the night that boy's drink was drugged? Call me paranoid, but I think someone tried to put something in my drink today. It's a sample, I thought you might have it analysed.'

'Oh, I see. I'll make sure he gets it, then. Was there anything else?'

He didn't think 'give him my love' was the kind of thing she meant, so he took out one of his postcards and pencilled a short message on the back. 'Just this,' he said, 'And thank you.'

Instead of going home, when he got back from the police station Dominic checked into the Cathedral Hotel. He'd been brooding on his plan all the way home from Paris, and now, rather nervously, he was ready to put it into practice. He put down his bag, made a truly horrible cup of tea and went online. Just as he had thought, there weren't that many escort services in the area, and it didn't take long to find Jake, appetising picture and all. He didn't want to register on the website, so he made a call on the hotel landline, and found he could make a booking for ten o'clock. Then it was just a matter of waiting for the boy to turn up, and hoping he still wanted to tell him what he never got a chance to say at Bitters.

He went out for dinner, which basically meant going home and making a salad, picking up his mail and then going on to the cathedral for choir practice.

'You're not exactly looking better, if I may say so,' Michael Taylor told him, 'I didn't know historical research was so dangerous.'

For a moment Dominic wondered what the choir master knew. Then he realised he still looked like he'd been in the wars from his encounter with those boys three days ago.

'I'm fine,' he said, 'Really. Look, Michael, you must know everyone here. What about people called Danvers?'

'Well, one of the senior partners in my father's law firm is called Danvers – they are Taylor, Danvers & Weir.'

'Yes, I've met him, I think,' Dominic said, unconsciously touching the bruise on his temple.

'And the rector of St Oda's used to be a Martha Danvers until recently,' Taylor continued, 'Nice woman, but she moved away. Why?'

'Just something that came up.'

'You're being mysterious. Are you sure you are all right?'

'Thanks, Michael, yes.'

'Not in trouble with that young fellow of yours?'

He couldn't think who he meant for a moment.

'Oh, Owen? No that's just–' What was it exactly? 'Fine,' he finished lamely.

Taylor shook his head, smiling. 'Maybe we just should go and sing, don't you think?'

Back in his hotel room he emailed his sister – still through his mother's account – to thank her for her detective work on the Danvers family, called the St Elizabeth's care home to make an appointment for the next day, and booked another ticket for London. The letter that had been waiting for him at home turned out to be a curt reply from James's former student.

> *Shortly after I had agreed the subject of my thesis with my tutor I was told in no uncertain terms to leave the chapter alone. I advise you to do the same. Please do not get in touch again.*

That was plain speaking. Another piece of evidence to add to DI Collins's hoard. Dominic was beginning to feel they were getting somewhere. Putting the letter aside, he turned to Blake's article on drugs and senescence. Dominic found the quotes from people spending their lives trying to live longer quite depressing. The article had been written at the time when Oblivion was still the promise of a panacea, but it was clear that Cloud Laboratories had been very cagey about it. There was no hint of anything dodgy going on, though, and Blake had said in his email that the people at Cloud Labs had been 'slightly scary, as these medical optimists tend to be, but mostly harmless'. Of course, Blake hadn't known about the connection with the chapter back then. After an hour or so, Dominic felt he knew more about drugs and senescence than he wanted to, and there was still no sign of Jake. He tried to tell himself he shouldn't force his own exaggerated sense of punctuality on other people, but surely being twenty minutes late for what was essentially work was going too far even for Jake. He hoped nothing had happened to the boy. Suddenly his stratagem didn't seem so very clever anymore. The last time Jake had come to see him he had ended up in hospital. Why couldn't he just have asked Collins to arrange a meeting, preferably at the station? He would call Owen now, ask him to make sure Jake was all right.

49

Detective Chief Inspector Flynn's small hand slapped down on his desk. 'Explain this.'

Under her spread fingers lay a photograph. It looked like a tourist ad, showing the Newmarket with the old guildhall looking handsome in the sun and people in summery clothes dotted around the square. And right in the middle of the picture there he was himself, with Jake's arms flung around his neck. The next photograph would have shown him swinging the boy around. Christ, Danvers moved fast.

'Well?' she said.

'I was glad to see he was all right. He was in hospital the other day, remember?' Collins said inadequately.

'Keep your distance, I tell you. Keep things professional. And what do you do?'

'Bridget–'

'No. Enough. I'm seeing the Chief Superintendent again the day after tomorrow. You have two days to bring this investigation to a good end. This investigation, and no other. No collar by Wednesday and I'm taking over personally, and you are out doing the legwork with Holmes and Dasgupta, and facing an internal inquiry. Understood?'

'Understood, ma'am.'

He felt crowded now, wanting to do everything at once. Two days, Bridget had said. He didn't know where to go with the murder investigation, he'd slipped up badly with Jake, he didn't know where Dominic was. Although DCI Flynn's disapproval stung, he didn't mind the possible inquiry, or doing the work of a constable. He'd gladly knock on doors for the rest of his life if he could make sure both Jake and Dominic were all right. He just didn't know how to do that. He recalled Daniel Wood's words: 'that helplessness, knowing that there is nothing you can do'. But if he couldn't do anything about it, he was in the wrong job.

He stopped by Sergeant Walter's desk on his way out. 'Anything useful from Charlie Howard's friends?'

Walter shrugged. 'I'm getting tired of hearing that he was such a nice bloke, he didn't have any enemies. None of them had. But they were all breaking the law, and practically everyone I've spoken to knew about it. What were they expecting?'

'They certainly weren't expecting to be killed by a client.'

'You think there's something in this trench coat story, then?' Walter asked.

'I was thinking of getting in some of the witnesses, trying out a few drawings.'

'It has to be worth a try.'

From Walter, that was practically ringing endorsement. They must be really desperate.

Late that evening he got a phone call from a number he did not recognise.

'Collins,' he said.

'Owen, I–'

'Dominic! Where the hell have you been?'

'Holland. France.'

'I've been calling you. I've been worried.'

'I kept my mobile turned off, I didn't want anyone to trace me.'

'It worked.' Owen realised he was being very unfriendly. 'It's good to hear from you. Are you all right? Why were you calling?'

'I was worried too. About Jake. Look, long story, but he should have been here an hour ago, and then I got this strange email...'

'Just tell the story,' Owen said, 'I'm trying to call Jake right now.' He dialled Jake's number on his landline while Dominic explained his stratagem for meeting the boy.

'... but he never showed up.'

'He's not answering his phone. But he usually doesn't, that nothing to worry about.' Owen didn't think he was managing to sound entirely convincing.

'I wouldn't, only he shouldn't have known this was me,' Dominic said, 'Surely he would turn up for work? And then I got this email from him on my university account. It was sent this evening, and ends in mid-sentence, as if he was interrupted.'

'Can you read it to me? No, forget that, just forward it. It's owendotcollinsat–'

The landline rang. He snatched up the receiver. 'Hello? No, sorry Dominic, just taking another call.'

'Sir, are you there?' It was Sally, sounding confused. 'There's been another shooting. Jacob Danvers, nineteen years old, lived on Oxford Road. I think he was on our list.'

'Right. On my way.'

Very slowly, he put down the receiver. *Jacob Danvers, nineteen years old.*

'Dominic? I have to go. Jake's been shot.'

50

The death of Barry Skinner should have been the last mistake, the abbot thought, the last time a threat like that would ever happen. It was usually one of the junior brothers who were sent out to deal with members of the public, but Skinner had taken them by surprise, and the prior, newly in office, had felt the need to deal with it himself. A stubborn young man, Barry Skinner had been, and an arrogant one. He had not been inclined to listen to reason. 'I'll publish and be damned, if it's all the same to you,' he had said, infuriatingly casual. He had not known the danger he was in, as the prior idly picked up the paperweight from his desk. He never knew the danger he was in, and two minutes later he was dead. They still had his unfinished thesis somewhere, a mass of messy typescript. The abbot knew the prior had read it, and had been appalled at how much Skinner had found out. That was when he had decided they needed to keep a much closer watch on who had access to information about the chapter. The prior had initiated a systematic search of libraries and bookstores, to make sure that there was as little as possible to be found. The brothers and sisters still made a point of buying Wright's and Poole's books when they came across them in second-hand bookshops, but unfortunately the writings of Lothar and Thomas of St Cloud were too well known in academe to suddenly disappear. Even so, the few students who attempted research on the chapter had been easily discouraged by the lack of sources, and until Dominic Walsingham had appeared on the scene, the campaign had been judged successful. So successful that the younger members of the chapter were used to treating 'hunting for Wright and Poole' as a bit of fun. They must be taking it seriously now, though. Silence got serious very quickly when the alternative was death.

51

'I think she is a bit lonely, to be honest,' the matron said, as she led Dominic along the corridor in St Elizabeth's care home, 'She has a sharp mind, and a sharp tongue, and the rest of them are simple souls mostly, or not as bright as they once were. She'll like having someone new to talk to.'

She knocked on a door indistinguishable from all the others. 'Good morning, dear. There's a handsome gentleman to see you.'

'Thank you,' Dominic said, as he stepped inside to meet Benedicta Danvers. He was still shaky from his late-night conversation with Owen, and he really did not know what to expect here.

'Hello? I've come to talk to you about the chapter,' he said to the upright old woman seated by the window.

She turned her clouded blue eyes on him. 'So you said. Please, come sit on my right side, I'm somewhat deaf on the other.' She shook his hand, her grip unexpectedly firm. 'I'm Benedicta.'

'Dominic Walsingham. I hope you can help me sort out some mysteries. I have found the chapter, um, rather elusive.'

'Since you have found me, I assume you know the Danvers family *are* the chapter,' she said.

'I guessed as much. Though it took me long enough to figure out. One expects celibacy, not primogeniture.'

'And one expects religion, too, of course,' she said. 'The church was always our best disguise. But the chapter's creed is agnostic.'

'What is the chapter's creed? I haven't been able to find out that.'

'There is no life but this life, and you shall strive to keep it,' she recited.

'That's all?'

'Is it not enough? It was enough to build our lives on for centuries,' she replied. He could see what the matron meant, she was sharp in every sense.

'But *you* didn't, you left a long time ago. Did you ever marry? I would never have found you if you weren't still called Danvers.'

'I shared my house with a dear friend for many years. Lydia Smith. We were happy. I never found it a hardship, living outside the order I grew up in. You must understand that the chapter is not a sect. Its members are rational, reasonable people who choose to stay or not as they find congenial. Being a member of the family does not mean you are in the chapter for life. I chose not to stay and I was not blamed or rejected, some of my brothers and sisters stayed in touch for years. There was no rancour.'

'But why did you leave?'

'Because I, too, was raised to be rational and reasonable, and I understood quite early on that although the chapter's creed is not illogical, most of my family were barkers. Eternal life, I ask you! Such a selfish, such a misguided wish. I do not want to live forever. Oh, it isn't 'unbearable' like you read in the papers nowadays. I'm as healthy as can be expected, I'm cared for. Lydia's niece brings her grandchildren to see me every second Sunday. I have the crossword and the telly – that Downton Abbey, I was there, you know, and it wasn't like that *at all*. But I was saying, life is fine for as long as it lasts, but one wouldn't want it to go on forever. Lydia died twenty years ago. She was seventy-nine, and we considered that a good old age. And look at me now! My family are mad, Mr Walsingham, all of them. I find the prospect of immortality quite horrible.'

She was silent for a moment, allowing this to sink in.

'Of course immortality was just what my uncle craved. He was a lunatic. A psychopath, I think they would call him now. And my elder brother was a weakling who was completely under his thumb.'

'That would be Isaac?'

'Yes, that would be Isaac. In another family he might have been a sweet, harmless man. Under my uncle's guidance he was a nervous heap of guilt. That was enough reason for me to leave, when I became old enough to see what was happening. I left at eighteen and I did not give the chapter – as opposed to my family – a thought for years. I had my own life; I taught at Lady Maud's College, you know. Then, in the fifties, a fellow of the college died. Alice Wright. I see you have heard of her, of course you have. It was never proved it was murder. They were clever. My uncle was an old man by then, and I could not believe it was Isaac. I used that as my excuse for not telling the police, even though they were all over the college for days. I didn't know for sure, did I? Perhaps the apple did not fall far from the tree, after all. That's what we must have told ourselves every time, we lookers-on.

'It was only after I retired, when I had time on my hands, that I started to investigate the claims made by the chapter. I am not an historian, but I knew the scientific method, and it kept me young to discover new territory. It had never occurred to me before to question our history.

But you know what I found at St Clothilde's, Mr Walsingham, you would not be here otherwise.'

Dominic nodded. 'The connection between St Clothilde's and the abbey of St Cloud is completely spurious.'

'Exactly. All the references to St Cloud in Clothilde's records can only be found in the seventeenth century transcriptions. There are no such references in the originals. None.'

'I know. And there's more, isn't there?'

She nodded approvingly, as if he were a clever schoolboy. 'You have checked the provenance of the Rule?'

'Nothing before 1627. It was cobbled together from various sources, most such rules are, but there isn't a scrap of text to prove it existed earlier than that, not even a mention in a catalogue.'

It turned out he had perfectly retraced Benedicta's steps, down to visiting the Bibliothèque Nationale, and they had come to the same conclusions. But she had been raised in the chapter, and there were a few things he could not have learned anywhere else.

'Really? There is still a Chapterhouse, the same house you grew up in?'

'Oh yes, it's been in the family since the beginning. Since what you and I know to be the beginning, that is,' she added with a hint of amusement.

'But why didn't you tell anyone about what you had found?' he asked her.

'I had a reason for that. You may not judge it sufficient. I spoke to a young man, a history student, during my research. He was a bright young man, not unlike yourself. We had quite a chat, and three days later he was dead. Murdered. Eternal life was never for me, but back then I badly wanted to keep the life I had for a little longer. I got the message. I didn't speak to anyone about St Cloud from that day forward. Not once until now.'

She looked at him gravely, an old woman made fearless by time. 'Aren't you scared, Mr Walsingham? The chapter may have mellowed in the last twenty-five years, but I wouldn't count on it. I always thought my great-nephew took after my uncle in everything.'

'Oh yes, I am scared,' Dominic said honestly, 'But it will not leave me alone. And even if I decided I didn't want to take the risk anymore, the police are on the case now. There's no way back.'

She nodded. 'Perhaps it is time to end it. I never thought I would survive the chapter. Unfair enough that I had the years my elder sister never saw. Evangeline. I was too young to understand what was said about her death at the time, but I have often wondered whether it was the chapter that killed her.'

He was silent, not wanting to add this painful knowledge to her already large share. But she could read his face. 'It was, wasn't it? You know.'

'Evangeline told one of her friends about the family, and the chapter. Your uncle decided that she could not be allowed to do that again.'

To his own surprise, it was he and not Benedicta who broke down. He buried his face in his hands, wet with tears. 'Nineteen years old. Killed for that ridiculous creed.'

He took a deep breath, wiped his eyes. 'Yes. It is time to end it.'

52

It was an unexceptional, tidy bed-sit. A table with a desktop computer – hadn't Jake told him he enjoyed online games? – a shelf with a few books, a poster of Ben Whishaw hugging Aloysius on the wall. A fine selection of T-shirts in the closet, a bloodstain on the floor. It made him want to sit down on the bed and cry. With relief, mostly. He could have kissed Sally when he arrived here and she said, 'I'm sorry, I wasn't quite clear on the phone. The victim's in hospital. He called 999 himself. Bullet through the shoulder, lots of blood, but nothing life-threatening.'

There wasn't much point in being here now. The SOCO's would do their work, and tomorrow he could ask Jake himself what had happened, and finally arrest his murderer. But after he had called Dominic to reassure him, Collins stuck around for a while, picking up things that had already been dusted for prints. Looking through the boy's paperbacks – why did he have a blue-covered one called *Wishful Thinking* squeezed between the fantasy titles? – waking up his computer to see that he really had sent an unfinished email to Dominic earlier that evening. The subject was 'Cloud' and it ended 'I only know what Bethany tells me, but–' and then no more. Jacob Danvers. Now he understood why Claire Althorpe's boyfriend had looked so familiar. If you gave the one a haircut or dressed the other in one of those narrow, V-necked tees, the brothers would look very much alike. He should have been asking Jake about the chapter instead of going on to him about drug-dealers. Or maybe Jake had been happy enough to go along with that. Not mentioning the chapter must run deep.

He was at the infirmary first thing in the morning. Jake was lying back against his pillows, looking very pale and very young. He opened his eyes when Owen sat down on the chair next to the hospital bed. 'Hey Jake.'

'I found out about Selina for you.'

Collins put down his paper-bagged piece of caramel shortbread on the bedside locker.

'Never mind about that. How are you? Does it hurt?'

Jake grimaced. 'Yes. They took out some bits of metal that shouldn't be there, and then they put in some other bits of metal to hold my collarbone together. And I bled a lot, apparently, I had to have a transfusion. Don't you want to hear about Selina?'

'All right, was there anything to find out?'

'I don't wonder she didn't want to tell you, but it's got nothing to do with your case, probably. Selina's known as a party girl, she's always got something, and she's always willing to share. There was a party a few weeks back, she gave some capsules of Oblivion to her cousin and the cousin's best friend. And now she's afraid people will always think of her as the girl who gave the drugs to Naomi Miller.'

'And seeing that you found out, that is what they do.'

It hardly mattered anymore. Selina could have saved him the trouble by just telling him, he wasn't going to blame her. Although Jake was right, it was understandable she didn't want to talk about it. Could it have been deliberate, though? Had he been wrong all the time, and was Naomi murdered? DCI Flynn's admonition still echoed in his ears 'this investigation, and no other'. Even if there was a measure of culpability in Selina Brinkmann's actions, it wasn't his case.

'Thanks, Jake,' he said, 'Well done. You ever consider a career in the force?'

'Does it lower the chance of being shot at?'

'Marginally. Who tried to kill you, Jakey? You know that's why I'm here officially, don't you?'

Jake looked away. 'He didn't shoot to kill.'

'Who didn't?'

'I'm not saying. He didn't shoot to kill,' Jake repeated stubbornly.

'Jake, for God's sake, it's not just you, you know! This man has murdered three other people already. I need to know.'

'It's not the same, really. He was just warning me, he didn't kill the others, that has nothing to do with it.'

'Who was just warning you, Jake? And why are you so sure he didn't kill the others?'

'They were nothing to do with the chapter, were they?'

He was beginning to see. Another shooting, of course everyone was assuming that it had to be the same perpetrator. But if it had been, Jake would be dead now. This killer didn't mess up his aim.

'He was just telling me to stay silent,' Jake insisted.

'And if you don't you're dead? Jake, if you tell me who he is, he'll be behind bars within an hour, no one's going to kill you.'

'I don't want you to lock him up.'

'It's someone you care about, isn't it?'

That got no answer. He tried again.

'What hold does the chapter have over you? Whatever it is, they shouldn't have, you know that.'

'They think differently.'

'Maybe you'd better explain a bit more, don't you think?' he said, '*Jacob*.'

'I know. Is Mr Walsingham all right?'

'Yes, he is, and rather worried about you, as it happens. Don't change the subject. Can you start at the beginning? What do you know about the chapter?'

'More than I want to know. And it's not changing the subject. You know they want to kill him?'

'Yes, I do. That's why I need to know.'

So Jake told him about growing up within the chapter, about its creed and its secrets, and about running away from it all. His family, Owen thought, it's his bloody family doing this!

'Is there anyone who should be told, anyone who'll visit you here, Jake?' he asked.

'There's you,' Jake said, and began to cry.

Owen saw no option but to gingerly sit on the edge of the bed and hold him. 'Of course there's me.'

'I should have known,' a familiar voice said behind him. He sat up straight, but kept his arm protectively around Jake.

'Bridget, what are you doing here?'

'DC Holmes called to say the victim was awake and talking.' She looked down at Jake. 'I'm here to question you, young man. Since it doesn't appear to have occurred to Inspector Collins here that he cannot be allowed to interview someone he knows personally.'

'It's no use, anyway, ma'am. This has nothing to do with the other shootings.'

'We'll see about that. Owen, playtime is over, you're back on duty as soon as you walk out of this room. Now,

Mr Danvers – can I call you Jake? – start at the beginning, please.'

Owen gave Jake a squeeze. 'You're going to tell her,' he said, 'All of it.'

'Okay.'

Sally was waiting for him back at the station. 'So who was it?'

Of course, she also thought Jake's assailant was their killer.

'No one. I mean, the man who attacked Jacob Danvers is not the murderer. No progress there, just another case.'

'Oh. Well, in that case. I looked at these descriptions, like you said to yesterday? Something bothered me about that, took me a while to figure out. I mean, you are right, they are all useless as descriptions. But they do have something in common. This man, we call him 'trench coat' because that's what he's probably wearing, don't we? I just thought: why? It's been blazing hot for two weeks now. Absolutely *no one* is wearing a coat.'

He looked out of the window, where shirt-sleeves and skimpy tops were much in evidence. What Sally said made sense.

'I know we can hardly arrest anyone just for dressing too warmly, but it struck me, I thought you should know.'

'Thanks, it's a good point,' he said absently. His thoughts were still on what Jake had told him. Was his assertion that the chapter wanted Dominic dead sufficient information for an arrest? It was still too diffuse, there was not enough harm done to charge anyone with. He kept staring out of the window at the lightly clad crowd. This idea of Sally's reminded him of something – 'huddled in his coat, even though it was a warm day' – where had he heard that recently?

He nearly had it, but DCI Flynn called, interrupting his thoughts. 'Apparently your boy was shot by his uncle to tell him to keep quiet about this chapter thing. It really has nothing to do with the murders.' She sounded disappointed.

He didn't say 'I told you so'. 'So are we going to pull in Danvers?'

'Eventually. Do you know how many Danverses there are in this town?'

'I have a fair idea. Did he tell you anything else?'

'Nothing pertinent. And this isn't our first priority. Collins, are we any closer to catching a killer?'

'Actually,' he said, looking out at a trio of T-shirted boys in low-slung shorts, 'I think we may be.'

53

Such scenes there had been when Jacob still lived in the Chapterhouse. He hadn't been at all like Stephen or Lucas, following meekly along well-travelled paths. He had been more like the prior, only in the opposite direction, questioning everything he was taught from the time when he was a little boy. Always asking why: why can't I talk about this? why won't you answer the question? why can't we be like other families? And it wasn't just a phase. The abbot recalled the prior threatening to give him a good thrashing as a teenager, and the drawled reply, 'Yeah, I bet you would like that'.

It was refreshing, someone who could think for himself, and the abbot regretted it when he left. But Jacob, with the narrow view of the young, had never paid much attention to his great-grandfather, and it was better for the boy himself, of course. He was more at home in the world than within the walls of the Chapterhouse. The prior had forbidden the brothers and sisters all contact with 'the runaway' as he chose to call him, but the abbot suspected that at least some of the younger members stayed in touch. They had mobile phones and Facebook like everyone else, they must be keeping track of their little brother. The prior himself probably felt safer knowing exactly what he got up to out in the world. And the ties with the chapter were not so easily broken, as Jacob had found to his cost. But in his attempt to rein in the runaway the prior miscalculated. For all that he had left them, hurting Jacob felt like violence against one of their own. The abbot was shocked that Lucas had agreed to it, and the thought of his great-grandson, so young and full of life, being frightened into silence, finally galled him into a decision. Fifteen-hundred years of silence were enough.

54

'Simon? Yesterday, the inspector said 'anything else your family may be involved in'. What did he mean by that?'

It had taken a while to gather the courage to ask that question. Claire wasn't sure she wanted to know the answer.

'All right,' Simon said, 'It was time I told you, anyway. Have you ever heard of the Chapter of St Cloud?'

That wasn't what she had been expecting. 'Of course. What has that got to do with anything?'

It was his turn to look stunned. 'You knew? But–'

'I know Dominic was planning to write a book about it. It was a medieval monastic order.' In her head she heard James's voice '... except that it still exists'. But it couldn't be, no, it couldn't.

'Walsingham is writing a book about us?'

She felt the conversation was spinning rapidly out of control. 'What do you mean?'

'My great-grandfather is the abbot,' he said, 'That is, we all are, in a way.'

She didn't see what he was talking about. Or maybe she just wouldn't. 'Old Toby? He's not a monk.'

'This is going to take some explaining,' Simon said, 'Let's get something to eat, and I'll tell you the whole story.'

'All right.'

They were back in town, mainly because Claire couldn't really stand being in the house with Simon's relatives at the moment.

She listened patiently while he outlined the early history of the chapter over a goat's cheese salad. She had the sense it was a well-rehearsed story, one he'd been told often from a young age onwards. It only became confusing during the main course.

'But why? It's not like you're aristocrats, why this obsession with lineage? Is the house entailed or something?'

'You don't understand. There has to be a son to succeed. And since Jacob–'

'Wait a sec, Jacob was younger than you, right?'

'Yes, but that's not the point, he might have grown to look more like dad and grandfather. But of course it became clear he wasn't likely to have children of his own.'

She stared at him. 'I think I'm missing something.'

Carefully, he explained to her the nature of the abbacy.

'Say that again, please,' she insisted, blowing on a forkful of cannelloni, 'The abbacy passes from father to son, but they always pretend to be the same person?'

'They are. The abbot has always been Simon Danvers. The members of the order always see the same man, who doesn't age or die. Right now it's Simon Peter who makes the public appearances, soon it will be my dad, and eventually, I'll be taking his place. Not that it matters these days, now the chapter is only the family. It's just, well, continuity I suppose.'

She tried to get her head around this.

'So that's why you call it the Chapterhouse. I did wonder, you know. But what's the point of it all?'

She could see he did not really get this question. She suddenly saw how the family worked, what they reminded her of. They were like medieval kings, absolutely convinced of their divine right, their superiority over lesser folk, the importance of their lineage. Asking Simon why was like asking the Lionheart where he got the right to rule. It was who he was.

'All right, forget that,' she said thickly. The cannelloni was surprisingly good. 'Tell me something else. When did you intend to tell me about this, if ever?'

'Soon,' he said, 'You'd have to know, wouldn't you? I mean, your son would be the next abbot.'

Reflexively, she put a hand on her belly. The idea that the future of her possible children had already been planned out repelled her. 'I need to think about this, Simon. This is too much, really too much.'

They talked about it again later that night, in her room. She hadn't needed time to think, not really. She made her decision then and there. But she needed time to put words to it, words that he would understand.

'I can't live with this, Simon. The thought that it was all planned. That there was this all the time we were getting to know each other. I hate the very idea.'

'But that shouldn't matter,' he protested, 'There's just us, you said so yourself.'

She shook her head. 'There was never 'just us'. There was always you and the chapter, watching me. Don't you see that? You didn't choose me for *me*. You did not fall in love. You *selected* me because you thought I would fit into the family. You *selected* me because you thought our children would have the right colour eyes and hair, the right kind of brain. And you have no idea how repulsive I find that. I fell in love with you, Simon. But I don't think that means anything to you.'

'Of course it does!' he protested,' You are everything to me, Claire. And it wasn't like you say – I think you are just right in every way.'

'And you think that's a lovely coincidence? My God, you are naïve.'

'Please Claire, what can I say to persuade you? I love you.'

'You think you do,' she said. She should have known better, oh, she should have known better all along. He was so young. And he did think that he loved her, he just didn't know yet what love entailed.

'Someone who loved me would have told me the truth from the start. I can't blame you, you've been under your family's influence for all your life, I couldn't expect you to act otherwise. But you cannot expect me to conform. It's over, Simon.'

He cried. She would have kept her composure perfectly through all this if he had not cried. Now she lost her temper.

'Did you never think it through? Did you really think we would be happy ever after – in this prison?'

'It's not like that,' he said, in a strangled voice, 'It was going to be perfect. We were going to be–'

'A picture-book couple like your parents? You think your mother is happy? You think your father is? No thank you. I am sorry, Simon, but this is it. Please leave.'

And so she ordered him out of the room in his own house, for the last time.

'Don't you care?' he asked in the doorway.

'I should have known better,' she said quietly, 'But I do care. That's exactly why.'

'Goodbye then.'

'Goodbye, Simon. I hope you find a girl who fits the picture better.'

55

Selina Brinkmann had proved more useful than she had ever intended to be, and like she had said herself, it was obvious once you knew. The trail didn't just lead from Howard to Whiteside to Wilson and stop there. It went on through Selina all the way to Naomi. Collins plucked DC Holmes from behind her desk and commandeered a squad car. He still knew the address.

'Sir, do you mind telling me where we are going? Sarge will kill me if I don't get that report done today.'

'We're on our way to arrest a suspect.' He quickly filled her in on what he had realised by combining her hunch with what he had heard from Jake and Dominic. 'And since you've been instrumental in discovering him, I thought you should be there when we arrest him. Ah, here we are.'

The weeks since the funeral had not been kind to Deborah Miller.

'Inspector,' she said in a flat voice.

'Mrs Miller, is your husband home?'

'You've just missed him.'

'Do you know where he's gone? I need to speak to him rather urgently.'

'I don't know. He just comes and goes, he doesn't tell me anything. I'm worried about him, to tell you the truth.'

'So am I. You really have no idea where he is? Did he take the car?'

'Yes, I believe so. Should I ask him to call you when he comes back?' she offered.

He ignored her suggestion. 'He's done this before, you say, leave without telling you where?'

'A few times. I was concerned at first, but he always comes back. He may be at the range, he used to spend a lot of time there, before, you know.'

He thought furiously. It was unlikely Miller had gone to the shooting range, but where would he have gone instead?

'Thank you Mrs Miller,' he told the bemused woman, turning away from the door.

He took out his phone and brought up the list Jim in narcotics had emailed him. He had forwarded it to Walter, never really looked at it himself. Miller could be after any one of these, or the people Holmes and Dasgupta had discovered on their night out, but one name jumped out at him. It really couldn't be anyone else – why hadn't he looked at this himself? The address was Grange Road, on the other side of town, twenty minutes' drive, at least. He turned back towards the house. Mrs Miller was still in the doorway.

'How long has he been gone? And what kind of car does he drive?'

'A quarter of an hour?' she said doubtfully. 'It's a grey Volvo estate.'

Fuck, fuck, fuck. No time.

'Sally, are you a reckless driver?'

'My boyfriend sometimes threatens to get out and walk, sir.'

He threw her the car keys. 'Good, you can drive us. You know the new development south of town, those posh houses at the edge of the nature reserve? I need you to get us there ten minutes ago.'

'Sirens?'

'Yes, we don't want to be a danger to the public.'

In the car, he called the station. He might be certain they were heading the right way, but that was no reason not to cover all options.

'Pardoe? I need you to send a team to each of the following people in the next five minutes. Doesn't matter who, anyone you can pull in off the street, just get them to these addresses. And warn them there is a small chance they may meet an armed man. Have them ring the bell, ask about the description of our mystery man. They won't get much response, that doesn't matter. But – this is important – they need to hang around afterwards, keep an eye on the houses until I say they can leave. Shouldn't be more than half an hour. Do it now.'

He reeled off the addresses while Sally took a roundabout at twice the allowed speed. His insides lurched as she headed off down the third exit. Good old Pardoe, didn't ask questions, just got on with it. He hoped he hadn't been too incoherent. And he hoped there wouldn't be young bobbies getting overexcited at the thought of meeting a gunman.

Sally overtook a lorry and wrenched the car into the right lane just ahead of an oncoming vehicle.

'Christ, woman,' he muttered, 'I want to get there alive.'

'You wanted to get there fast, sir.'

'All right, all right. Turn off the sirens, will you. I don't want to give him advance warning.'

The next exit brought them to the new development.

'Which number?' she asked.

'Fourteen. Should be the next but one.'

She brought them to a stop in a graceful swerve on the gravelled drive of a brand-new villa. There were two other cars parked out front. One was a grey Volvo estate. Gotcha. He was out and running before she killed the engine. No use ringing the bell. Round the back, warm day, garden doors would be open. People never bothered about security when they were at home. He swung himself over a low wall and crossed the lawn. He halted by the entrance, trying to listen over the beating in his ears. Yes, there were voices somewhere inside, that was good, wasn't it? That meant at least two live people. He stepped inside quietly and looked around. It was a large room, with an open spiral staircase in one corner. The voices were coming from upstairs. He started to climb, very quietly, trying to make out what they were saying. Two different men, he thought, and one voice sounded familiar.

'You killed my daughter.' Yes, he knew that querulous tone.

'I don't know what you are talking about.' The other voice sounded posh and panicky. Danvers.

With his head just level with the landing, he identified the probable source of the conversation, a room on his right. He could feel the shift in the stairs as Sally stepped on the first tread.

'You killed my daughter,' Miller repeated, 'Your filthy drugs killed my little girl.'

Collins edged his way forward on the landing and looked round the door. Miller stood turned away from him, his gun trained on a terrified man in a chair by the window. Collins shook his head minutely but emphatically, trying to tell Danvers not to let on he was there. But the man was much too panicked to think rationally. 'Who are you?' he demanded in a high voice.

Miller turned around, pointing his gun at the intruder. Collins knew he must recognise him, knew Miller must know the game was up. But he saw the man's shoulders tense, saw him reach a decision in a fraction of a second.

He didn't lower his gun. Collins threw himself forward as Miller swung back towards Danvers, his finger on the trigger. He could see himself flying through the air before he collided with the older man's body. He could hear a long drawn out 'Noooo', that must be Sally coming up behind him. Then it was all lost in a loud shattering sound. Too late, he thought, as he and Miller hit the floor together, knocking the breath out of him, too bloody late. There was a moment that was filled only with his own beating heart and laboured breath. Then, 'Thank God,' he heard Sally say.

He held Miller to the floor with his own weight and looked up. The window had cracked crazily around one small, definite hole, and below it Adam Danvers sat staring, mouth open, white as a sheet, and alive.

'Drop the gun,' Collins said tersely, before levering himself up on his elbows. 'Sally, handcuffs.'

She snapped them shut over Miller's wrists.

'Harold Miller, you are arrested on suspicion of killing Sean Whiteside, Lisa Wilson and Charles Howard. You have the right to remain silent...'

He turned back to Sally when he had finished cautioning Miller. 'Do you have another pair?'

'Handcuffs? No.'

'Well, we'll just have to hope he comes quietly, then.' He got up and stood in front of Danvers' chair. The man hadn't moved through all this, he still sat staring wordlessly at Miller.

'Adam Danvers, I am arresting you on suspicion of the manufacture and sale of illegal substances...' He went through the whole rigmarole again, with DC Holmes standing by looking very surprised.

'Miller was after people who supplied Oblivion,' he explained to her, 'Lisa and Sean led him to Charlie Howard, Howard led him here. So I reckon Mr Danvers must be a pretty big player in this field. Could you call back-up? We can't take them both to the station in one car. I'll stay here to make sure Mr Danvers doesn't run.'

He could hear her talking downstairs as he remained in the study with his two suspects. Sound carried well in this house, he noticed. Or maybe his senses were still alert from too much adrenaline.

'Chandra? We need a car at 14 Grange Road. Yes. No, Collie's only gone and caught our murderer. It was Harold Miller, we caught him red-handed. Yes, he's in cuffs, but then the DI went and arrested the victim too. No, of course he's not dead. Look, just send a car, will you? We'll explain later.'

Collie, he thought. Well, it could be worse.

Bridget Flynn was waiting for him in his office, sitting behind his desk.

'Owen Collins, this place is an absolute tip.'

'You sound like my mother.'

'There's an envelope with a sodden napkin in it sitting next to your keyboard.'

'Oh fuck, I forgot to send that to the lab. Never mind, I'll do it today.'

He picked up the eraser and, with great deliberation, started wiping the whiteboard clean.

DCI Flynn was silent for a moment. 'I hear you've caught your murderer.'

Satisfied that the whiteboard was gloriously empty, he sat down and gave her a detailed summary of the afternoon's events.

'I see,' she said eventually. 'Well done, you. Just don't do it again.'

'What?' He had hoped for a little better than that.

'Collins, when you have information that an armed man with intent to kill is at a certain place at a certain time, what have you been taught to do?'

'Evacuate the area and call armed response. Bridget, do you think I would have been in time if I'd done that?'

'Probably not,' she admitted, 'You were barely in time as it was. We've had two reports of dangerous driving by a police car this afternoon.'

'Sally's a star,' he said, 'I would have been nowhere without her.'

'We haven't room for another sergeant,' she said automatically.

He hadn't meant it as a plug for Sally's promotion, but he knew to beat the iron when it was hot.

'It wouldn't surprise me if Walter put in for a transfer one of these days. We don't have room for another DI either, and he knows that.'

'We'll see,' was all she would say, 'Now this man Danvers you say Miller was threatening, you've brought him in as well?'

'Harold Miller was looking for the source of the Oblivion that killed his daughter. Naomi was given the pills by a friend, who was a flatmate of Lisa Wilson. Lisa bought them from the barman of the Hollow Crown, who regularly got them from Charlie Howard. And Howard got his supplies straight from the source: Adam Danvers. In effect, Miller's done our work for us.'

'You're very certain Danvers is our man.'

He supposed it wouldn't cut much ice with her that he automatically suspected anyone called Danvers.

'Oblivion was originally produced by a company called Cloud Laboratories. We've been assuming someone else started making it since the first batch went missing from Cloud Labs, but I think we were wrong there. Adam Danvers is the owner's son. They are simply still making it, and making a good profit, too, probably.'

'We'll send in Walter and Pardoe with a search warrant,' she decided. 'Now, you have suspects to interview, I think. And you'd better send this to the lab.' She handed him the squishy envelope.

'Of course.'

He couldn't wait to tell Dominic he had caught a Danvers.

56

'All right, you first,' Dominic said, after they had talked through each other for a full minute in their haste to give each other their news. He was sitting in the late sun on his tiny balcony, feeling pleasantly tired after three busy days.

'I've arrested our murderer today,' Owen told him, sounding like he shared that mood, 'And I should say thank you. I would never have realised who it was if you hadn't been so observant.'

'Me? But I've had nothing to do with that case.'

'No, but you noticed Harold Miller, whose grief made him huddle away in his coat. He was still wearing it when he tried to shoot Adam Danvers this afternoon.'

'Wait, wait. Naomi Miller's father killed these other young people?'

'They were the people who supplied her with the drugs. She was given them by Selina Brinkmann, who got them off Lisa Wilson, who bought them from Sean Whiteside, whose dealer was Charlie Howard, who got the Oblivion straight from the source.'

Dominic tried hard to see the connections.

'So Adam Danvers…?'

'Works for Cloud Laboratories. I've arrested him too, while I was at it. First Danvers behind bars.'

'What about the one who shot Jake?'

'I can only be in one place at a time, you know. We'll get him, too. And then they can explain exactly what they think they are up to with this chapter of theirs.'

'Speaking of which...'

'Yes, your turn.' He could hear the smile in Owen's voice.

'The chapter doesn't exist.'

It was a shame they were on the phone. He'd have liked to see Owen's face when he said that.

'I think I may have misheard you there. The chapter – what?'

'Doesn't exist. There are no references to the chapter *anywhere* before the 1620s,' Dominic explained, 'For all those centuries, it just wasn't there. And don't go quoting the 'absence of evidence' thing at me. In this case it won't wash. There is no chapter.'

'You mean it's all a fantasy? But what did the other historians write about, then? What about the Rule?'

'There was an abbey of St Cloud, to be sure, but there never was an order. That first house joined the Cistercians in 1169, and became defunct in the 1500s, and that was all there ever was to it. So what we call the chapter didn't start in AD 550 but more than a thousand years later, in the seventeenth century. I told you about the philosophers and the early scientists. I forgot that another kind of enquiring mind flourished at the time: the antiquarian. The son of Bishop Danvers became convinced he was a descendant of the Simeon d'Anvers who was abbot of St Cloud in 1200. That in itself is an odd thing to get into your head. Bishops and priests may have fathered children at the time, but Cistercian abbots usually didn't.'

'I'll take your word for it,' Owen said, 'Go on.'

'Danvers must have based his claim on the similarity of the name and the occurrence of the crossed nails in the arms of his ancestors. Like I did, he probably thought they were a reference to St Cloud, but it was almost certainly just coincidence. But once he had hold of the idea, nothing short of recreating the original chapter would do. He cobbled together a strange set of ideas from Lothar and Thomas, making the quest for eternal life the central tenet of the order – which it certainly wasn't for the original house called St Cloud – and set up the society of philosophers to put it into practice.'

'And then he taught it to his children.'

'There was a lot to teach, and he had a long life to teach it in. They may not be immortal, but they are a long-lived lot, those Danverses. But it's amazing, all the certainties, all the usually cited facts about the order go back to the bishop's son. Remember the Priory of St Bernard? Simon Danvers wrote about the ruins, there is even a drawing of what the priory would have looked like in the fifteenth century. But the site was excavated in 2006, before they built that new development. There's nothing there, never was. Just Simon's lively imagination.'

'And the secret the current chapter are protecting? Or is that it?'

'I'm not sure, but I'm going to find out. From what Benedicta said, they do believe the story themselves. There were still associated organisations as late as the sixties, and perhaps even people who believed the abbot to be hundreds of years old. The office passes from father to son, but they all pretend to be the original Simon Danvers. Or at least they did in Benedicta's time. And it is still immortality they are after, though the people at Cloud Laboratories aren't saying that in so many words.'

'I see, I think. But who's Benedicta?'

'Evangeline's younger sister. I went to see her today. It's quite a story, isn't it? And it isn't finished yet,' Dominic said, 'Look, now you've caught your killer, does that mean you have more time? I've made an appointment with Claire, you see, for lunch at the Chapterhouse tomorrow. Practically invited myself. And I asked if I could bring someone. I'll feel safer with an officer of the law along.'

'Of course I'll come. It's high time I talked to your Claire's in-laws, anyway.'

It took a moment for Dominic to realise that this shouldn't make sense.

'Hold on, how do you know about Claire? I didn't tell you about her, did I? And I only found out about the old bishop's palace being the Chapterhouse from Benedicta.'

'Ms Althorpe and her fiancé came to see me on Monday, with information about the murder case. Pretty useless information, as it turned out. But it means I've met one of your Simons already.'

'And here I was being so proud of my detective work,' Dominic said, 'While you stumble across Danverses right, left and centre.'

'I did explain about Jake, didn't I?'

'Yes, you explained about Jake,' Dominic said contentedly, not minding hearing it again, 'How is he?'

57

Claire packed her bags, slowly and methodically. She hadn't told anyone yet, not even Simon senior when she met him at breakfast. He had looked preoccupied anyway. That was a look she had come to know well, and she had almost asked him if he was all right. But she would soon be rid of this family, she thought, it didn't matter anymore. She would call Gina and Bryony and Julia later today, organise a proper girls' night out, to bitch about their men and forget about this mess.

She did a systematic tour of the house, looking through all the rooms she had spent time in in the last ten days. How freely she had spread her belongings! She had felt at home here, for a short time.

She was in the library, wondering whether this copy of *The Sense of an Ending* was hers, when Simon's aunt Sarah appeared, the one who looked so much like Esther. She calmly locked the door she had come in through and walked over to the other one, without saying a word.

'What are you doing?' Claire asked, trying to get to the door before Sarah did.

'I think you'd better stay in here, for the time being.'

'What do you mean? Let me go, please.' She tried to push past Sarah, but Simon's aunt grabbed her wrist and twisted her arm up her back.

'Ow! What are you doing? Let go!'

'I said you'd better stay here,' Sarah repeated, pushing her back into the room. Sarah's other hand went down the pocket of her skirt. For an instant, Claire thought she'd met the final indignity of being groped by her ex-boyfriend's aunt, but it was her phone Sarah was after.

'Give that back!' She fought to get loose, but Sarah was surprisingly strong.

'We can't have you calling for help.'

Sarah suddenly let go of her by giving her a violent push, and slammed the door shut behind her while Claire stumbled to her feet. She heard the key turn in the lock just as she twisted the door-handle.

'Let me out!' She shook the door-handle uselessly.

Claire cursed herself for being so careless. She had got so used to feeling at home here and safe with Simon, even when they had talked about the murders she had never considered there might be a threat to herself. Dispiritedly, she tried the other door, which was just as closely locked, and looked out of the window, which at least opened. She was one storey up, which she would have dared to jump in almost any other house, but here, this being a stately bloody home, was a frighteningly long way to the ground. She sat on the floor with her back to the window. They had locked her in the library, at least she wouldn't be bored. Why, though? What were they going to do with her? There must be something important going on, something she wasn't allowed to witness or talk about, but which only concerned the chapter. Had Simon agreed to this? If he had, she was well shot of him. At this thought, Claire began to cry. She had loved him, really loved him. But the Simon she thought she knew was just a fiction.

Far away, the doorbell jingled. That must be Dominic. She wondered what they would tell him. Probably that she had been taken ill, or, given her final words to Simon yesterday, that she had left. The minutes ticked away.

Once she heard voices in the distance, and she tried calling for help, but they didn't hear, or ignored her. She was getting hungry, and she needed to pee. Be resourceful, she told herself, don't just sit here allowing things to happen to you.

She was trying to force the lock on the library door with a pen-knife when there was a determined knocking on the window behind her.

58

It felt oddly formal to Collins, meeting Dominic for their appointment at the Chapterhouse. The last time he saw him had been in Dominic's bedroom, naked and sleepy. Now they hesitated about how to say hello, finally settling for a hurried kiss. There was a friendly wolf-whistle from Sally, just coming out into the car park with Dasgupta.

'You're bringing back-up?' Dominic asked.

'Constables Holmes and Dasgupta are going to follow us in a squad car, in case I have to make an arrest. Or several. And for the same eventuality, you'd better carry these,' he handed Dominic two pairs of handcuffs, 'Don't want to be short again.'

Dominic put them in his bag and got into the passenger seat.

'Sally, just follow us in the car, I'll call you if we need assistance,' Owen told her.

'Right, sir.'

'Does your friend Claire know what her fiancé is involved in?' he asked Dominic when they were on the road, 'Or are we going to give her a nasty surprise?'

'I don't think she knows. She's not the kind of woman to put up with much nonsense.'

'Well, she knows *something* is going on. She and her Simon were convinced it was cousin Lucas killing off drug-dealers.'

'Really? Where did they get that idea?'

'Something about a missing gun, and all the victims being known to the family. Of course, the missing gun–'

'Was used to shoot Jake?'

'Yes, I've only just thought of that. Here we are.'

The bishop's palace came into view, looking splendid at the end of its long drive.

'Oh,' Dominic said, 'Somehow I had been expecting something more sober.'

'It does look as if there's an entrance fee, doesn't it? Remember you were invited.'

A car tore past in the opposite direction, narrowly missing them. That woman could teach even Sally a thing or two, Owen thought. He parked his own car out front, next to at least a dozen others.

'Lots of people here,' he remarked, getting out.

'It's the seventh today,' Dominic replied, in a tone that suggested he had only just realised.

'I believe so, yes.' He didn't see what was so special about the seventh.

'St Cloud's day. The general chapter. Owen, every Danvers you've ever wanted to meet is here today.'

'Right, then let's go and meet them.'

The tall front door was opened by a boy of ten or so.

'Hello,' he said politely.

'Hello. I'm Detective Inspector Collins. I'd like to speak to the abbot, please.' He had decided on the direct approach. It really was time to get things out in the open.

'And I'm Dominic, I'm here to see Claire Althorpe. May we come in?'

The boy nodded solemnly. 'My name is Titus.' He turned around. 'Auntie Rhoda! There's a policeman here to see great-grandfather.'

A middle-aged woman came to the door. She wore her hair in a bun. Could this be the Roddy Danvers who had worked in the library?

Owen repeated that he was here to see abbot Tobias Simon Danvers.

She frowned. 'I am afraid that is not quite convenient.'

'And I fear a murder investigation will not wait on your convenience. Could you please ask him to speak to me?'

'I'll see what I can do.' She didn't seem very put out by the mention of murder.

'Could you find Claire for me?' Dominic asked the boy, who was still hanging around curiously.

'I'll try.' He ran off.

'Strange family,' Owen said, when they were left alone together in the hall, 'I'm glad I asked Sally and Chandra along.'

The squad car was parked squarely in the middle of the drive, and it wasn't going anywhere soon.

59

It was the day of the general chapter, and they were all gathered in the Chapterhouse.

The prior called the roll of members in order of seniority. The abbot, Tobias Simon. Sister Abigail. Brother Solomon. Joseph and Dorcas. His own wife, Edith. Austin. Bennett and Maisie. Rhoda. Simon Stephen and Anna. Esther. Sarah. Brother Adam was absent, detained by the police. Timothy. Martha. Lucas. Young Simon. Judith. Bethany. Rachel.

They were so few now.

'Welcome to the general chapter of the order of St Cloud,' he told them, 'Before we proceed to the usual business, we have an urgent matter to discuss. As you are probably aware, the silence of our order has once again been threatened. I assure you measures are in hand to contain the situation and keep our knowledge confined within these walls. I need not remind you that what is said here should not go further. Brother Lucas has made sure that no information will be released by the runaway, and–'

'What do you mean? What have you done?' Bethany asked.

'A warning shot,' the prior said tersely, 'Please, no interruptions.'

'You shot him?' the girl said incredulously.

Anna's chair scraped back violently. 'You!' she said, rising, 'You've hurt my son? You're standing there just–

How can you say that? You–' she sobbed. 'I'm leaving. You're mad, all of you. I'm leaving. My poor boy.'

'Anna–' Edith said. But it was already too late, the door had slammed behind her.

'She made her choice,' the prior told those remaining, 'Respect it.'

He resumed his account, but Anna's outburst had left them restless. When Sarah told them young Simon's girlfriend had been secured for the time being, Brother Stephen spoke up.

'What have you done to Claire?'

'Nothing,' Sarah replied impatiently, 'She's locked in the library. Really, Stephen, don't be so soft.'

He was already on his feet. 'I'm going to let her out right now.'

'Simon Stephen, it is not your choice,' the prior warned.

'It certainly wasn't hers,' he said, 'I'll get her out.'

'What are you going to do, take the keys from me?' his sister asked calmly.

For a moment it looked as if he wanted to try. But Brother Stephen was not a violent man. 'I'll think of something.' He strode out of the room.

'Shouldn't we try and stop him?' Brother Joseph asked.

'No, let's proceed. These are minor distractions. Our real problem, and I will not deny that it is a problem, is the historian.'

The sound of the doorbell interrupted. He looked around the circle of faces. 'Are we expecting anyone?'

'I'll go and see who it is.' Rhoda got up.

'Claire had a friend coming over,' young Simon said, 'I forgot.'

'Rhoda will get rid of him,' Edie said dismissively.

'How could you make an appointment like that, for today?' Dorcas asked Simon, shaking her head, 'You young people, you never think things through.'

'It was just a colleague of hers, Dominic something-or-other. I thought he could keep her company while I was busy here.'

The prior looked at his grandson in pure disbelief. 'You've asked *Dominic Walsingham* to come to this house?'

'Yes, that was his name. Shouldn't I have?'

'Are you aware that this man is intending to write a history of the chapter?'

'So Claire said. Oh.' Understanding finally dawned. 'Is that why we're here?'

'It may be our chance,' Sarah suggested, 'If no one else knows he's here. Who would miss him?'

'Dangerous, though,' Dorcas said, 'How do we make sure of that?'

Rhoda came back, a serious look on her face. 'Father, there is a policeman at the door, wanting to speak to you. He asked for the abbot, specifically. I told him it is not convenient, but he insists.'

'Good,' the prior said, 'It's not Walsingham, then. Send the officer away, Rhoda, and we can continue here.'

The abbot rose. 'Of course I'll go and speak to him, it's only common politeness.'

'You can't!' the prior protested, 'May I remind you that this is the general chapter?'

'Yes, and I am the abbot of this order. I make my own choices, thank you, my son. Rhoda, where do I find this policeman?'

'In the hallway.'

'Show him to the morning room, then, please.'

The abbot slowly walked out of the room.

'Right,' the prior said. But before the door fell shut, the boy Titus stuck his head around it, though he had been told he wasn't allowed in here.

'Simon? I can't find Claire anywhere and there's a man to see her. Where is she?'

Martha got up from her chair. 'Claire is not here, darling. Come, you shouldn't be here either.' She held out her hand to her nephew.

'I'm sorry, father. I think I'd best take him away.'

The prior crossed his arms. 'Is there anyone else who wants to leave?' He looked around the diminished circle, daring them. The young ones would stay, he knew, Judith and Rachel and Lucas, and so would his own brothers and sisters. They were loyal to the chapter. But young Bethany rose.

'Yes, actually. Mum, dad, I'm sorry, I should have left ages ago.' She closed the door behind her with a gentle click.

'That leaves us,' the prior said, 'This chapter meeting is suspended until we have dealt with our visitors. Sarah, please go and see if father is all right. Joseph, come with me. The rest of you: stay here.'

60

'DI Collins? Please come through.' Rhoda Danvers had returned.

'Should I come too?' Dominic asked.

'Better not,' Owen told him. Why hadn't he thought about this beforehand? Of course he couldn't bring Dominic on a police job. 'You just talk to Claire, see what she can tell you.'

He followed Rhoda into a light, high-ceilinged room.

'Father? This is Detective Inspector Collins.'

'Inspector, sit down. What can I do for you?'

He had half been expecting to see the abbot of the pictures, still the same chap in his thirties. But Tobias Danvers was an elderly man, who looked quite frail and didn't get up to shake his hand.

'Let me establish some facts first,' Collins said, sitting down across from him, 'You are the head, the abbot, of the organisation which calls itself the Chapter of St Cloud?'

'I am. And my father and great-uncle before me.'

'Then you can tell me what happened to Alice Wright in 1954 and to Barry Skinner twenty-five years ago?'

'Yes, I can. I can also tell you what happened to Alfred Poole and Nathaniel Cottington. We have long memories here.' The abbot spoke in a quiet voice, but with great deliberation. 'I have wanted to tell this story for a long time, but I've always doubted whether I should.'

'Father...' Rhoda began.

'No, my daughter, it is time now. Do you want me to start at the beginning, Inspector? Or with the most recent events, with Jacob? I think you care about him, I'm glad someone does.'

'Please, start with Jacob.'

'My son had him shot. It was Lucas, I believe, who actually did it, but the prior told him to. Lucas was never very good at thinking for himself. Perhaps few of us are, when it comes down to it.' For the first time, the old man looked troubled by what he was saying. 'But hurting Jacob was wrong whichever way you look at it.'

A woman entered without knocking. The abbot looked up sharply. 'Sarah, please do not interrupt.'

'Father asked me to see if you were all right,' she said, in a tone that made clear who she chose to listen to, 'I hope the inspector is not tiring you.'

She sat down in a chair by the window, clearly not going anywhere.

'Ms Danvers, if you do not have anything to tell me, I'd prefer it if you left us alone,' Collins told her, irritated by her presence.

'That is not going to happen,' she said simply, 'I'm afraid there isn't much any of us will tell you.'

'You'd be surprised, my daughter,' the abbot said, 'We do not all live according to the prior's will.' He turned back to Owen. 'As you have gathered, it is my son, Simon Peter, who thinks he is in charge here.'

But before the abbot could continue, there was a quiet knock, and the door opened once more.

61

While he waited for the boy to reappear with Claire, Dominic looked at the portraits in the hall. He was getting quite sick of that face. Attractive enough in itself, perhaps, with those striking blue eyes, but once you'd had it spying on you in various guises for a few weeks, it started to pall. He wondered if susceptibility to historical *idées fixes* was as genetically transferable as dark hair and blue eyes, and how you would go about finding out.

'Mr Walsingham, please do exactly as I say.'

He turned around to face a current incarnation of both, and all his flippant thoughts were gone. The man, a stern-faced Danvers in his sixties, held a gun pointing steadily at Dominic. He gestured imperiously with his other hand. 'Come with me.' Behind him like a shadow stood another man, who didn't look like a Danvers at all.

Not knowing what else he could do, Dominic took an unsteady step forward, then another, until they stood in front of a closed door.

'In there,' the man said, 'Your friend the inspector is talking to the abbot. I think it is time we put an end to that conversation. Go on, enter.'

'And you are?' Dominic managed to ask, stalling.

'The prior. I am surprised to find you here alive and well, Mr Walsingham. You have proved irritatingly resilient. And you are trying my patience.'

Dominic didn't feel resilient at all, he felt as if his legs could give way any minute. He knew what would happen when he went in. There would be a hostage situation with only one unarmed police-officer present, a police officer who was personally involved. He wished he had a means of letting DC Holmes and her colleague know that things were going wrong here, but when he moved his hand to his pocket to feel for his mobile, the prior rested the gun against his back.

Seeing no other option, Dominic knocked weakly and turned the handle of the door.

62

Owen knew he had fucked up badly when he saw Dominic's face, even before he saw the gun.

'Don't move,' the man holding it said, 'I'm going to explain exactly what I want you to do. Joseph?'

He was followed into the room by another unknown man, who stood silently by the door. 'Good. Rhoda and Sarah, please stay where you are. Now, Inspector, since you do not appear to know when to back off, I'm going to tell you once and for all.'

Despite the attempt on Dominic's life, despite the attack on Jake, he had not been expecting this. He knew Dominic hadn't either, or he wouldn't be here. They had been so used to the chapter acting on the quiet. He should have known that, after centuries of this, they would not be afraid to act boldly.

'Who are you?' he asked the armed man, while he slowly got to his feet.

'Stay right there. I am the prior, that is all you need to know. Now, in a minute you are going to leave here, knowing that if you ever speak to anyone about what you have learned, Mr Walsingham will die.'

Owen looked at Dominic. There was no question that they both believed him. This man would not stop at anything, and he had killed before.

'Dominic, I'm–'

'No discussions,' the prior interrupted, 'You will go out, and tell your subordinates there was nothing in it after all.

You will go home, and do your job, and forget all about the Chapter of St Cloud.'

'And then you'll let him go?' This wasn't right, not Dominic, this shouldn't be happening. Owen tried hard to recall his training. Keep talking, he thought, stay calm. Don't provoke.

'I will let him go, with the same bargain regarding you,' the prior replied.

'Why is our silence so important?' Collins asked, wondering whether he should just do as he was told. If only he could be certain they would not hurt Dominic anyway. 'Why does it matter so much?'

'I have no obligation to explain myself to you,' the prior said.

'Excuse me?' a tremulous voice cut in, 'I think you have forgotten I am here. Simon Peter, put down your gun.'

'Father, don't interfere,' the prior said impatiently, without looking at him.

'Put down your gun,' the abbot repeated.

Owen saw Dominic staring, wide-eyed. He looked around cautiously.

The abbot was holding a gun of his own, both hands pointing it at his son. His aim wasn't steady, but at this range it was unlikely he would miss.

'It is finished, my son. Put down your weapon, and I'll continue my story to Inspector Collins.'

For a moment, in his surprise, the prior lowered his gun. Then he shook his head, smiling grimly. 'No. You couldn't. You never were strong enough. You never killed a man.'

'No, I haven't. But what have I got to lose? You cannot threaten me, or harm me. I have lived too long. Let my last deed be a good one.' The abbot opened his mouth, and on his tongue lay a blue-and-white capsule. Oblivion, Owen thought, what else?

'Please, give it up, Simon Peter. This cannot go on.'

'No,' the prior said, 'The only thing that ends here is the historian's life.' He raised his weapon again, finger on the trigger.

'Brother, no!' Rhoda cried. Owen moved impulsively towards Dominic, hardly knowing he was doing it. There was a loud, clean crack, and the abbot sank to his knees.

'An end,' the old man gasped, biting down on the capsule. Owen saw him swallow.

63

He remembers. He remembers all he has been taught to remember, by Simon Isaac, Simon Joseph, Simon John, by all the abbots who were taught by those who went before them. He remembers what he taught his son and grandson, and what they taught in turn to theirs. It stretches back far, this chain of memories.

What if they had cooperated with Barry Skinner? What if they had let Cottington publish, to hell with the consequences? The chapter as it is now would no longer exist. He cannot, at the moment, with his eyes closing over a deep weariness, remember why that would have been a bad thing.

What if Alice Wright had been in, that day he visited?

There is nothing but this life. That is the first thing they are taught. There may be a God out there, there may be forces we cannot comprehend, be that as it may. But for us, there is nothing but this life, and it should not be wasted. Decisions must be weighed carefully, and then regret has no place.

Speculation is useless, there is no alternative to a choice once made, things are as they are, we can only make the best of it. A philosophy that has served them well. Every man and woman responsible for their own actions, and theirs alone. Fine words.

Fine words that did nothing to lessen his father's terrible guilt, his grandson's doubts. The nature of their office meant that inevitably the sins of the fathers were visited on the children. The forged charter, the broken lamp, the rope that hanged Evangeline, the poisoned tea, the heavy paperweight, it was as if his hands had held them all. He had tried to make amends, between his father's guilt and his son's fanaticism. He had tried to shield the youngest Simon from these memories, to put a twist in the long inevitable concatenation of events that has brought him to pull the trigger on his own son. He fears he has not succeeded. Simon Peter's voice has always carried more conviction than his own, and the youngest Simon is neither subtle nor strong. His only hope now is that his grandson is free.

He had loved words once, and the things they could do.

What if Clothilde had chosen the knife?

But it does not matter. In that long moment before memory ceases altogether, he knows there is no reckoning, there is an end.

64

As soon as the prior dropped to the floor, Dominic was free to move again. Simon Peter had fallen backwards, a dark stain spreading over his shirt. His father's aim had been true. Following Owen's example, Dominic moved in the direction of the fallen abbot, wanting to help.

'Stay where you are!'

It was the prior's daughter, the one he had met in the library. He had quite forgotten she was there at all. She picked up her father's gun, and in the same movement kicked the one her grandfather had used into the corner, out of the inspector's reach. She came up with the weapon once again pointing at him.

'One wrong move, Walsingham dies.'

'Look, at least allow me to try first-aid,' Owen pleaded, down on one knee, a hand still reaching out to the dying old man.

'He made his choice, he can die,' she coldly replied.

'Or call an ambulance, for God's sake!' He rose to face her.

'No. There's enough of you here already.'

'Then what? What do you want? More deaths?' He was looking at her now, a puzzled frown on his face. Dominic looked anxiously from the one to the other. Her aim was still straight at him, and she was frighteningly close.

'You can just leave. Leave us alone. We can deal with this.'

'Sarah – it is Sarah, isn't it? – you don't have to deal with this. You don't have to deal with the mess they made. Please don't make it worse.'

'Leave.'

Dominic stood there, eyes on the gun, listening as Sarah and Owen talked themselves into a stand-off. The other people in the room were so quiet they might as well not be there. They certainly weren't interfering. Dominic didn't know whether he should speak or stay silent. He hoped Owen knew what he was doing.

'What's going to happen Sarah, do you think?' the inspector asked, 'If I go now, there'll be other officers, and they'll have a crime to charge you with.'

'Just go.'

She gestured impatiently, just like her father had, and came a step closer. Dominic's eyes flicked from her to Owen, but he could not read the inspector's face.

'Sarah, you're a smart woman. Think about this, think about what's going to happen.'

She didn't like this. 'Of course I've thought about it. Have you thought about it, inspector? Have you thought about what it will be like to have him bleeding on the floor?' She was angry now, and the pistol moved from him to Owen and back.

It looked to Dominic as if Owen grew physically smaller as she took another threatening step towards him.

'It's simple, just go, and it will never happen.'

Owen moved slowly backwards, towards the door. Sarah's eyes followed him, and for a moment left Dominic.

'Please, Sarah,' Owen said, resting his hand on the doorknob, 'Think. What would you gain?'

She looked at him with narrowed eyes, seemed to hesitate for a moment, marginally lowering the gun, and in that instant Dominic stepped forward. He grabbed her wrist and forced her hand downwards as she pulled the trigger. He felt the recoil as the bullet tore through the back of an antique chair, and as she staggered backwards he jerked the gun out of her hand.

'No!' She made a grab for it, but he was already holding out the weapon to Owen.

'Here, you probably know how to put the safety on, or something.'

Owen took the gun, white-faced. 'Don't *ever* do anything like that again.'

Only then did he realise that Owen really had been going to leave just to make sure that she didn't shoot him. They stared speechlessly at each other, the seconds stretching, while Sarah knelt on the floor, in tears. Then the inspector sprang into action.

'Dominic, cuffs. You, what's your name, Joseph, please pick up the other weapon and hand it over. Rhoda, call 999. Now.'

Dominic scrabbled in his bag for a pair of hand-cuffs, and Owen put them on the sobbing Sarah. 'You are under arrest,' he told her, 'You have the right to remain silent, but you are going to tell me right now who else is in the house and where I can find them.'

'In the dining room, all of them,' Sarah said bitterly, 'At least those who stayed.'

'An ambulance is on its way,' Rhoda Danvers said quietly, 'But I fear it is too late.'

Owen nodded at her, his phone to his ear, 'Sally, I need you both in the house right now. And call back-up, at least two cars.'

They waited for the constables to arrive, the hand-cuffed woman and her aunt, with the bodies of the abbot and the prior on the floor between them, the wooden Brother Joseph, who hadn't spoken a word yet, and the police inspector who cautiously put down both guns on a cabinet and finally turned to look at him again.

'Dominic, are you all right?'

Owen put his arms around him, and he realised he was shaking.

'They are both dead,' he said, trying out the reality of it. He held on tight.

'Yes. And you are still alive, thank God.'

65

Claire hitched up her skirt, swung her leg over the window sill and climbed down the ladder while he held it steady. 'Thanks for coming to the rescue,' she said at the bottom, 'And sorry to be such a damsel in distress. Your bloody sister– in fact, your whole bloody family!'

'I know,' Simon Stephen said, 'I'm afraid she still has your phone.'

'Never mind that, I'll buy a new one. Just get me out of here.'

'I figured that. I brought you this.' He handed her her packed overnight-bag.

'Thanks.'

She looked around her. They were standing on the south side of the house, the steps to the rose garden were just to the left. 'What made you come and find me?'

'Anna just left.'

He said it in a way that made it clear he didn't mean 'gone out for a while'.

'She never had much interest in the chapter, just let it be,' he explained, 'But now they've hurt Jacob– I don't think she'll be coming back.'

'Jacob? You mean he's alive?'

'You don't think they really meant to kill him?'

They looked at each other uncomprehendingly. There was a loud noise from the other side of the house, which they ignored.

'No,' Claire said, beginning to see the cause of the confusion. 'Anna said 'Jacob's not here anymore' oh, ages ago, and I thought she meant he was dead.'

'Oh no. He left home two years ago, when he was seventeen. Didn't want anything to do with us. Not surprising, really.'

'And now someone, your father, I suppose, tried to– what? silence him?'

'Shot in the shoulder. But he's going to be fine, apparently.'

'So that's what Lucas needed the gun for. Jesus, how we got it wrong, Simon and I.'

'You do seem to know more than you should.' He looked at her half-admiringly. 'I hoped this business could be kept from you. I didn't want you and Simon complicit. I wanted you to walk free.'

'I think maybe Simon was trying to keep himself innocent a little too hard,' Claire said, 'He should have seen this, knowing your long history. And there isn't a 'Simon and Claire' anymore, you know. That ended yesterday.'

'Like Anna and me.'

'So what are you going to do now?' she asked, ignoring the implications of that for the time being.

'Leave, I suppose. There's the house in Nogent, I always go there when things get too much for me here.'

'Don't you want to go and see Jacob?'

'I will, but not today. Anna will be with him now.' He shook his head sadly. 'I haven't done well with my children.'

'They are their grandfather's children more than yours, I think.'

'Yes, I lost Rachel and Judith long ago. And I just told Titus he's going on a sleep-over at his aunt Martha's tonight, she knows it is time to take him away from here. Jacob removed himself. There's only Simon. I was so glad when he found you, Claire. You are strong. I thought my son could have a life unlike mine, an independent life.'

'But he is in there with the chapter,' Claire said, 'And you are out here with me. What about *your* independent life? If your children do not keep you here, what does?'

'Nothing,' he said. 'It's not only your bag I've got here. I packed my own.'

'Let's go, then,' she said, making for the corner of the house. 'We'll take my car.'

He grabbed her arm to pull her back, then hurriedly let go. 'Not so easy, I'm afraid. There's a police car blocking the drive. It showed up just after your friend and his partner arrived. No one's going anywhere that way.'

She'd completely forgotten about Dominic, and she vaguely wondered who 'his partner' was. But he could take care of himself. 'So what do we do?'

'There's a bus stop at the end of Drovers' Lane. We can cut through the park.'

She picked up her bag again. 'Right.'

It was September seven, St Cloud's day. A deceptively normal day, as bright and sunny as the day she arrived. The air smelled of late roses, the wail of a distant ambulance kept it all from becoming a charming cliché, and she was walking out of her life with a man she hardly knew.

'There's something I have to tell you,' she said, as they reached Drovers' Lane, 'A secret of my own.' She took a long, steadying breath. 'I think I'm pregnant. I'm not certain yet, but I'm a week late and, well...' she tailed off, not even sure why she was telling him this.

'Oh Claire, with my son's child? Now you've left him? You must feel...'

'...strange,' she completed. 'On the one side I'm thrilled. I've always wanted children. I think I wanted Simon's until a few days ago, but now?'

'I suppose I should feel pleased,' he said honestly, 'But I'd hoped the chain was broken. I don't want to be a grandfather.'

No, of course not. Not with the example of Simon Peter before him. She understood he didn't want all that again. But maybe–

'Is it too late to be a father again?' she asked. She could almost feel the heat of burning bridges on her back.

'Do you mean that? Yes, you do, I can see.' His face broke in that typical, charming Danvers smile. 'All right, then. But for God's sake let's not call it Simon.'

She took his hand. 'Anything but Simon,' she agreed, as they left the Chapterhouse behind.

66

'What kept you?' he said to Holmes and Dasgupta, 'You must have heard the blasted gun-shots, you should have come running.'

'Oh,' Sally said, 'Was that what it was? We heard this cracking noise, but there was a gardener who came by with a ladder just then, we thought it was him.'

'We were questioning Beth– Ms Danvers,' Chandra said, looking like he would have preferred to go on doing that rather than face DI Collins in this mood.

Apparently Bethany Danvers had walked out of the general chapter straight to the police car and offered to tell Holmes and Dasgupta everything she knew.

'Good work,' Owen said, 'But there are others waiting to be interviewed. As far as we know, all the family who are currently in the house are gathered in the dining room. Please go and take their names and the addresses of those who don't live here, and ask them politely to accompany us to the station.'

He stepped aside to let through two ambulance men, 'Don't move them once you're sure they're dead,' he told them in passing, 'Crime scene.'

'Then why bother to call us?' one of them grumbled.

'I've been known to be mistaken. Dominic? Christ, you're still white as a sheet, maybe they should have a look at you instead.'

'I'll live. You're not looking too good yourself.'

'Never mind about that. I'm afraid you'll have to come back to the station as well, this is going to take some explaining.'

Dominic nodded. 'I'll wait in the car, shall I?'

'Yes, all right.' Owen would have liked to come along and just hold him, but he had to call Bridget, and see how Sally and Chandra were doing, and put Sarah in the back of the van that had just arrived, and see to a dozen other little things.

'I think you would like to put this one under arrest, sir,' DC Holmes said, gesturing at one of the men sitting in the dining room. 'I think he's the one who shot Jacob.'

The word 'uncle' had led him to expect someone middle-aged, but Lucas Danvers was his own age, a man who gave a fair impression of what Jake would look like when he grew into himself. After being told the reason for his arrest, he said, 'Did he tell you it was me? Why would he do that?'

For a moment, Collins thought he was saying he didn't do it. But Lucas Danvers simply did not seem to understand that Jake had told on him.

'But he's all right, isn't he? I made sure I did not kill him.'

It was the closest Owen Collins had ever come to hitting a suspect.

'He's in hospital with a shattered collarbone and the trust in his family in tatters. No. He is not 'all right'.'

He was glad DCI Flynn could not hear him right now. He was showing too much emotion over Jake. But it broke his heart, it really did, that creeps like these were all the boy knew of family and loyalty. He was just making up for it.

Back at the station, he handed Lucas over to the custody officer, who no longer appeared surprised that this one was also called Danvers – 'collecting the whole set, are you?'. The next few days were going to be one big puzzle, with so many suspects to interview and so many different crimes. Especially if they wouldn't talk or started covering up for each other. He wished he could just throw the whole charge sheet at the family collectively, but the law didn't work like that. They had in the cells right now a young woman who had drugged her brother; a middle-aged lady who had tried to kill a stranger in a French café; an underage girl who had played havoc with privacy laws, but at her grandfather's – now deceased – insistence; a perfectly reasonable solicitor who had paid a couple of youths to beat up a passer-by; and a woman who had locked up and threatened her nephew's girlfriend and then aimed a gun at Dominic. He was sure he was forgetting others, it was such a tangle. The murder case, by contrast, was all done and dusted. Harold Miller had admitted killing Whiteside, Howard and Lisa Wilson. It was not a result Collins could feel much pride in. Miller was still the same broken, empty man he had seen at the funeral, and now some other lives were also broken and empty. Fanatics like the Danvers family you could dislike and prosecute and feel you had done something worthwhile. Men like Miller just made him feel sad and useless.

Alone in his office, Owen hunted through the stacks on his desk for the Barry Skinner file, which he needed to see if any charges could be brought now Jake's grandfather was dead. Where did all this stuff come from? Pathologist's report on Charlie Howard, the employees' questionnaire that should have been returned last week, a list of names he didn't recognise but thought might be the scholarship students who had to be told there was no dinner at the

Chapterhouse tonight, detailed summary of the effects of Oblivion on the human body, photo of himself and Jake... right, Barry Skinner. There was also a postcard he was sure he'd never seen before, showing an illuminated initial O. He read the back.

Owen,
Sorry about not getting in touch,
had to disappear for a few days.
Interesting news from France. Will call soon.
x Dominic

It was dated two days ago. O, indeed. He'd really messed things up recently, hadn't he? Quite literally in this case. And he couldn't even explain to Dominic, because DCI Flynn had sent him home, and had instructed Owen not to talk to him about what had happened until they had given their statements, *separately*. He understood why, of course, but he hated it.

Before he went home he stuck the postcard up on his whiteboard with one of the little magnets, and the photograph of the Newmarket next to it. That looked nice. Maybe if he got some other pictures to go on there he wouldn't have to use it anymore.

67

Dominic spent most of the next morning and a large part of the afternoon in an interview room with a DCI Flynn, being questioned about what happened at the Chapterhouse. He didn't quite understand the tenor of her questions, he just kept going over the same events again and again, dutifully answering. It was only when he told the story of the abbot's suicide for the third time that he understood that it wasn't about what he had seen and done, or even the abbot's intentions. She was trying to find out whether Owen was in any way to blame. Two violent deaths with a police officer present couldn't easily be explained. And he realised that Owen wasn't busy interviewing suspects, as he had thought, he was being interviewed himself, and probably having a tougher time of it than Dominic.

'Thank you, Mr Walsingham,' Ms Flynn finally said, 'Your statement will be ready for you to sign tomorrow. And I hope this means the end of trouble for you. It cannot have been easy, with the chapter dogging your steps. We got the lab results this morning, by the way, from that sample you left for us, and you can thank your lucky stars you never drank that hot chocolate. The stuff in there is what Oblivion is before they dilute it and put it into capsules to make it human-friendly. Pure death tasting of artificial sweeteners.'

She walked him to the door and shook his hand. Apparently she expected him to go home and leave it all behind him, but he couldn't do that. He was glad to run into DC Holmes downstairs.

'Sally? Sorry, I mean, DC Holmes, do you know where the inspector is?'

'In his office, I think. I'm sure I heard the door slam.'

Taking this as permission to go through, Dominic walked back up the stairs. Owen was sitting behind his desk, apparently not doing anything in particular.

'Have they finished with you?' he asked cautiously.

'Hey, Dominic. I think so. For today, anyway. Chewed me over and spat me out. Are you finished here, too?'

'Yes, I told DCI Flynn everything I know. I probably told her things I don't know, come to that. But it will be all right, won't it? For you?'

'I hope so,' Owen said doubtfully, 'I should never have brought you along to the Chapterhouse, though. That shows a culpable lack of judgment, endangering innocent bystanders.'

'I asked you to come,' Dominic said indignantly.

'Yes, but that I brought Sally and Chandra means that I knew there was appreciable danger. I should have told you to stay away instead. And then there's two people dead…' Owen sighed. 'On the other hand,' he added, more like his usual self, 'I've also solved at least five separate crimes in one go, they'll have to cut me some slack.'

'I think you've done all right. More than all right.'

'Thanks,' he smiled at Dominic, 'Really, thanks.' He got up from behind his desk, picked up his jacket. 'I was going to the hospital to visit Jake, see how he is, keep him posted. Would you like to come along?'

A well-groomed woman in her forties was sitting by Jake's bedside. She looked familiar.

'Look, you have visitors. I'll leave you alone with your friends. Don't eat all the chocolate at once.' She gave them a friendly nod as she left.

Dominic was getting used to feeling bewildered, but this he really hadn't expected.

'What was Laura Garnett doing here?' he asked.

'That's my *mum*. You're not going to arrest her, are you?' Jake asked Collins.

'I'm afraid I'm going to question her, but probably not arrest her, no. I think she may be the only member of your family who hasn't actually committed a crime.'

'I haven't,' Jake said, with a sly look from under his fringe.

'You,' Owen said, 'Have *so* been withholding evidence. You didn't have amnesia at all, did you, after you were drugged? You knew all the time it was your sisters.'

'And that the drug was meant for me,' Dominic put in, 'What on earth possessed you to switch our drinks?'

'I didn't want them to hurt you,' Jake said. It was an answer to Dominic's question, but he looked at Owen when he said it. Owen just shook his head and gave his good shoulder a gentle push. 'Silly bugger.'

'You could have just knocked over the glass,' Dominic said, 'That worked the time your, um, great-aunt, I think she is, tried to kill me.'

'I'd taken Oblivion before, it's no big deal.' Jake tried to shrug and winced painfully.

'What did I say? Thinks he's immortal,' Owen said.

'It must run in the family.'

Even Jake found this funny. 'What's going to happen to them, though?' he asked.

'That depends. Your father has disappeared, he and Ms Althorpe–'

'Are in France, I think,' Dominic put in.

'Oh?'

'I got an email from her this morning,' he explained, 'Back to the chapter's beginnings. This time is going to be different, it said.'

'Your father is in France with Ms Althorpe,' Owen resumed, apparently past being surprised, 'I don't know whether he's actually guilty of any crime, but we'll need him as a witness. Your aunts and sisters will appear in court for various minor offences. We'll probably forgive young Titus the burglary, but I'm going to throw any possible charge I can at your uncle Austin. Lucas will go to jail for shooting you, and we'll have to see if anyone was complicit in your grandfather's murder of Barry Skinner.'

'Oh,' Jake said, taking this in. 'Who's Barry Skinner?'

'You can explain that one,' Owen told Dominic, sitting back and helping himself to some of Jake's melting chocolate, 'You always tell a good story.'

'My God, I'm tired.' Dominic stretched his shoulders in the hot sun. 'You know there are people who think the life of an academic is utterly boring? They should try historical research.'

'Whereas the life of a detective inspector is completely unexciting, of course,' Owen said. They grinned at each other happily. 'You did a lot of research for nothing, though. Now there's no book for you to write,' he added, as they strolled down Infirmary Road together.

'Not the academic tome I intended to, no,' Dominic said, 'But it's an interesting story, maybe there's a popular book in it. *St Cloud: the History of a Fiction*. What do you think?'

'I'll read it.'

They turned into Woolweaver Street, companionably silent. There was nothing to explain anymore, Dominic realised. No murders, no mysterious chapter. The only question left was walking right next to him, looking rather pleased with himself. Was this it, then? Case closed, nice knowing you, see you in court? Dominic hesitated on the corner of Flanders Alley, wondering how to frame the question, while Owen strode confidently ahead. He looked over his shoulder to see what was keeping Dominic.

'Aren't we going home through the cathedral?'

So that was all right.

Bibliography

Adams, Robert, *The Great Crossroads: Alchemy and Science in Seventeenth-Century England*, London, 2001.

Althorpe, C., 'Queens of the Cloister: Noble Abbesses in the High Middle Ages', in *Medieval Queenship: Lords and Ladies*, K. Sanders and J.S. Webb (eds.), Oxford, 2010.

Garnett, Laura, *Wishful Thinking*, London, 2007.

Garnett, Laura, *Two is Company*, London, 2009.

Garnett, Laura, *A Silver Lining*, London, 2010.

Levitt, M.D., 'Mothers and Daughters: Patterns of Monastic Filiation in the Medieval West', in *Proceedings of the Third International Conference on Monastic Life in the Middle Ages*, Linda Norman and Tyler Watts (eds.), Kalamazoo, 2011.

McLaren, B.A., *The Construction of Noun-Phrases in the Indo-European Languages*, Cambridge, 2008.

Poole, Alfred J., *The History of the Monastic Orders*, Edinburgh, 1879.

Pritchett, Marjorie (ed.), *The Letters of Beatrice 'Baby' Cavendish 1921-1951*, London, 1998.

Sutherland, James (trans.), *Thomas of St Cloud's* De Vita Sancta, Harmondsworth, 1973.

Walsingham, D.S., 'Monastic Rule in History and Memory: Creative Contradictions', in *Proceedings of the Third International Conference on Monastic Life in the Middle Ages*, Linda Norman and Tyler Watts (eds.), Kalamazoo, 2011.

Walsingham, D.S., St Cloud: the History of a Fiction, forthcoming.

Woods, Helen (trans.), Charlemagne's Thinkers: selected writings of Theodulf of Orléans and Lothar of St Cloud, New York, 1989.

Wright, Alice, Forgotten Visions: the Life of Judith of Paris, Oxford, 1952.

St Oda's Bones

Three decades on, everyone who was there has long accepted their own version of events about the night Kester Johnson disappeared. But when an unexpected find lands the case on DI Collins' desk, those certainties start to crumble, and life in Abbey Hill suddenly becomes a lot less peaceful.

Owen Collins has never been very good at keeping the personal and the professional separate, and even a murder from long ago can cause present-day complications. The first person he sees at the scene of the crime is his former lover. The mother of the victim appears to care less about the case than he does. His star witness is also the best friend of his boss. And then there is Jake, lost in a world of his own. With nothing to go on apart from what people choose to tell him, it looks like he may never unravel the mystery of St Oda's bones...

Printed in Great Britain
by Amazon